KUNMA

KUNMA

Frank Corsaro

A Tom Doherty Associates Book
New York

KUNMA

Copyright © 2003 by Frank Corsaro

A Forge Book
Published by Tom Doherty Associates, LLC
175 Fifth Avenue
New York, NY 10010

www.tor.com

Forge® is a registered trademark of Tom Doherty Associates, LLC.

Library of Congress Cataloging-in-Publication Data

Corsaro, Frank.
    Kunma / Frank Corsaro.—1st ed.
        p.   cm.
    ISBN: 0-765-30472-4
    1. Psychiatric hospital patients—Fiction.   2. Demoniac possession—Fiction.
  3. Mythology, Tibetan—Fiction.   4. Psychiatrists—Fiction.   I. Title.

PS3603.O6894K86 2003
813'.6—dc21
                                                                    2002045460

First Edition: June 2003

Printed in the United States of America

0   9   8   7   6   5   4   3   2   1

*Dedicated to a remarkable human being,
my friend and mentor*

David Greenbaum

Acknowledgments must be made to several friends
and advisers close to my heart:

First, to my dear wife, Bonnie, who lived, listened, and
commented smartly on the text as it developed.

Second, to Al Miner, a walking Baedeker of information,
whose astute comments clarified many aspects of this book.

Third, to Randy Behr, who introduced me
to that most amazing author and now friend Chelsea Quinn
Yarbro, who is really the ultimate fairy godmother,
edging the book toward publication.

Last, but hardly least, to Pat LoBrutto, the magician editor who
helped juggle the pages into the final form that follows.

PART ONE

August 1981

The sky split apart as a flash of lightning struck the earth, Route I-95, overlooking Bridgeport's Immaculate Conception Hospital on the New England Thruway.

A black Mercedes emerged out of blackness and skidded to a halt on the rest area overlooking the hospital. A tall, elegantly dressed man emerged from the car as rain lacerated the highway, momentarily imprisoning him in its impenetrable sheets. He was completely drenched in seconds. As he lurched forward onto the highway, he stopped some twenty feet from the Mercedes and looked up into the lashing storm, luxuriating in its punishment.

A screech of brakes and the man was impaled in the headlights of a Volkswagen.

"Jesus Christ, man, I could have killed you." The driver took off his glasses and cleaned them rapidly against the rough material of his coveralls, which bore the legend "De Santis Construction." Replacing them, the young man peered through the eddies of rain curdling on his windshield and saw that the man outside was staring into his headlights with unblinking eyes. The driver was about to offer help when the man removed his jacket and tossed it at his idling vehicle. The jacket hung precariously on one of the headlights, then fell off. The man's white shirt shimmered eerily and seemed stuck to him like a second skin. A sudden gust of rain blurred this vision. When it reappeared, the sodden man had started to scream.

Completely unnerved, the driver pressed down on his accelerator and swerved past.

"Look, honey, it's only a little past eleven. I'm here till midnight when my relief comes—you know that." Camilla Watkins, the nurse in charge of emergency at Immaculate Conception, listened attentively as her lover rambled on.

"Well, it's been a pretty slow night here too, sugar—what with this weather . . ." As she spoke, she played with the gold chain round her neck, with its flat, pendent crucifix. Camilla had met Jimmy Del Ray at a Baptist church affair only a month ago—and the next day this gift was at her station. At twenty-four, Camilla Watkins was indeed fortunate to be in her position at Immaculate and to have met the man of her life.

"Just honk and I'll be ready for you—quick as that." Their muffled guffaws of anticipated pleasure overlapped, as Camilla casually looked toward the entranceway.

The man seemed to have appeared from out of nowhere. A tall, handsome white man in shirtsleeves—dripping water onto the floor. He kicked off his loafers, wrenched off his socks, and, unable to unbutton his shirt, tore it in one downward move.

Camilla heard the sound of buttons hitting the linoleum as she hung up, then watched as he stripped down until he was naked as the day he was born.

"Please help me!" he pleaded. "I'm burning up! I'm burning up!"

His fingers pummeled his flesh. Bloody lacerations oozed as he dug at himself. Camilla Watkins, transfixed, watched the grotesque pantomime in disbelief. Was this a bad drug trip or what? Outside, the storm punctuated the fantastic scene with a sudden outburst of thunder and lightning. The man spotted Camilla. "Nurse! Help me—I'm burning!"

Camilla punched in several numbers on her switchboard and wondered if she could be heard over the man's wrenching screams.

"Emergency team needed in the lobby. There's a man here—" Camilla managed that much before she felt the grip of his hands on her shoulders. As she forcibly yanked herself free, their eyes met for an instant. An animal-like snarl broke through the man's lips, and Camilla fled to the safety of the office behind her and locked the door.

She listened over the sound of her pounding heart to the commotion of voices filling reception. Shortly, she heard the squeaking wheels of a stretcher as the man was rushed out of the area. When she reemerged, the clock read 11:35 P.M. Jimmy would be ready for her in twenty-five minutes. The storm outside was beginning to play itself out, headed eastward. An intern was picking up the burning man's apparel, strewn haphazardly over the floor. Piling the clothes onto a cart, he stopped.

"Did I hear right? Did he say he was burning up?"

"Burning up, my ass," Camilla rejoined fiercely. "His hands were cold, man, and I'm saying ice-cold."

"Well, there are new strains of virus showing up all the time," he said almost merrily, and wheeled his burden off. Camilla stood there massaging her shoulders and elbows. She also realized she was trembling—not so much from the physical assault. She had never seen anything quite like that look before on any living being—in or outside the hospital. She poured some lukewarm coffee into a paper cup—and noticed her sleeves bore the imprint of his blood. The cup fell from her hands, staining her shoes and stockings.

September 1981

David Sussman stepped out of the shower and picked up the phone after seven rings. On the other end was Dr. Lacey, recalling their Park Avenue days at the Psychiatric Institute. Lacey lost little time and got to the point. Would David consider a consultation with one of his patients? The name, Laurel Hunt, did not ring a bell, but Lacey persisted, "That is, if you still handle that sort of thing." David wondered what sort of thing he meant, but before he could frame the question, an appointment had been made for Mrs. Hunt for the following day at eleven.

David had just returned to his aerie apartment on Riverside Drive from a desultory summer and had not yet arranged a schedule with his own private patients. Usually any kind of referral by a colleague massaged his ego, but as he hung up, he felt an old anger previously generated by this same Dr. Lacey. It had been another summer's return. From India—eight years ago—the termination of a pilgrimage made to study with the great guru Rajneesh. What David had discovered on that journey had made it difficult for him to resume his place among the pundits of psychoanalysis, and their comfortable solutions. He'd presented the Psychiatric Institute with provisos for his return. The board, with Lacey as its president, had convened to consider them.

Tom Wright, at thirty-five the youngest member of that august body, had sat opposite David at a small table at the Plaza Hotel. Tom squirmed uncomfortably in his institutional gray suit, sparked by a yellow bow tie with small red dots. A slight quaver was in his voice as he spoke.

"Frankly, I felt like the defense lawyer in the case. I even pulled out your résumé and started from the top: Columbia graduate, top honors, first man chosen for Kennedy's mental retardation project—"

"They put you through all that?" David said with some asperity, and removed the cherry from his margarita.

"David, your provisos were just too rich for their blood—too exotic." Wright's fingers drummed against his untouched glass of chardonnay. "Asking them to incorporate Buddhist principles into the practice. What could you have expected from them? Hell, I had to tell them how to pronounce *Rajneesh*, for God's sake."

Wright sipped his wine nervously, then blundered on, "It was the use of drugs, and I quote your letter, 'other mind-altering substances,' that really got to them."

David savored the lingering sweetness of the cherry as a palliative against Wright's negative report.

" 'Exotic,' I like that," David responded with a lame grin.

Wright leaned forward and dropped his voice in a conspiratorial whisper. "You know, I'd really love to schedule a lunch with you and hear more about the effect of those drugs—"

"Then I gather you disagreed with them?" David looked sympathetically at his soon-to-be-late colleague.

"I did what I could, but in the end, Lacey steered things his way." Wright's fingers tightened round his glass.

"I await the coup de grâce with a steady hand," David quipped, and finished his margarita.

"Lacey said, and I quote, 'I think it perhaps wiser for Dr. Sussman to set up his own practice outside the purview of the Institute.'" It was all out at last, and Tom Wright hung his once-tussled head and finished his wine in one defeated gulp.

"Tom, let's have another round to celebrate that decision, shall we?" And David smiled, catching the waiter's eye.

The scene had replayed itself for David. Throwing on his terry-cloth robe, he went into the kitchen to put out the day's rations in the kitty bowl for Sam, his pet Siamese. He went back to the bathroom, and while he shaved, his mother's voice unexpectedly sounded in his ears in a familiar yet comfortable tape loop.

"Look at you, almost tall—five feet eight is almost tall—and with your dark hair and blue eyes—a regular Jewish movie star, so why aren't you famous?"

"Fame isn't everything, Mama."

"So then why aren't you married with three kids?"

She was right about one thing—he should have been settled down, more so than he was. Dr. Lacey's referral had recalled the scene of his dismissal, unfortunately exacerbating a chronic low self-esteem. He looked at himself guardedly in the mirror—his summer tan had made his blue eyes even bluer while covering up two months of subtle depression. At least he'd present a rested face to his patients. Otherwise he was the same old self—the Polish-Russian Jew whose high cheekbones suggested that someone in his family tree had traveled farther east than Moscow. He dutifully pursued the ministrations of dental floss that preserved his near perfect teeth.

"How long will they last?" he asked his reflection. The ears he could do nothing about—the slightly pointed tops reminded him of Franz Kafka. But a small dimple in his chin could charm, and he patted his flat stomach, willingly accepting his mother's estimation of him with kind indulgence. Combing his jet-black hair with nary a sign of forty-four years visible in it, he paused and thought of Lacey again. He had to thank him for one thing, at least. Freed of his constraints at the Institute, David had developed the process therapy he had evolved out of his East-West experiences. It was ironic that Lacey and some of the other old boys of the ancient trade occasionally called him in "odd cases." Amongst them he was affectionately known as "the karma bum." So be it. Yet David detested the Gypsy, tea-leaf, tarot-card mentality of those recommended his way. David didn't doubt that Lacey's present referral would be another such case. Why, oh why, did he let himself in for such put-downs?

Next day, punctually at eleven, Laurel Hunt arrived—in all her grave, apologetic beauty. In her middle thirties, with a Madonna-like face, wearing a half-cape and no makeup, she could have stepped out of a Victorian novel. Fair skinned, blond, with strands of gray, she exuded a natural beauty. Only a flickering Mona Lisa smile hinted at secrets. David offered her tea, which surprised her. Three years of strict Freudian analysis had not prepared her for niceties, at least not from a shrink. Charmed by the offer, Mona Lisa became the girl next door. The smile so enchanted David that for several moments he did not speak. She was dressed in an old-fashioned, beige dress with a string of pearls accentuating the lacework round her décolleté. She seemed avidly interested in David's special approach to therapy. Her own analysis—scrupulously carried through with a female analyst two years earlier—had rung down its curtain after a bitter coda. Unfortunately, Dr. "Mama" had not righted the wrongs of the past, and Laurel Hunt was still smarting from the feeling that she had been scientifically taken. David thought of Lacey and nodded in complicity. All this she revealed in a neutral voice so modulated it could be describing someone else.

As she spoke, her eyes searched the walls for the insignia and diplomas of David's credentials. Finding nothing but two primitive watercolors of flowers, she smiled ruefully, looked directly into David's blues, and asked if he believed in karmic destiny. David was squatting cross-legged on a pillow, smoking a filtered cigarette. He was wearing freshly laundered khaki pants, a bright orange shirt, athletic socks but no shoes. A small votive candle burned in a dish nearby, while behind him on the floor a single daylily rested in a blue vase.

"Well, let's see, karma—according to Eastern thought—is the sphere of influence that rules man's daily existence. Theoretically it is made up of the acts and events that occurred in a previous existence. I said theoretically—"

"You obviously must accept the principles of reincarnation?"

"Well, no, I don't exactly accept it as a belief—if that's what
you mean."

"How do you accept it then?"

"Oh, I guess as part of the materials of psychic history," he
concluded lightly.

He had just pinched out the guttering flame of the votive
candle when she said, "As a piece of psychic history, do you
believe in the existence of malevolent forces? A force operating
above and beyond individual karma?"

As David replaced the candle, he smiled. "What did Dr. Lacey say? What did he tell you about me?"

"Only that you might be able to help me."

"Help you—how?"

"Perhaps you may have read the newspaper account?"

David looked blankly at her. He had canceled his *New York
Times* subscription for the summer and had not renewed it.
Opening her purse, Laurel Hunt produced two cleanly cut
newspaper items. As she handed them to him, he saw her nails
were polished a pale pink. David recognized the "Notes on
People" column. She handed him the one dated August 12.

> Last night an unidentified man in his
> middle to late thirties arrived in shirtsleeves
> during a thunderstorm at the Immaculate
> Conception Hospital in Bridgeport, Con-
> necticut. He entered the reception area rip-
> ping the wet clothes from his body
> screaming, "Please help me! I'm burning
> up!" He collapsed and was promptly sent to
> emergency and put under sedation. His pic-

ture appeared on the local television news, prompting an immediate identification as Hugh Caswell Hunt, the prominent art dealer residing in West Haven. Examination by the medical staff confirmed that nothing of an organic origin explained Hunt's condition. Although tests continue, the patient remains under sedation. Mr. Hunt's reputation as a connoisseur in art circles was established early in his career. He was responsible for the rediscovery and reclamation of paintings belonging to the symbolist movement that sprang from Eastern and Central Europe during the turn of the twentieth century with such artists as James Ensor, Charles Mangen and Leon Spilliaert, among others. His adventurous spirit continues in his search for fresh, new American talent.

The other item was from the London *Times* and was dated August 14. He read through it hastily—it concerned a gruesome murder of one Charles Kirkwood Palfrey, acting head of the Hunt Galleries in London. Palfrey's pajama-clad body had been discovered in a London hotel suite. His tongue had been ripped out of his mouth at the roots. His remains had been flown back to the States for burial. David said nothing as he handed the clipping back to her.

"They're connected," she said.

"What's connected?"

"The murder and my husband's condition—they're connected."

"In what way?"

"The same thing that killed Palfrey is after my husband."

"How do you know that?"

"He told me so."

"He?"

"My husband, Hugh. He's still under observation at the hospital. He's afraid to talk about it to the doctors there for fear they'll think him mad."

David, watching her, thought, *She's not out of Thackeray but Brontë.* "And in your estimation is he? Mad?" David said solemnly.

"No." The answer came back with a snap. "He was driving alone on his way home when he began feeling there was someone following him. He even looked through the rearview mirror—until he sensed the presence right there in the car with him. That's when he first felt the burning sensation in his body and the certainty he was in the grip of something—something monstrous."

"Did he actually use that word, *monstrous*?"

"What would you think, Dr. Sussman? Surely nothing human could have done that to Charles Palfrey."

"I still don't quite understand—what do you expect from me?"

"I don't know. Dr. Lacey merely said your experience would offer some solution."

David put out his cigarette, blew out the last puff of smoke, and squinted at Laurel through the cloud. "Mrs. Hunt, do I look like a witch doctor to you?"

"A witch doctor?"

Growing piqued, David rose. "What about the hospital—surely by now there must be some diagnosis explaining his symptoms?"

"Do you think Dr. Lacey would have called you if there were?"

"I guess not. Well, to answer your question first. No, I do not believe malevolent forces exist—as independent entities or collective ones for that matter."

"Please, I'm sorry if I put things so crudely."

David, arms akimbo, looked at the lady and sighed. *She really believes this garbage.* "Where is Mr. Hunt now?"

"Still at the hospital. He's safe there."

"Safe?"

She looked up at him with startled eyes, and for the first time David saw that they were gray, flecked with a fascinating mixture of blue-green.

"And I suppose you'd like me to see him?"

Laurel Hunt shut her eyes against the taunting offer, then opened them quickly. "I'll make it worth your while."

David walked away, then turned to face her. At that precise moment, he recognized the scent of her perfume. Tatiana. Denise's own brand. How could he have forgotten so soon? What fate had brought this lady into his life at this precise moment? Mumbling something about thinking matters over, he promised to be in touch with her, then politely ushered Laurel Hunt out, closing the door more abruptly than he'd intended.

Just before the summer, he and Denise had parted—angrily, bitterly—and now with this whiff of Tatiana, he realized he'd been mourning her absence in his life. He had coveted Denise too completely, demanding faithfulness while offering no other stability than sex. He still had her last letter from Paris before the summer. He'd kept it in his desk, moving it from one cubbyhole to another. Hopefully he would toss it one day. He had spent a dismal summer trying to get over her.

On top of his own amorous disaffection, what was he to make of this rich lady in distress, ready to slum in the fulsome pastures of the occult? Many con artists were around panhandling Kali and Co.—some even friends and acquaintances. After all these years the whole psychiatric establishment had continued to distort the evidence of his travels to India. On impulse, he was tempted to pick up the phone and give Lacey a good lacing. Instead, forgiving himself his pun, he decided a walk up to Grant's tomb would do his heart and his psyche a world of good.

Poor Beauty, he lamented, thinking of Laurel Hunt—all that expensive couch time and still insisting on magical solutions to life. The best way to get back at the Laceys of the world was to undo their mischief wherever and whenever he could. In truth, it was one of his driving passions. So it came as no surprise to him that he would undertake the deprogramming of this latest derelict of psychoanalysis.

Back in his apartment he first renewed his subscription to *The New York Times,* then systematically called his patients back to resume their own bouts with life's uncertainties.

October

The Immaculate Conception Hospital was a grand relic, built just before the turn of the century. The working staff mirrored the trimmings, a mixture of nuns from a local order and a heterogeneous assortment of interns and students from nearby universities. It had taken David weeks to organize his own practice, and only then had he called the chief of staff and, on the basis of a request for a "second opinion" on the part of the patient's wife, had secured an appointment to see Hugh Hunt. The interview would take place in the psychiatric division where the patient had been transferred.

Hugh Hunt, head of Hunt Galleries Ltd., a multimillion-dollar enterprise with branches in New York, London, and Paris, had until now managed to project a low profile among the piratical ceremonies of Sotheby, Parke-Bernet, and the rising new ateliers of the fine arts. The man who was led in to meet David appeared cool and collected. Only the eyes gave him away—an occasional fluttering behind the irises like tiny wings of terror taking off. The small, bare meeting space, ordinarily an examination room, was pungent with the smell of ammonia and other chemicals—layers of sweet nausea that had accumulated over years, causing the green walls to flake in resignation. Hugh Hunt's patrician bearing was an anomaly in this mean setting of a table, two chairs, a sink, and an old, empty white cabinet. Hunt was lean, blondish, of average height but hardly average good looks. David saw that he was slightly taller than himself. Hunt's thin, tight mouth evinced a bitterness that belied the rest of him. Long lashes framed deep-set, green eyes with a dark dot that lent them an air of mystery and allure. His tapered fingers and high forehead seemed emblematic of a refined intellect and the man's affinity for his chosen profession. David guessed him to be two or three years older than his wife. He wore an expensive black robe of oriental design over his hospital garb. A long, thin yellow dragon with furling tail dominated the back of the garment. The entire impression was unexpectedly theatrical. Hunt's first concern was whether David was "another one of these meddlers," a term embracing policemen and psychiatrists alike. David, playing his advantage, confessed to being neither and offered Hunt a cigarette.

"I thank you. You know smoking is not permitted in the ward." The voice was baritone, cultivated. As David went to light Hunt's cigarette, he noticed the man's hands shook. Hunt inhaled deeply, choking slightly on his next words.

"That's good, that's very good. For this relief much thanks."

"Bernardo to Francisco, *Hamlet,* first scene," David chanced.

"Francisco to Bernardo," Hunt corrected, "which concludes, ' 'Tis bitter cold, and I am sick at heart.' "

David conceded, beginning to feel encouraged by this unexpected bit of confraternity. Shakespeare was one of David's icons.

Hunt inhaled tensely. "Anyway, this will help neutralize the smell of formaldehyde or whatever it is in here. The entire establishment reeks of it."

"Ammonia, primarily."

"Oh! Well, do you suppose it has anything to do with its being a Catholic organization? Sin, bodily corruptions, and disinfectant?"

"Quite possible—although I'm afraid it's the bona fide hospital smell."

"I've never been in hospital before." Hunt's eyes narrowed

and his lips were drawn to a taut line. David's measure was being taken, and he permitted it, with no show of discomfort. "What kind of doctor are you, Dr. Sussman?"

"Well, that's not easy to answer—in so many choice words, that is."

"If you don't minister to the mind or the body, what else is there?"

"The soul—to borrow a catch phrase," David responded blithely.

"Does that imply a belief in a deity?"

"No, not in any mystical context. God as a more generic view of the energy force that balances mind and body, you might say." Hunt was suddenly staring at David with a flat, metallic expression. "I just wanted us to have a little chat." David, beginning to feel a tiny lick of uneasiness, turned on his most beguiling smile.

"Whatever it is, you're wasting your time. I've told them all they need to know—Dr. Whatever-his-name-is in charge here can show you the necessary data."

Hunt's eyes were now positively unnerving. His skin had tightened around his jaw and forehead. A slight smile crept across his face—a smile so slow in completing itself, so stylized in its final effect, as to seem almost separate from the man himself. What was Hunt seeing? David wondered, and continued with some little effort in meeting this chilling scrutiny. Suddenly, David raised his head sharply, acutely aware that a sweet odor had insinuated itself into the chamber. It rapidly grew in density until it reminded him of—yes, the wild and improbable sweet stench of charred flesh. In India, David had witnessed several instances of "suttee," but here? Now? David felt a lump welling at the base of his throat and automatically looked around the room. Hunt's cigarette had fallen from his fingers to the cement floor, but David could see his pajamas and robe had not been singed. Just as suddenly, the sickly disinfectant reasserted itself in the small chamber. A slight shiver passed through David.

"You know, of course, your wife came to see me," David said, breaking the silence. His uneasiness was still evident in his voice—a live nerve end gradually subsiding. He drew on his cigarette and waited for Hunt's response. Another long silence hung between them before David's words penetrated. The mask became a face again—darkening now in a rush of feeling, and forgoing all former effort at composure, Hunt started to moan. An attendant stationed outside opened the door to investigate. David made a commanding gesture, waving him back. David now watched as Hunt put his head down on the table beside him and gave in to a deep-seated grief. As David waited, he began to light up another cigarette. When he struck his match, Hunt looked up and watched the blue-yellow flame with curious fascination. He raised his hand weakly and David offered him another Marlboro. Hunt's hands were now so out of control that he tucked them under his thighs to prevent their shaking. With some difficulty, David placed a lit cigarette into Hunt's mouth. He began to hunch over, rocking himself back and forth. A web of tics flickered across his cheeks and forehead in a relay race at cross-purposes. David lost no more time and, bending over the swaying figure, asked, "Is it true—what your wife told me?"

Letting go an agonizing wail, Hunt looked up at David with a haunted expression. He opened his mouth to speak, but he was now shaking so visibly that the cigarette fell from his lips to the floor. Reaching over to recover it, Hunt lost his balance, and his chair toppled over as he fell. Huddled over as he was, the curving dragon on his back seemed to have taken sudden life: the garment was bunched up over his shoulder so that the creature appeared to be crawling over Hunt's neck toward his chest. Hunt grabbed a table leg to steady himself and continued his rocking motion like a child. Spittle began oozing from the sides of his mouth.

Fearing a possible epileptic seizure, David knelt down in an effort to lower the man to the ground and pry loose the rigid jaw. With a quick lurch Hunt rolled away and collided with the wall nearby. Recoiling from the impact, Hunt started to roll back toward David, and his right cheek accidentally contacted the still burning cigarette on the floor. A frightened-animal snarl resounded in the closed-off chamber. In the next instant, the attendant was grappling with Hunt and found himself flung against the peeling green wall. Two other interns appeared and managed to subdue Hunt, who in his agony was literally bouncing up from the floor, emitting the same animal grunt over and over. David saw them finally slip a straitjacket over him. When they lifted him off the ground, Hunt's mouth was a rictus through which no further sound was heard. He was bundled off into the corridor of the third-floor ward followed by the shaken attendant. The passenger elevator opened as the interns carried their burden. Inside, three nuns, Sisters of Mercy, crossed themselves before stepping out.

David perused the hospital report with mixed feelings. Usually pathology of some sort is evident in such cases of psychic trauma. Yet organically there was absolutely no reason to explain Hunt's condition, nothing pertaining to possible grandmal, brain, or glandular damage, in fact, no dysfunction of any kind. Hunt had been put under pretty heavy sedation for three days—an IM injection of Thorazine, one hundred milligrams repeated every four to six hours as needed. A restraining device had become essential prior to injection. The dosage had been cut to a third thereafter. Three days later the burning sensation disappeared, and Hunt was apparently himself again. Three days after Hunt was admitted into hospital, according to the dates of the London *Times* report, his partner, Palfrey, had been done in. A coincidence, David reasoned, but hardly supportive of occult intervention as Laurel Hunt had intimated. It would have had to be a busy demon. After all, Palfrey had been killed while in London—question: Do demons need visas?

From a psychiatric point of view, Hunt had been examined by a prominent specialist, Hakim Arrabal. Wooing Arrabal from his Menninger Clinic obligations must have taken considerable influence and money.

Dr. Arrabal's summation was simple: he clearly placed Hunt in the incipient stages of a paranoid-schizophrenic withdrawal—and only time would indicate the extent of the problem. Meantime, Hunt was to remain in hospital for further observation.

The psychiatric ward was silent. The attendant at his desk sat reading the local sports column. Hunt was resting quietly, but the effects of the injection were gradually wearing off. A distant smile formed itself gradually across his lips. It lingered briefly, then suddenly erased itself again. If anyone were to sit long enough by his bedside, it would be evident that much was taking place inside the now still body. Hours later the small quickenings signaling the invasion of some savage energy force subsided and finally ended. Hunt's eyes opened widely and seemed to pierce the darkness surrounding him. What they contemplated was a vast stretch of blue sky and the threat coming toward him through its expanse.

Saturday morning found Seventy-second Street and Riverside Drive an almost deserted outpost of the city. A clear sky and empty streets. As he returned from his early-morning walk, David's eyes went up to his eagle's nest of an apartment and the protective heraldic figures—bearded Titans and enchantresses born of Stanford White's imaginings—gracing its upper reaches. In the sunlight, the building's ocher surface with the burnt-umber stripes running up its Georgian facade made a singular old world impact in contrast to the silhouettes of steel and chrome looming against the Jersey sky beyond.

A Mercury Zephyr was parked in front of the Chatsworth. A window was lowered as he passed by. David guessed who was at the wheel.

"Dr. Sussman—I was frantic. You saw my husband yesterday, why didn't you call?"

He stood there at the curb looking in on Laurel Hunt, and there it was again—the scent of Tatiana. He saw she was wearing a blue sweater over a gray shirt; her blouse had the imprint of little blue flowers.

"How could you be sure I was home?" David asked, quite bemused by this encounter.

"I even stopped along the way and called."

"I'm afraid I'm expecting a patient," David lied.

"Patients on Saturday?"

"The psyche doesn't know about the Sabbath."

"Oh, of course, you're Jewish." David, caught in his own contradiction, wasn't quite sure what that was supposed to mean. "Süssman," she pronounced it in German, umlauting sweetly.

"Sussman," David corrected brusquely.

"Whichever way, it is supposed to mean sweet man." She turned from the wheel and looked at him covertly and sighed. "You're angry at me. Why?"

"Why not?" The lady disturbed him. Why?

"I'm sorry." She blushed. "Your doorman said you were out on your daily walk, so I've been waiting here patiently for the last half hour."

David opened the door of the car and sat down beside her. "I have twenty minutes," he said curtly. "As for your husband, he is a very sick man," he concluded bluntly.

"Is that all you have to report?"

"He's not sick in the way you think, however. It's obvious he's had some kind of psychic breakdown. It may be temporary or it—Look I know nothing about him beyond his medical report," David put it squarely.

"What is it you need to know?" Laurel responded gently.

"Well, besides being a tycoon of the arts, who is he?"

"Do I have to go all through that again," Laurel said tiredly.

"No, you don't—"

"Hugh was born in Shanghai," Laurel began with a heavy sigh. "His father was Lewis Caswell, a rare-book dealer, who met his wife in China while searching out an encyclopedia of some ancient dynasty or other."

"Caswell?" David queried. "Where does the Hunt part fit in?"

"His mother was an American, working at the embassy in Shanghai. Caswell took his family to America and then abandoned them for another woman. Hugh was barely six at the time—"

"Would you mind if I smoked?" David asked, pulling out a pack of Marlboros.

"On the contrary." Time was taken for both to light up from a single match. David tossed it out the window.

"So then?" he asked, cracking open the window by his side farther.

Laurel exhaled resignedly. "Yes, well, although Hugh loved his mother very much, she became an alcoholic and within a year was dead—a suicide. Hugh was placed in a foster home, and a year after being admitted, he was adopted by a wealthy Midwestern couple, Wendell and Katherine Hunt, who, and I can recall Hugh's own words, were middle-aged, childless, and looking for a perfect adornment." She exhaled and shut her eyes.

"Did he ever make contact with his actual father after that?" David now seemed caught up in the story.

Laurel brightened for a moment. "Just before his twenty-first birthday, his father unexpectedly showed at Hugh's graduation from Harvard. That was the first and only time. He met his death while crossing the Himalayas in pursuit of some other rare artifact."

"Like father, like son, eh?" David flicked ashes out the window.

"Yes—Hugh became interested in painting and rare objects. By his early thirties, he had acquired, and still possesses, a genuine Turner, previously unlisted in the artist's catalog."

David breathed deeply. "An incredible acquisition. Was it one of his impressionist paintings?"

"Yes." She looked at him. "You have knowledge of such things then?"

"My share"—he smiled graciously—"only don't talk to me about Picasso beyond the blue period."

"I know what you mean." She smiled, wanly, for the first time. "Well, subsequently Hugh's parents helped establish him in his profession. They both now live in Zurich and there's only formal contact."

"What about yourself in all this?"

Laurel put out her cigarette. "We met at a party—and between us, we have produced one child." She persisted in grinding out the cigarette in the car's tiny disposal bin.

"Produced?" David was puzzled. "Odd way to put it."

Laurel leaned back in her seat. "I'd rather not go on with this any longer, if you don't mind. May I ask you a question? Do you agree with the diagnosis presented at the hospital?"

"You were lucky to have Arrabal as a consultant. Who managed that for you?"

"Dr. Lacey, of course."

"Lacey—good old Lacey." David continued flicking ashes.

"Why, is there anything wrong with that?" Laurel's voice had a tinge of alarm in it.

"No—Dr. Lacey commands formidable connections, and frankly, having read Dr. Arrabal's report, there's nothing I can add." David glanced up at her turned-away face in the mirror. Mona Lisa was behind the wheel. "Sorry," he added sympathetically.

"I'm much more sorry than you. I thought you would be able to see what the others, including Dr. Arrabal, are incapable of seeing."

"Mrs. Hunt, my work has to do with the things of this world. That's hard work in itself, believe me," David said tautly.

"But didn't you tell me that Buddhist thought has had great influence on your process technique?"

"Sure, because Buddhism is chiefly about illusion—"

"Illusion?"

"—which in my own flat-footed way means games people play."

"Ah, I take it then everything we do is a game . . . ?"

"Everything. God, the devil—and all the hordes that come from such beliefs. The guilt game being the worst, and the pleasure one the most valuable. That's what my work is about."

"In a nutshell," she taunted. "And the rest?"

"What rest? Oh, ghosts, you mean? That's just imagination, the biggest parlor game of them all. So, in essence, I'm afraid I concur with Arrabal's conclusion." In a subliminal flash, the stench of burning flesh insinuated itself in the car. David turned his face toward the window.

"Perhaps, after all, you have been misrepresented to me, Dr. Sussman."

"Well, it certainly looks that way, doesn't it," he answered flatly.

"So, it's imagination that pursues Hugh Hunt. Imagination that tore out Charley Palfrey's tongue?"

David turned to her, and her scent struck him. The Tatiana was more tantalizing than ever.

"You saw Hugh—and you can still say it is only his imagination?" Her voice rose in challenge.

"A sick one, yes. And as for Mr. Palfrey's death, we have only your husband's supposition, his feelings—and feelings are not facts."

"What did he say to you?" she demanded, her knuckles white against the steering wheel.

"As a matter of fact, very little. Within minutes of starting our interview he had to be forcibly restrained."

"Imagination," she said wearily.

"Fear is a powerful and devastating enemy."

"Did he say anything about me?"

David turned and saw a small vein pulsing rapidly in her temple. The rest was all eyes. Without thinking he said, "Look, I'd like to recommend someone who might be of help. His name is Ara Havakian. He's a psychic reader. One of the best in the field and, well, sort of a friend of mine."

"I thought you didn't believe in such things?"

"I don't, but you do. In his own way, he's helped many people open up doors to their—"

"Imagination," she completed his thought. David felt the hot hand of shame. Why was he twisting this poor, unhappy woman around? He had never recommended anyone to Havakian or his ilk before on any basis. What had provoked this absurd decision? The remembered stench had unsettled him, and Havakian's name had popped up from out of nowhere. He hesitated a moment, but then scribbled Ara's number on a sheet of memo pad and handed it to her.

"You will send me your bill—with expenses included, of course."

"As you like."

"You have my address," she said with a trace of scorn.

"Teach not thy lips such scorn," he quoted in his head, *"for it was made for kissing lady."* Was Richard III to be proved right again? But then look at what had happened to Lady Anne.

David had not spoken to Ara Havakian for over six months—not since the last get-together of the old team. David, Ara, and Peter Mendoza—the three "wise men"—had traveled from separate destinations to meet, not in a stable in Bethlehem, but at an ashram in Pune, India, run by Rajneesh, India's renowned guru. Each had absorbed his wisdom and created new lifestyles. Peter Mendoza with Spectra, an occult bookstore in Greenwich Village, David his therapy on the pleasure principles, and Ara—well, Ara was Ara.

David did not contact Havakian until nine-thirty the next morning, with five minutes to spare before the arrival of his first patient. He had to wait through Ara's unctuous recorded greeting before he could leave his message. "Hello, boychick," Ara responded immediately on hearing David's name. When David announced the reason for his call, Ara practically clapped his hands over the phone. "I knew you had a warm spot in your heart for me, lover, and a real 'name' you give me, too." David suggested that Ara join him for a drink the next day. Having made this faux pas with Havakian, he was intent on getting a square deal for Laurel Hunt.

Ara Havakian was a pint-size (five feet three inches) Levantine Jew who sported custom-made clothes of Edwardian cut. A wart-frog dandy with sparkling eyes and a fabulous set of pearly teeth, he easily dominated any group. At Rajneesh's feet, he had learned that the English poet Swinburne had figured in one of his past-life incarnations. In that light Ara later attributed his psychic gifts as the poetry of his life, much to David's amusement and Peter Mendoza's chagrin. Ara flung himself across his battered couch and flicked on his telephone device. Each move he made was punctuated by one broken spring or other beneath him. "Let's have that drink, boychick," Ara chortled, and waved in the direction of the windows. David located some Drambuie in a pile of otherwise empty bottles, including one of a green liquid detergent. Since divorcing Elsie a year ago, Ara had taken over the housekeeping, which consisted of his rearrangement of the debris from room to room. Elsie's piano, which she had intended to move out to her new home in Meredith, New Jersey, was now barely discernible under the mound of junk on and surrounding it.

How do his clients react to all this? Do they think it "glamorous" or don't they even notice? David wondered. Fortunately, some clean drinking glasses could still be found in the kitchen.

David handed Ara his drink, and the little man flipped the rewind button, clicked in, and there was Laurel Hunt's voice asking for an appointment, with David as reference. Ara studied David's face intently while they listened, and at the conclusion of the message, he winked. He picked up the phone and dialed the Connecticut number she had left. David knew it was hers, because Ara prided himself on never returning long-distance calls, figuring if it was important enough, they would call back. The sofa springs sang discordantly as Ara waited for a connection. David looked away from Ara's Cheshire grin and peered out the window at the boarded-up brownstone across the way. Laurel was instructed to bring photos of her immediate family and several other personal artifacts. David turned to face Ara as an appointment was made for Tuesday, two weeks hence at 11 A.M. "It's the best I can do, boychick." Ara beamed.

Then hung up and dialed a local number. In a flash the original Tuesday client at eleven was shifted to a later date at five. Ara hung up amidst an audible flurry of protest from the other end. The psychic trade was obviously on the upswing if he could afford to be this cavalier with his clientele. David always marveled at Ara for one thing: he kept no appointment book, no scraps of paper. He was a one-man UNIVAC.

Ara flashed a smile. "So, bubee," he asked, "are you still shtupping the French broad?"

David temporized, "Actually, we're temporarily separated. Denise went back to Paris to be with her mother."

Ara nodded in condolence. "Watch out, bubee, she's a high-stepping shtupper. All Frenchies are like that." Ara winked and downed his Drambuie in one gulp.

"Do you speak from experience or what?" David sipped slowly, almost poker-faced.

Ara laughed. "I forgot how jealous you are, lover. No, never had her pleasure."

Jealous? Have I been that transparent?

"So what's the story, boychick, with Laurel Hunt—what gives?" Ara asked amiably.

David filled in Laurel's situation with as much discretion as he felt it warranted. His visit to Bridgeport elicited a raised eyebrow from Ara, who otherwise listened with both hands joined under his chin like a postcard of a Victorian angel framed in a frosted border.

"She believes her husband is being pursued by some 'malevolent' force, as she puts it."

"Has she been visiting Gypsies? Those people stop at nothing with their chicken feathers and voodoo stuff." Ara frowned.

"I don't believe so. This is wrapped up in 'karma' business, or so she says—you get the picture." David felt like some sleazy fortune-teller himself as he rose to fill his glass of whiskey, which needed no refilling.

"So what do I say among my other things," Ara conjectured. "Do I say, 'My dear Mrs. Cunt, there's a dark, blue-eyed man lurking to comfort your karma'?"

"Same old Ara," David said as he picked up the bottle.

"Bubee, you're fucking beautiful. You're turning me into a psychic pimp. But after all, we've got to fill separation with something—nu?"

David tried to drink, but it went down the wrong pipe and he sputtered and coughed.

Ara rose from his chair. "I'll tell you what I'll do," he said, pummeling David's back. "I'll make up a copy of the tape of my session with her. Leave it to me. A friend in needy is a friend indeedy, deedy."

David lost his restraint. Shrugging Ara's hands away, he turned on him in cold fury. "Havakian, you've become a fucking insensitive rug merchant. Drop dead!" Slamming his glass on the bar table, David started for the front door. Ara caught the door before David could slam it. David was about to shout some further obscenity when Ara did an extraordinary thing: he leaned against the wall in the hallway, put his baby-fat hand to his checkered vest, and started twitching his lips as if he were a fish out of water. He closed his eyes for a moment and his face went chalk white. When he spoke, it was a single word.

"What?" David shouted belligerently. And Ara repeated it again, slowly, deliberately.

"Kunma."

"What are you talking about?"

"I don't know. The word came into my head just now while you were shouting at me." Ara was still in his pose against the rose-colored wallpaper, but his eyes were now opened. At first David conceived of this as Ara's little trick of turning the tide. Yet Ara's face remained pasty while his lips were faintly drawn back over his teeth. The sight was grossly sexual, a demi-fop in psychic transport.

No doubt about it, David concluded, Ara was working on him (and for free).

"Kunma—remember that," Ara admonished.

"Okay," David played along momentarily. "What is it, for God's sake?"

"Kunma has nothing to do with God." This said, the color returned to Ara's face.

"What, then? Some indigestible Armenian dish?"

"I don't even know what it means, or what language it is. I only know you must beware of it." The elevator had arrived, and of course by now the wind was out of David's sails.

KUNMA

It was past midnight by the time he made it back home. The apartment felt chilly and David turned on the heater before lighting his last cigarette for the night. Sam jumped up on his lap and David sat there stroking him. Involuntarily, he glanced at the phone on his desk before switching it off. He was half-expecting Ara to call, telling him it was all a perfect put-on. But there was no call, and he would not try to dissuade Laurel from seeing the mighty mite. He rose, feeling the need for a cup of tea before retiring. He felt achy and feared he was coming down with a cold. The silly name came back to him as he waited for the water to boil—"Kunma." What in hell is a Kunma?

The next morning he called Peter Mendoza at his occult bookstore. If anyone would know what *Kunma* meant, it would be Peter, who prided himself on keeping a private dictionary of arcane terms and their definitions. Mendoza's answering device indicated he was out of town and should be back by the end of the week. David left his message anyway: "Peter, when you get back, check out the name or term *Kunma* for me in your dictionary and give me a ring. Thanks."

He had marked Laurel Hunt's appointment with Ara in his own daily diary: November 15. David duly noted it and worked with unusual concentration on that day, taking minimum breaks between patients. Yet the recurrent thought that had plagued him for weeks returned. Had he made a mistake not calling off Laurel's appointment with Ara? Downstairs in the mailbox was a single card from Denise—now traveling the Greek isles—hoping in her insinuating way that she remained "nymph in his orisons." (David had taught her to appreciate

Shakespeare, among other things.) Nymph indeed. David kvetched and, thinking of Greek manhood, he muttered, "Shish kebab," wondering how many Greeks she'd managed to skewer so far.

Oddly there were no calls that morning, so by lunch break David impulsively dialed Ara. David got the answering machine and hung up immediately. During session breaks, David tried again, but he still got the mechanical device. At five, after the last patient for the day, David decided he would wait another half hour for Ara to call and then catch a hamburger on the corner. He needed a break. Between his own and his patients' woes, the collective vibes of the day had become overpowering. Even Sam was acting skittish.

At around four-thirty, Dr. Richard Filer was just about to make his checkup round the psychiatric ward at Immaculate. He was rereading a letter describing his sister's wedding in Buffalo. A tall, morose man of forty-odd years, he was placing the letter back in its envelope when he noticed the screens around Hugh Hunt's bed were vibrating, as if someone or something was shaking them. Filer looked around. None of the others in the ward had noticed this. The patients were either asleep, reading, or lost in their own thoughts. By the time he stood by the bedside, the folds of the screens had ceased their oscillations. Hunt was, of course, still lying there. The intravenous apparatus continued its ministrations. Hunt's left hand moved impercep-tibly, doing flip-flops like a fish in its death throes. Probably in the middle of a dream, Filer thought, but hardly the cause for the movement of the screens. He looked around for an opened window, but there was none. He studied the sleeping man and observed that his head had taken up where the hand had left off. It was beginning to loll back and forth, and the eyelids were starting to flutter—a sure sign he would momentarily awaken.

Ten minutes later, when Filer was about to leave the ward, he saw Hunt sitting up at the side of the bed where a nurse had just completed her examination. As Filer came to the nurse, who was writing down her report, Hunt suddenly hissed like a snake and stuck his tongue out at him. Filer stopped in his tracks for as long as Hunt's tongue was extended. The nurse, preoccupied elsewhere, was not aware of this. Filer had a double reaction: first, that there had been rapid character deterioration during Hunt's coma, and second, that, rather than an affront, the tongue seemed a formal gesture of some kind.

After a quick hamburger at the corner, David started to walk along Riverside Drive. Still tense after his last patient, he would keep going until he was tired, then try Ara again from a phone booth. The weather, slightly brisk up to now, was turning chilly. David began wishing he had on an overcoat instead of just his suede hunting jacket. Indeed, he had eaten nearby with no other plan than that of returning to the eagle's nest.

By the time he had reached Ninety-fourth Street the sky had darkened. The steady rush of black clouds jutted fanglike against the fading light of day. The clouds gathered mass and spread like a hair shirt over the defenseless city. Concurrently, the slumbering beast of an early winter roused itself and roared. David almost recoiled against the blast, but buttoning up, he bent forward and plunged ahead. Above him the naked trees had started warfare. The cracking jousts caused David to look up. He could not believe that those overhanging snakes were the same branches that blessed the city come late spring and summer. He was held by their hideous intertwinings and by the flat slate deadness of the river beyond. David made it to a telephone booth just as the hailstorm hit the streets. Protected in his little shelter, he watched the area being rhythmically pelted by tiny diamonds. He thought of the Beatles and watched the puddle gathering round his feet. The icy darts seemed to be hitting the booth from several directions at once as if he were a special target for their wrath, and the trees continued in their inchoate frenzy. Remembering why he was huddled here in the first place, David dialed Ara's number, but hung up in mid-digit. He couldn't have heard Ara's voice if he had gotten him at the other end.

Ara's place was situated between West End and the river, and there was no canopy, just a skeleton frame of one, chipped and pitted, emblematic of an ongoing decline on Riverside Drive. The West Indian doorman scrutinized David with a heavy-lidded languor. He seemed a sleeping creature in a rumpled maroon uniform, who had scuttled out of the storm to find refuge here himself. No, he had not seen Mr. Havakian either entering or leaving the building, but then he had not been at his post until noon. Some mail was still waiting to be picked up. David glanced at a dark-stained baronial table holding a large package from the Literary Guild (four books for one dollar each—that's Ara's alright) and a roll of letters trussed together by a large rubber band.

The lizard grudgingly set his coffee container down and rang the intercom up to Ara's apartment, but there was no response. David, hanging about the lobby radiator in a fruitless effort to dry himself, remembered Ara saying something about dinner tonight with his former wife. It was just past five, and in all likelihood she would be driving in from New Jersey for their weekly get-together. No, the doorman had not seen her either. David picked up the package of mail and suggested he act as Ara's friendly deliveryman. The lizard blinked disinterestedly.

Ara probably never tips, David concluded, and as the man returned to his coffee, David rang for the elevator. A tight irrational thread of fear began lacing itself up David's spine. As the indicator slowly moved down toward the lobby, his dread escalated. He was forced to put the package down outside Ara's door and take deep breaths—one of his prescribed exercises to induce tranquillity. After ten attempts, David was sufficiently calmed down to proceed. He knocked on Ara's door. Nothing. He looked up at the mezuzah screwed into the doorframe. Behind him the elevator had gone into motion. David tried the doorbell; no sound. He knocked again, then listened at the door. He reached for the knob and turned the handle. Ara's door was open. If Ara was not in, why had he left the door unlocked?

He rang once more to be sure and listened again. Nothing left to do or think, David turned the knob and entered the apartment. It was dark. The rain guttering at the window seemed to be inside the apartment, beating its tattoo over the messes. He listened a long time, then, feeling foolish, turned on the lights. David tentatively called out Ara's name, then set the mail down on a small table next to a dried-out cactus plant. He moved out of the foyer into the living room and on from room to room, calling out before switching on the lights.

The kitchen—"Ara?"

The bedroom—"Ara?"

The den—"Ara?"

"Are you here? Bubee—!" He smelled it as soon as he opened the office door, the unmistakable odor of shit.

The next thing he knew, David found himself retching down a toilet bowl, heaving and splattering the tiles around him as he gagged. His own smell rivaled the one in the other room in human putridity and helplessness. Finally spent, he stretched out on the floor and lay his head against the cold tiles, closing his eyes against the sight now indelibly fixed in his mind's eye.

PART **TWO**

He was in bed with a fever climbing sometimes to 104 degrees—a dangerous place for a grown man to be. For several days, he was vaguely aware of what was going on around him. Mostly he slept; occasionally he drank hot soup delivered from the Famous Deli down the street. The wind seemed to be eternally howling outside his bedroom—echoing in a sinister, shrill key, recalling another time and place. Fleetingly, he worried about his patients. On the third day toward sundown, he had a dream. In it he was digging frantically in the ground with a shovel. Finally Ara emerged, eyes shut—a malefic smile on his face. David placed Ara on his knee and smoothed his tie. Ara then opened his eyes for the first time and said, "Kunma"—like a ventriloquist's dummy. David woke up, touched his cool forehead (the first break in his illness), and thought of the tiles in Ara's bathroom he had begrimed. The memory forced him back into the comforts of sheets already soggy with the worst of his fever. His eyelids hurt as he closed them. Another time he woke feeling a dead weight all over.

Peering down from his splotched pillow, he saw Sam at the foot of his bed—his pupils dilating rapidly in concern for his old man.

He had called the police from Ara's apartment—not daring to go back into the office where the body lay. Later he was taken to a police station, where he was interrogated.

First they took his fingerprints. Next—and this he had never seen or read of in any book or movie—they meticulously scraped his fingernails of all matter onto a sheet of paper, which they carefully sealed in an envelope. The white overhead light hit him then.

"Open your mouth, please," someone said.

"My mouth—you're joking."

"If it's a joke, Mr. Sussman," the voice droned on, "this examination might supply us with a punch line. Open please." *The precinct's obligatory wit,* David thought, and complied. His teeth and gums were studiously probed for further "incriminating debris." "Personally, I could never eat brains," another man's voice was heard from somewhere behind him. "My wife considers them a delicacy." It took everything for David to keep his mouth open.

A large plainclothesman hovering in the shadow of the lights' glare, took up the questioning. "You didn't turn on his office light right away—is that right?"

"No—er—Mr.—"

"Scarpino."

"No, I saw—him—Ara seated with his back toward me. He sat rigidly. He was surrounded by his equipment." And a hand passed over some black coffee in a paper cup.

"How did you know what it was if it was so dark?"

"Ara and I go back many years." As David sipped the coffee, his fingers sought warmth from the cup.

"We can explore that later." Scarpino pursued, "Let's just stick to the moment, Doc."

Doc—they had been calling him Doc, like the benign old codger in a small-town-USA movie.

The interrogator stepped into the light. David looked up at him. The man pulled back his lips in what seemed to David some characteristic gesture, exposing a space between his upper front teeth. He then shut his lips again. "Just tell us what happened next, Doc," he cajoled.

David put down his cup. "Well, I . . . approached Ara. I called out to him, but he didn't answer. So I touched him on the shoulder."

"Why did you do that?" Scarpino leaned forward in a friendly gesture.

"The swivel chair Ara sat on seemed to turn by itself." There was a long pause as David began sipping at his coffee cup. Again, he suddenly became aware of the other men arranged round the room in a classic police tableau of feigned indifference. David swallowed.

"Ara's head seemed to separate from his body . . . and . . . it fell . . . landing at my feet. He . . . the head was looking up at me. I think there must still be traces of his blood on my shoes." Someone stepped out of the tableau and gently removed his shoes. David could only hope that his socks had no holes in them. His feet touched a cold surface beneath them.

Scarpino repeated his lip bite and nodded for David to continue.

"Ara's mouth . . . was opened . . . and," he stammered, "there . . . there was no . . . tongue in it."

"You could tell that, even in the dark? Doc, you got some pair of eyes." Scarpino rubbed his chin.

"Yes, oddly, I do. And Ara's own eyes were wide-open. They were glassy, in fact."

"So what did you do?" Scarpino said quickly.

"I just . . . stood there." The policeman who had examined David's shoes was now whispering something in the ear of Scarpino, who in turn readdressed David.

"Doc, it looks like there's more than blood on your shoes. What could that be now?"

David's mouth went dry.

"Did you notice anything else?" Scarpino continued.

"Yes. Ara's bow tie was still . . . gracefully knotted to his . . . neck."

Later David was driven home, wearing a pair of oversize slippers found in a locker. His shoes had been retained as evidence. He was told not to leave town while the investigation continued. Until proven otherwise, he would be considered a suspect in Ara's murder. Motive: professional jealousy.

Oh, God—Lacey, Laurel Hunt, and now this unthinkable insult. Emotionally drained, David managed to laugh weakly at the farrago confronting him, but no one in the car was sympathetic.

On Friday morning, David was completely out of danger, but his brown suede jacket and pants, soaked in the rain, were almost unsalvageable. His evidentiary shoes had been returned, spit-polished, and summarily dumped down the incinerator. The week's newspapers had piled up during his illness, and the gruesome murder had naturally usurped the headlines. David was apparently off any suspect list. Most ominously, the forensic report implied that something other than a human agent was at work. The mouth and cranial damage had helped establish the time of Ara's death to be around 4 or 4:30 P.M. (David had literally just missed meeting the killer or killers face-to-face.) An autopsy reported no internal pathology. A medium amount of alcohol was found in Ara's bloodstream. There had been no forced entry (the door was opened), no attempted robbery, no sign of struggle. Ara had "soiled" himself (*The Times* spared no details) and Ara's skull had been cut through "as if it were a grapefruit"—the animal-like nature of the assailant was suggested by the canine-like incisor marks left on the brain. No blunt instrument or weapon of any kind could have caused the head wound without leaving residues of blood and cranial matter in the immediate vicinity. The severed parts of the brain had not to date been found. The image of huge ivory teeth insinuated itself in David's mind—where, oh, where, had he seen them?

Unfortunately, since Ara had kept all records of his activities in his head, it was impossible to trace the identities of the patients who had sought his ministrations on the day of the tragedy. The police commissioner made a plea in the local newspapers to all people who could be helpful with information leading to the apprehension of Dr. Havakian's killer. The only valuable discovery lay in a cabinet full of cassette tapes recorded by Ara during his interviews.

David wondered if Laurel Hunt had kept her appointment with Ara that morning. And if so, would she "declare" herself to the police? David switched on the phone extension in his bedroom for the first time in three days. The answering service was swamped with messages, but David's first call was to the Immaculate Conception Hospital, where he contacted Dr. Filer on his last tour of inspection in the psychiatric division. Filer informed David that Hunt's burning sensations had reoccurred but had left his body on Monday evening, and for the moment his condition was stable. David hung up feeling weirdly apprehensive. Monday. The third day he was himself again—as with Palfrey. And . . . ?

By Saturday noon (his first full day on his feet), all of David's patients were contacted and ready to get back to the fold in the upcoming week. By lunchtime, a new wrinkle presented itself to the convalescent. It came in the form of a call from Precinct 24.

"How yuh doin', Doc? Sergeant Scarpino here."

"And to what do I owe the honor of this call?"

"Well, we been kinda worried about you. I mean, you didn't look too good that night when we had you down the—"

"I appreciate your concern, Sergeant Scarpino."

"Like I said, no hard feelings. I hope—"

"Well, I don't quite know how to answer that. I suppose if I hadn't been detained, I might not have fallen ill and lost a week's work."

"Jeez, I'm sorry about that, Dr. Sussman," Scarpino replied in his best professional manner.

"Suppose I could sue the city, send them a bill—who do I address it to?"

"Well, sure, Doc, you could try."

"That means I wouldn't get very far, would I?"

"No, but I know what's the next best thing."

"What's that?"

"How would you like to work for the city?"

"How would I what?"

It seems Elsie Havakian, née Stern, inveigled to help sift through Ara's tapes and decode the material, had broken down after several days and found herself unable to continue. On her recommendation, David (as Ara's reinstated friend and colleague) was being pressed into service.

"You name the fee, Doc, and I'll take it up with the commissioner." Against his better judgment, David accepted.

David shared a large can of tuna with Sam, and only after washing the dishes and smoking his first cigarette in days did he decide to call Laurel Hunt. There was no answer at either of her numbers. An hour later he reached a maid in Connecticut who did not know where her mistress was. David left no message. He paused before rising: the scent of Laurel's Tatiana had once more beguiled his senses. He had no idea what message he would have left.

Sunday was not to be a day of rest for David. By 10 A.M. he was flying on high energy—the first return to his former self. He would face his initial bout with Ara's tapes that afternoon. But now, spread out in front of him was the centerfold of *The New York Times Magazine*. He had let out a whoop of astonishment, for there it was in living color—the illusive image he'd been connecting with Ara's murder. The Tolos monster! Someone from Asia House, spurred on by a description of Ara's death, had dug up a reproduction of this ancient god of wrath and forwarded it to *The Times*. The scene, of Tibetan origin, comprised part of a temple mural. The detail reproduced isolated a mythic half-man, half-beast, savagely gnawing on a man's skull while he lay insensate in the monster's grip.

Some snappy editor had done a little chapter-heading re-search, and accompanying the reproduction was an abbreviated history of cannibalism as practiced by a pre-Buddhist sect known as Bon Po. David felt enormously relieved to have his scattered pieces of nightmare coalesce into a tangible whole. He was uncertain where he had first encountered the vision, seeing it now in comparative miniature. Since Ara's murder it had assumed gigantic proportions in his mind, almost as if he had witnessed it in the flesh. The original fresco now rested in a museum in Peking. David had never been to Peking, so how could he have seen it? A reproduction perhaps? Certainly. He had first attached the memory in an Aztec context. The beast's headdress suggested plumage of some sort—instead of an ivory collar. But Aztec ceremonies centered around the heart—that scalding muscle ripped out of human chests by priests with obsidian knives. Strangely, the heart did not seem to figure prominently in oriental butcheries.

Considering cannibalism as a whole, he conjectured, was the tongue the pâté de foie gras of some religion? The tongues of buffaloes were considered high-grade stuff among the American Plains Indians. What about the female breast, the male cock—who ate those? His anthropology was shadowy on these points. It was certain that the parts were eaten in an attempt to gain their intrinsic power by ingestion. Quasi affectation in the over-all scheme, for the cause-and-effect principle underlying can-nibalism was pure hunger, not the metaphysical variety but plain old starvation—lack of manna, animal meats, fish, etc. Besides, what better way to thin out the population and, accordingly, competition? There was always some method to otherwise unexplained madness—and since mankind was ever resourceful and quick to exculpate itself for its primal hungers, it invented deities to take the brunt of the blame.

As if in an unexpected close-up, the Tolos monster's mandibles sprang at him. He even imagined the black streaks of decay marring the ivory's surface and was forced to look away from this hallucination.

By the time David had plowed through a dozen of Ara's taped interviews, he was convinced the little toad was a genius. Ara could have made a fortune writing paperback thrillers, so fecund and serpentine was his mind at improvising and constructing past lives . . . at $125 a throw. Ara's method was not to make his clients aware they were being recorded. A duplicitous technique, but then anything goes in the underbelly of occult industries.

By the end of the first day, working in a cluttered office set aside for him at Precinct 24, David had supplemented Elsie's skimpy report with three yellow pads of his own. Somewhere in these stacks would be a little plastic tale bearing Laurel's name.

The next day, his own name was in the morning papers: "Dr. David Susman, friend and colleague of the deceased, has been brought into the case to apply his expert knowledge in"— etc., etc. Friend and colleague indeed. Worse yet, they had misspelled his surname. For some reason, he thought of Denise. He wondered if she might come across the item somewhere in her travels. However erratic she was in her human relations, she was punctilious about her *Herald Tribune,* which in her wonderfully egocentric way she considered her personal tie-line with friends throughout the world. Never mind, the *Times* article with the misspelled name had a good picture of him, so he'd send the clipping to his mother in Baltimore, who would show it to his three married sisters, who loved him, didn't believe he was past forty, and thought anything he did was glamorous, therefore better.

By early evening, Laurel's tape had not yet shown up, and Ara had been running a dry spell—too many monks, frustrated painters, Chinese shopkeepers, and practically every other client was from Atlantis.

By the time David reached home around 3 A.M., he was exhausted. He was sitting in his kitchen, warming up the last of the chicken soup, when the phone rang. Instinctively he knew who would be calling.

"Doctor, I'm sorry to call so late, but I've been trying to reach you all day."

"Well, you've reached me."

"I need to see you. It's important." Laurel Hunt's voice was low, urgent, as if she didn't wish to be overheard.

"I have a cancellation tomorrow at three."

"Thank you. I'll be there." She hung up.

Automatically David knew it had something to do with the tapes. He couldn't help wondering, in any event, would the meeting be another prelude to more cock tease?

Do I invite such behavior? he thought. *Of course I do. I always have—and, face it, I thrive on it.* A connection had been set up between Laurel Hunt and himself. A connection not related to her as a patient.

Laurel arrived in pouring rain. David watched from the window as she parked across the street. She sloshed through a puddle before hitting the Chatsworth lobby. David suggested she remove her shoes and stockings and allow them to dry while they talked. He went into his bedroom to fetch the heater, and while he poured hot water over the tea leaves, he did his breathing exercise to quiet himself down. At the first sight of Laurel, Sam went into the kitchen and remained near his litter box, watching David critically. Somehow the sight of the little animal's disdain did the trick, and within minutes he was pouring with great aplomb.

Laurel had tucked her legs under her large pillow on the floor. Progress, David observed. He had not quite finished pouring when she spoke.

"I saw your—Mr. Havakian. As he requested, I brought some photos. A picture of Hugh, my son Chris, my father." David heard her voice drop. "And another of Hugh and myself together." A meaningful pause. "I've never been to a psychic before. Mrs. Feinninger would die if she knew." Laurel buried a quick blush behind the back of her hand. "In fact, I've never been to any of these—I was about to say *charlatans*—but I suppose I would mean it in the classic sense." Naturally, David wondered if he was included in that pantheon.

She took two deep swallows of tea.

"I must admit, Dr. Sussman, I felt angry at you for putting me in this situation. Palming off the hysterical rich lady. Yes, I'm sorry, but I did think that, and several other unmentionable things. After all, when you consider your friend—and his way of living—I thought, frankly, I was in the midst of some prearranged charade."

Somehow the confirmation of her snobbery, rather than having a dampening effect, excited David more. It intensified an air of intimacy that was gathering between them.

She uncurled her legs languidly; to David, it seemed provocatively. *My God,* he thought, *the connection he had felt toward her was mutual. He was certain of it. Or was this merely her usual behavior around men?* She continued in her cool, level manner, "He explained about listening to my voice and commenting as he saw fit. I didn't know what he meant or where to start. I wanted to blurt out everything, my fears, my disgust at being there even, but, as always, I hedged, went schoolgirlish, started that silly résumé of my life.

"You know what I mean—and before I knew what was going on, he started talking about my past lives. I hope you won't take offense, but what was I to make of this incredible parade of nuns and queens I had been?" She had obviously brought out the worst in Ara.

"He even designated times and places, everywhere from Spain to the Near East. I was embarrassed for the poor man."

"Just an overactive imagination," David proposed kindly.

"Ah, we're back to that again." She laughed her sad laugh and looked away. "Finally he asked to see my photographs. He looked at all of them collectively, then, pointing to one, he said, 'Eighteen fifty-nine.'"

"Did that strike any bell?"

"No! I couldn't even see which picture he was referring to. I thought I was going to be in for another historic revelation."

"Instead?" David urged her on.

"He did something funny with his lips—comic really—closed his eyes and said . . ." Long pause.

"What? What did he say?" David's heart skipped a beat.

"I don't know. Something odd—beginning with a *C* or *K*—"

"Kunma."

"How did you know?"

"What else did he say?"

"That I was to become involved with this Kunma person or thing."

The little bastard, exploded in David's head—Ara had been putting both of them on. "Is that all he said?" David resumed quietly.

"Yes. And by this time I had absolutely no desire to ask his help in any other way."

"What did you do?"

"I left. I just couldn't take any more of it. He kept grinning as he made these ridiculous pronouncements. How could I take him seriously? The next day I read about the—the tapes. Isn't that rather illegal?"

Not a word about the murder. What was she hiding? "So you never got to the heart of the matter?"

"You haven't answered my question. How did you know that name?"

"I'll tell you when you tell me what really happened."

"Could I have a cigarette?" She stalled and, uncurling her legs again, drew them up, rested on her knees, and struck a pose. David, encouraged, lit her cigarette from his own. Their fingers had touched and lingered together briefly before she leaned back. *Amazing*, David thought, *how much one can read in a touch as brief as theirs.*

"What makes you think there was something more?" She spoke as if there had been no break in their conversation.

"Well, then, why come back to me if that's all there was to it? You sounded urgent last night."

"Did I?"

Another long pause. He wanted to reach out and touch her again. Find any excuse to do so, but he could find none. Instead, he bantered foolishly, "And, right now, a pause is a pause is a pause."

" 'Rose,' she said."

"What?"

" 'A rose is a rose is a rose.' Gertrude Stein."

"She was a lesbian, you know." *What a stupid thing to say.*

"What difference does that make?"

"No difference. Go on."

"He said something rather silly." She smiled aloofly and lifted her cigarette. "Yes. He said I'd been having an affair."

"In a past life? With a lesbian?" David smiled sheepishly. *More stupidity. Stop it.*

"With a dark-haired man of medium height."

David was not sure whether he should feel apoplectic at Ara's shade, or thankful. *I'll start believing in such stuff if I don't watch out. But do I want to watch out?*

"Was that Spain? Or the Far East?" he played on.

"Neither. Manhattan."

"Ah—1859?"

"No—1978."

"I see—you managed to get that far? 'Seventy-eight—'79—"

" 'Eighty," she interrupted. The trapped angel was becoming defiant. He could feel her wings fluttering all around him. "It was another one of his revelations you see."

"And, was it true?"

"What difference would it make?"

"Well, you brought it up."

"No, he brought it up."

"Look, you obviously get your morning paper delivered to your doorstep? Isn't that why you came?" Still no mention of Ara's death. David was determined to find that tape tonight, if it took all night.

"Then you've heard it," she said simply.

"I'm afraid so," he lied.

"Where is it now?"

"In my office at police headquarters."

"Has . . . has anyone else . . ."

"Not yet." She looked up, poised to strike. He looked levelly at her. "I wanted to talk to you first."

"Charley Palfrey meant absolutely nothing to me—he was simply there, and he was sympathetic."

"Palfrey." He hid his shock. " 'Seventy-eight, '79, '80. Pretty steady for a—"

"Charley was bi—not that it matters anymore, poor darling. Oh, he'd admitted his ambivalence to me—and the fact he'd always had an unrequited passion for Hugh. That's what kept him devoted to the galleries and . . ."

"To you."

"Yes." She drew the word out hesitantly. "He knew all about Hugh and me. The kind of nonlife we led—separate when together, together when separate. I met Hugh in Ottawa of all places. He'd come to check the single Turner canvas they have in their little museum up there. The thought he would come there just for that amused me vastly. And some musical occasion was being celebrated at the French embassy. Hugh took mercy on my shyness and started telling me how the embassy building we were in had originally been designed for Peking, China." *Peking again*, David thought. "Instead Peking got the building meant for Ottawa and vice versa." She paused, lost in the memory. "We were married three months later in New Mexico where Papa Champ, my father that is, lives."

"When did it go wrong?"

"Up until Christopher was born, it was almost perfect. By then, we'd even been around the world two times."

"Why did the boy make the difference?"

"It's hard to say, but it did. Hugh's a very good father, yet very strict, very demanding. His high standards of being a gentleman he's bestowed on Chris. And yet, it's as if Chris must be everything else Hugh fears he's not."

"And that is . . . ?"

"Strong, aggressive."

"Hugh isn't then . . ."

"He is—and yet, he isn't. I suppose it's his way of ensuring his own son's destiny in a way his was not."

"I take it you don't approve?"

"I love Chris, but you see—a year after his birth, Hugh stopped sleeping with me . . ."

"Enter Palfrey?"

"No—he—that came later. Funny, when it did, I had this terrible feeling I was being drawn to him because of his love for Hugh."

David raised his eyebrows.

"Yes. I didn't realize it then, until the analysis."

"Of course."

"As for the rest of it . . ." She closed her eyes against whatever it was and clenched her jaw. For a brief moment, she resembled Hunt before his seizure. Suddenly her face flushed a deep crimson. She picked up her stockings and, turning her back to David, put them on.

"I hope they're dry." David said, and automatically turned away, in some vestige of modesty. "Where will you be around midnight, tonight?"

"At my apartment in town, why?"

"Wait there, till I call."

They looked at one another, collusion riding the air between them. And something else, which caused David to swallow hard. Laurel was out the door before another word was exchanged. Only then was he hit by the full implication of what he was planning to do. Sam was looking up at him, his paws on his trouser leg, a sure sign he wanted something—but then, who didn't?

Within two hours after resuming his duties at the precinct, David had Laurel's tape in his hands. He had been rifling through the remaining cassettes, starting and stopping almost instantly, till he found the right one. Anyone looking in at him through the dirty glass partition would have had the impression the room contained a whirling dervish. But it was a slow night and his redoubled activity went unnoticed. When at last he had it in hand, he sat down not quite knowing what the next step should be. He knew he meant to steal it, and the repercussions laid a cold hand over his heart. If he took it, he would be guilty of withholding vital evidence that could just about ruin him—if he was caught. And why? Admit it. For a woman he'd become attracted to. Was he imagining he could buy her favors with this ludicrous bit of Mylar? He felt like a lousy baritone villain in some Italian opera. Had he turned that desperate? In obsession there was no temperate zone, and besides, Laurel Hunt was a married woman. Was he setting himself up for another awful letdown? Was that to be the continuing regimen of his life? And this tiny cassette, the beginning of the next spiraling downward? He was terrified as he contemplated the questions that could eventually undermine the foundations of his life and the tenets of his work. He suddenly sat down at his desk at the impact of his next thought. He had just seen the true nature of his "connection." Attraction was sharpening into something more involving, and even threatening.

I wish I could tear myself up sometimes and rescramble the pieces, he thought, and slipped the cassette into his briefcase.

Filling in his report for the evening, he pleaded fatigue and bade good-night to the sleepy officer at the front desk, hours before his usual 2 A.M. curfew.

Back in his apartment, David locked himself in his bedroom, turned on the heater, and prepared himself to face the real Laurel Hunt. Strange that he would suddenly be attributing the word *real* to anything concerning Ara's work. But he had been caught up in the tide of events, and something inside him was already prepared for the worst.

He had gone through a half pack of cigarettes by the time he'd played through the cassette twice. Keeping his voice under control, he dialed her New York number and told her she could come by immediately.

From the evidence of the tape, Laurel Hunt, victim extraordinaire of a failed marriage, had systematically celebrated its failure in an orgy of promiscuity. This knowledge suddenly threw him into an inexplicable torment. Not even Denise had evoked such a strange mixture of tenderness, desire, and plain fury.

The moment Laurel entered his apartment, he struck her across the face. He was appalled at his reaction, but there it was. Laurel didn't seem a bit surprised. She was almost relieved. The anticipated blow had finally fallen. She sobbed, making a series of low self-debasing sounds at the base of her throat. The anguish was deep, convulsive, the fruition of a hundred little preliminaries tapping at a well of despair. A trickle of blood appeared at the corner of her mouth, and it was David's turn to become unstrung. He had never struck a woman before, even Denise, who had provoked him most of all. He hustled Laurel into his bedroom, sat her on the bed, and fetched a wet towel from the adjoining bathroom. Laurel sustained her weeping as David wiped her lips and chin. Laurel grabbed him around the waist and buried her head in his belly. She tried to get up, but David was easing her down. She made a furtive grab at him and suddenly both fell backward onto the bed. Sam, who had been lurking in the background, just as quickly leaped up beside the fallen pair. Laurel let go her grip on David for a moment and flailed out at the Siamese. David, his anger erupting in full fury, spun her onto her back, pinned her down by the shoulders—forcing her to look up at him. The gray-green irises were clouded with fear. David covered her mouth with his own. Automatically, his tongue pushed its way past the pearly teeth and did its intended business.

David, inflamed, handled Laurel as if she were a lifeless man-

nequin. His hands worked on both their garments simultaneously. The mannequin, who had clearly given her consent, lay
there, waiting, her head turned away. David's erection, freed of
the final constraint of undershorts, literally slapped his belly.
Laurel's hands leapt forward and covered his genitals completely, holding him throbbing against her palms as if to draw
out their energy. Slowly, Laurel slipped down, under David's
body, and began her private litany of pleasure.

David had not been with a woman since Denise had deserted
their little pretend nest, but where Denise was a calculated and
efficient Baedeker of the available manuals, this little Catholic
girl was all unthrottled instinct. He had not experienced anything so all-encompassing since India.

The tables had been reversed. He who had started to ravage
was, in turn, being ravaged. Her slim, pink nails brushed his
skin and her steady, pulsing tongue darted and caressed. Her
mouth was everywhere. His skin tingled as his belly spiraled in
the first bloom of release and a startled sound escaped his lips.
In response, she leaned back and slowly spread her legs under
him. She had been prepared for this, even before her arrival at
his apartment. David's attraction had, indeed, been mutual.
How mutual? But the future of such speculations was overwhelmed as he moved against her, his mouth embracing her
nipples. They moved easily against one another and her hands
held his buttocks in a firm grip. He withheld his charge against
all of life's disappointments and cruelties until she leaned over
the bed, her head dangling, hair flowing, and only then did he
pulse home.

———

Afterward they lay there, listening to the wind moaning off the river.

"Strange," she murmured.

"What?" His cigarette glowed in the dark.

"I was thinking of my marriage."

"Thank you very much."

"No, it's just that Hugh would never permit what happened tonight between us to take place."

David passed the cigarette over to her.

"Funny, we never ever discussed sex—in any way. It was all . . . well, as if it were part of the organized schedule of his life, so much time allotted and no more." She inhaled and the smoke curled like tiny wraiths toward the ceiling. "Yet, to look at us, our life together, we were like a wonderful piece of porcelain. Only the most practiced eye could discern the indiscernible crack."

She exhaled again. "Gradually, as I learned about his background, I began to understand a little more. He tried to keep all that a secret, but Hugh, it seemed, told my father things about himself he would never mention to me. I found that odd."

"Really? I find it rather typical."

"Of what?"

"Marriage."

"Is that meant to comfort me?"

"No. It's true. Perhaps your husband regarded your father as a surrogate parent figure. That often happens in marriage, too."

"Well, I wouldn't know. I don't know much about marriage.

Least of all my own. I have no women friends, no one that I can really talk to about such things. Oh, I'm on a lot of committees but . . ." The sentence was completed by a sigh as she handed back his cigarette.

"The summer always brought out the best in Hugh, at least at the ranch. Somehow the open air suited him. That is such an anomaly for a man who spends most of his time in galleries and art sweatshops. If I go out into the sun, I have to arm myself with lotions, big hats, and things. My skin can't take the sun." David reached across and caressed her buttocks.

"Hugh insisted I go with him everywhere while we were in New Mexico. Then when we got to wherever, he'd leave the car and go exploring in the mountains while I remained in the station wagon. Have you ever experienced the August sun in New Mexico?"

"I've never been to New Mexico."

"It's an extraordinary place. The air in the mountains is so dry, so thin, and the sun so blistering."

"I'd stay inside the car with you"—David smiled in the dark—"with the air-conditioning on."

"I used to think I knew all the ins and outs of Peso d'Oro— that's part of the Sierra range. I was brought up in its shadow. But toward the last weeks of summer, Hugh would always ask me to pack a lunch. He'd work his way deeper into the hills than I'd ever been, then suddenly stop in the midst of what seemed nowhere, grab his camera equipment, and scramble up to the mesa. This happened three summers in a row."

"What was up there—the treasure of Sierra Madre?"

"Condors and vultures."

"Vultures?"

"He spent hours photographing them in their native habitat. Places I didn't know existed. He'd already filled several large scrapbooks with very artful studies of these grotesque creatures. Once I put on my hat and decided I'd climb up with him and watch. My heart was in my throat. I'll never forget the sight or smell of those scavengers. Creatures herded together in a kind of restless harmony—totally unmindful of the solitary man moving cunningly into their midst to study and record. After that first time, I just waited in the car till he was through. Soon enough I'd hear a booming sound and I knew that meant the flock had taken off—to some distant carnage somewhere, I used to imagine. Then Hugh would come back dusty and smiling and we'd have our drinks in the car."

"Was it a hobby or . . . ?"

"Well, I suppose you could call it that. Later on the Smithsonian and *National Geographic* people saw some of his pictures and featured them in their magazines. I think Hugh was prouder of that than when he acquired a new Pissarro or Sisley. God!"

"What's the matter?"

"One of those summers when Chris was six years old and Hugh had insisted on his going on one of these expeditions . . . Well, Chris told me later that he found the high croaking sounds the birds made to be rather funny. Playfully, he started to throw stones at them—at six you're afraid of nothing. And so he ran toward one of the huddled mass of birds, tripped, and fell. His knees were bloodied, and as he lay there on the plateau, crying in pain, his father was forced to rescue him from a group of birds who were moving in."

"How did he do that?"

"I forgot to mention that Hugh brought a rifle along with him on these occasions. It must have been ghastly. Poor Chrissy. Poor baby. Since that time Hugh never returned to that spot. In fact, he never came back to Taos again."

"When did this happen?"

"Six years ago. I think the incident frightened Hugh. Chris, after a little disinfectant and a Coke, was very much himself, but his father went around for days looking as if he'd seen a ghost. He could hardly wait for us to pack and leave. That winter was when I started feeling totally superfluous in his life. Of course, being Catholics, divorce was impossible. Yet we determined to stay together for Chris's sake. Out of duty for our son's welfare. It was then that it—well . . ."

"Ah, it happened, 'the winter of your discontent made glorious summer by this sun of York.'"

"What's that supposed to mean?"

"I was referring to Palfrey—and the start of your . . ." He didn't add *adultery*. She hadn't recognized the quote from *Richard III*. Shakespeare with Denise—soon with Laurel, he hoped.

"Hugh started to stay away on business trips most of the time after that, and I had stopped imposing myself on him that way. Charley Palfrey took over the New York gallery about then."

Laurel went silent for a long while and David did not press her. All during her bizarre recollection, one thought kept surfacing and resurfacing in David's mind: Ara's murder and the tape. Not once had she mentioned either.

"Last summer Chris was away at camp," she resumed. "Hugh was abroad so I decided to spend August with Papa Champ. Nothing was working for me—in any department—and I'd become deeply depressed. My analyst had gone off on vacation and I was in no mood to talk to a surrogate doctor. I was at the ranch only twenty-four hours before I told my father everything." Her rueful sigh was complemented by the rattle of the exhaust fan in the john played on by the wind.

"How did he take it?"

"He told me I must find a way to 'manage.' As if I hadn't been doing exactly that. He simply set his jaw and wouldn't pursue the conversation. When I tried to, he went into his den, slammed the door, locking me out."

"What's his problem?"

"My mother. But that's another long story. The point is he would hear nothing negative said against his favorite son-in-law. I went completely hysterical and then he opened the door and warned me he'd cut me off without a penny if I did anything to threaten the security of my marriage."

"How much of this does Hugh know?"

"I'm not sure. God, once I casually mentioned the infidelity of a business acquaintance. He absolutely petrified me by his reaction."

What would he make of this present situation? And a shard of guilt hit David squarely. In complement, Laurel's voice continued her complaints: "It's all my fault. You see, everything that's happened to Hugh is my fault!" She went pale, and her voice suddenly rose to a high wail, thinning out to nothing. She struck at her naked flesh with her fists. She rose precipitously and huddled in the armchair nearby.

"It will happen to you, you know. What's happened to the others. What happened to that terrible little man with his silly visions—oh, God!"

There it is at last.

David sat up and put out his cigarette, his eyes trying to pierce the shadows where she remained hidden.

"What do you want me to do with the tape?" David asked with forced deliberation.

"Give it to the police. Let everyone know."

"You don't mean that."

"Yes! It will be a relief." Her voice was filled with self-loathing. She suddenly rushed out of the shadows into David's arms.

"No! No! I don't. I don't. Hold me, David. Please hold me." He cradled her tenderly.

"What are we going to do?" David murmured in her ear. "Will this be it—or what? What?"

She pulled back and looked at him with fierce eyes burning into his. "This is not just it, and we both knew that from the very first day." She then dug her nails into his shoulders and sobbed. The sound was of a lost child finding herself home again.

David kissed her gently, then placed a finger on the side of her mouth, where she had bled. "Forgive me. I will never do that again." After a while she was quiet and they made love before she fell asleep.

The wind had subsided and an unexpected mist was thickening outside the bedroom windows. The river had all but disappeared under its mantle. He trembled both in his own nakedness and for her. They had both put deep claims on one another, and yet, she was operating on the lowest level of superstition imaginable, learned in childhood. It could eventually drown her if she permitted it to. He emptied his head of all thought and climbed into bed. He kissed her gently on the cheek and imagined himself her champion-to-be in some as yet unknown contest. Comforted by that thought, he fell asleep almost immediately.

David awakened like a shot. Laurel was not lying beside him. She had gone. Her scent rose up at him from the sheets and he felt the kick of his longing. On the table by her side of the bed was a note: "You'll be with me all day. L." As he placed the note on his desk, he caught sight of the tape resting on its edge by the armoire.

Christopher Hunt stood staring down from his bedroom window into the tangle of bushes and trees adjacent to the big house. From the second floor he could see the large pond that separated the Hunt estate from the dense woodlands of an adjoining property long gone to seed. Somewhere in its thickets was a rambling Tudor manor. No one had lived there for as long as Christopher could remember. It was early twilight and Chris was squinting against the rapidly setting sun. He was big for his twelve years—big, but light of build, with his mother's tapering oval face and pale green eyes. His blond hair was thick but unruly. He wore his maroon shirt outside his tan corduroy trousers. It was the style at the West Haven Academy for young gentlemen of good families. The influence of his father and the training at school had produced a sterling example in Chris.

He had put on his loafers and gone down to the pond soon after Tripp had left. Chris had beaten him in three straight sets of Ping-Pong, and rather than face another shellacking, Tripp had taken off for home, claiming an overload of homework. Tripp was Chris's best friend, his only friend and sole defender

against the guarded and often open taunts of the other boys—
gentlemen all. Yet the newspaper accounts of his father's
"mysterious" illness had made of Chris a fair target for their
mischief. As soon as Tripp had left, the loneliness of the big
house had settled in again with its oppressive, if familiar, grip.
Chris's mother had called from the city, apologizing she would
not be joining him for dinner that night. His mother had been
staying away for two or three days at a time—sometimes in the
New York apartment, other times in Bridgeport—to be near
his dad. Therein lay his biggest trouble. Chris missed his dad.
Since his illness (the nature of which still confused the boy),
Chris had not been allowed to visit his father at the hospital.
Had he done something wrong? Was he in any way responsible
for his father's condition? Chris worried about that. He had
been aware for some time of the rift between his parents, although their behavior in front of him was exemplary and, in
truth, Chris was grateful for that. He respected their concern
for his well-being and loved them the more for it. His sadness,
however, had been growing out of proportion, and this afternoon he had needed to go down to the pond and unwind. The
tears of frustration that welled up out of him mingled with the
squawks of a new visitor to the pond—the northern shoveler,
which had migrated to these and surrounding woodlands. Chris
had identified it in his Audubon album.

It was an unusually still day for December and freezing cold.
Ice was already forming over the pond—soon it would be
Christmas. As the boy wept, he couldn't help feeling he was
betraying his father at their favorite spot. His father would certainly not countenance such unmanly behavior if he knew.

During the warmer season, whenever his father was at home

in Connecticut, Chris and he would spend hours together fishing. Their being together had increased since the end of the summer when Hugh had been forced to shoot the huge condor back at Papa Champ's out West.

It seemed so enormous, a monster with the most incredibly malevolent beak and eyes. A wild croaking, lunging thing that had suddenly folded up like an oversize accordion with its pinion feathers thrashing the air. Then, the simultaneous thunder as the rest of the creatures took off while the echo of the gun blast ricocheted through the mountain passes. For an instant it seemed to Chris that the entire flock was about to descend on him. They were hovering like a low, ominous cloud. In the next instant their ascent was so rapid it belied their lumbering frames. They climbed swiftly, trailing thin, unearthly screams. That was the last time Chris had cried in his father's presence. The resolute, even cold, expression in Hugh's eyes as he'd picked him off the ground served its own warning. At least then there was his bloody knee as an excuse, but Chris had seen that look glitter in his father's eyes before, and at such times he realized that he feared his father as much as he loved him.

Chris had only been back to see Papa Champ once since that summer six years ago. Papa Champ he loved totally and unequivocally. He simply was what he was: a big, forthright bear of a man with a summer smell about him even in winter. No less a gentleman himself, but of a rugged cast of some other manner born.

Even though it was against the law to shoot the condor, Papa Champ's immunity against such things ensured protection. Papa Champ then had it stuffed and mounted in his animal trophy room—already full of mountain lions, eagles, and other exotic things. Chris remembered he wouldn't turn round in the station wagon all the while they drove back to the ranch with the condor in back. He was afraid if he did, he would find its baleful eyes staring back at him. That thought was replaced by the look of pride in his father's eyes as they all stood confronting the winged nemesis in its stuffed glory. Chris felt strong and confident at that moment—secure that he was as he should be again in his father's eyes. He had canceled out his fear. Now still sitting by the pond, he smiled at the memory. He missed his father so.

David decided to burn the tape rather than chance other avenues of disposal. He did not play it again. He pulled the tape loose from its casing, cut it into large strips, and burned it piecemeal in a large metal ashtray. He watched the miniature pyres dissolve—thinking it would mean a breakthrough in his life. From what to what? He was uncertain, but then uncertainty was a major factor in his process work—almost its only stabilizing certainty. He had committed a crime—punishable by law. This was the one incontrovertible fixity in his life at the moment. He would take it in his stride. One misdemeanor does not a criminal make, he rationalized. Yet some part of him bristled with the excitement of having done it with impunity.

Next, David took Denise's letter from its cubbyhole, wished her luck, and gently placed it into the wastebasket. A faint trace of scent still clung to the pink notepaper. Instinctively he sought the comfort of the right side of the bed. He rested his head on the sheets and breathed in deeply. Now it would be Tatiana with Laurel. He pulled the coverlet gently toward the pillow, hoping that way to trap Laurel's scent between the sheets. For this and for all small blessings to follow, David quietly thanked Ara, dialed Laurel's number, and reached her at her apartment:

"Laurel." Direct, no edging.

No response.

"Are you there?"

"Yes, I'm here." And he felt that warm spasm in his groin.

"I wanted to tell you two—or three—things. Are you listening?"

"Of course." The pathos was present, but so was the rest of last night.

"One: I burned it." He heard her gasp. "Two: I want you to meet me for lunch. And three, I'll tell you when I see you. How soon can you meet me?"

They made love slowly in the afternoon. The sensation of being within one another was beyond mere pleasure. His tongue again found her nipples and nuzzled them. As they distended, David's tongue shifted to the base of her neck, an especially erogenous zone for this lady, whose arms and legs held him in tight embrace.

She nestled deeply against his remarkably hairless body, so unlike other Jewish men she had known, admiring him for his perfect submissiveness and his equally firm domination. The Janus head of love incorporated in one splendid human being. David had become more than a lover now. He was her protector. Sensing this, David savored all the permutations to come.

Outside, Sam had been locked out of the bedroom. He resented not having the run of the whole house—his runway on weekends when no patients came and went. He knew they would emerge sometime and then he would have his chance. Meanwhile he contented himself resting on the window ledge, watching for stray birds that might alight there.

David had just completed his last report at Precinct 24. He was treating himself to a Scotch and water when the phone rang. The kindly voice at the other end immediately summoned the man himself. Peter Mendoza had finally returned to his book-shop, Spectra, from Spain, where he had sold property belonging to his long-dead wife. For David, Mendoza would always be Mr. Chang in the film *Lost Horizon*. In figure and manner he resembled the actor H. B. Warner, who had created that venerable character in the film. Peter Mendoza was almost six feet tall, thin, with a slight stoop befitting his sixty-four years. Reverential and soft-spoken, he exuded an older world's charity and grace. His gray, slightly lidded eyes could sparkle in sympathy or squint judgmentally, as the occasion required. The last of the Pune Trio, outside David himself, his first words concerned Ara's death, which he had read of in a copy of the *International Herald Tribune*. After due consideration of that, and a long-drawn-out sigh, his subdued voice asked, "Davie, I don't know why I'm asking this, but could this Kunma in any way be connected with Ara's death?"

David paled somewhat. The intuitive Mr. Chang had gotten straight to the point. "Strange that you should ask that, Peter. It was at Ara's that I first heard the word *Kunma*. Who but you would know of such things? Then it's in your dictionary?"

"Everything is in alphabetical order. The word *Kunma* is nestled under *Koor-Bash*—a whip of heavy leather used as an instrument of torture. Origin—Turkey."

"How does that relate to our word?" David bantered nervously. "Frankly I thought it was one of Ara's jokes."

"Well, it's no joke, Davie, no."

"So what sort of thing is—or was it?" David protracted his levity.

"Kunma is a thief," Peter said in his most confidential voice.

"A thief—you mean like a garden-variety, through-the-back-window thief or what?" David's jaw went slack in disbelief.

"It wouldn't be in my dictionary if it were," Peter kindly admonished. "The Kunma is a thief of the soul."

David swallowed the rest of his Scotch and asked after its origin.

"Tibet," Peter said. "That remote and poor invaded country, not the Tibet of Capra's film."

David was silent as he absorbed this information. The Tolos monster, and here was Tibet again. He was now fully alert.

"David, are you there?"

"I'm here, Peter," David responded tensely.

"So when do we see each other to discuss further and pick up where we left off? Six months is a long time between meetings, Davie." Peter chuckled.

"Let me check my schedule and I'll call—and welcome back, Peter. I've missed you," David said with some feeling. And they hung up on each other, both sensing that some major event was pending that would reunite them in a search beyond the one offered in India.

Unlike David, neither Ara nor Peter had been invited to become part of Rajneesh's inner circle. Ara was gone. Peter, the oldest of the three, had learned to mine the knowledge of a past incarnation that had always simmered in his imagination. Rajneesh had made Peter aware that he had lived the life of a judge during the Spanish Inquisition, which had ruled and terrorized the Church in the fifteenth century. In his present incarnation, Peter had opted for a more modest occupation, and as the creator and manager of the bookstore Spectra, he now cherished what he had once consigned to the fires of righteousness. Human victims, mostly heretics and Jews, had been interspersed alongside the pages of seditious literature. Sometimes during the day, the cries and screams outside on the streets of his Third Avenue establishment reminded Mendoza of those former times. Hearing such echoes, Peter would put his palms together and daven in thanksgiving for God's ameliorations of his earthly condition, if not the ironic reversal of his religious affiliation.

As that former inquisitor, Mendoza retained a memory for arcane information. He had compiled his dictionary, which spanned time and civilizations—an alphabetic collection of a mostly profane nature, forming a vast encyclopedia of pain. He could find little evidence that such was not still the universal state of mankind today. He had made his peace with that condition. So while Ambrose Bierce had his *Devil's Dictionary*, Mendoza had his own "Mal"-orum, as he called it.

About to return to the aerie, where Laurel was expecting him, David mulled over Mendoza's information. The Kunma was a stealer of souls. What an impossible idea. How can one steal a soul in Tibet, or anywhere else for that matter? The soul was a tantalizing, still unproven myth. It was a word that often came easily to the tongue, chiefly because its highest commendation lay in that it was the reputed seat of love. As for those simple words *I love you,* he said them, often, to so many people—all day long. The firm currency of his work, if not entirely his person. His kind of love was impartial, meant to heal, but also somewhat clinical. The real article stretching out from gut level could be annihilating. Yet it was there that he longed and needed to be. Love was the most dangerous of games played between people. A game without a goalie, one might say. You were simply there, unsure of your next move—the fool in the tarot card about to plunge over the precipice, smiling all the way down to his destruction. But say it he must. Tonight—to Laurel—a married woman. He would risk it.

As he left the precinct to hail a cab, he instructed himself to get off at Broadway. Oscar's was the only place open at this hour for one of the small necessities of life, challah bread—the bread of his fathers made the best French toast in the world.

In David's apartment, Laurel must have fallen asleep, for only gradually did she become aware of another presence in the room. Time had just slipped by, and now a patch of moonlight was stroking the window, outlining the big leather chair and part of the desk in its glow. Like a Magritte canvas, she thought, in the brief instant after opening her eyes. She was chary of keeping them opened longer for it would spoil the fun. David had come home and, finding her asleep, was undressing. Even now he was moving cautiously toward her. Her exposed flanks had chilled in the unheated room. Soon they would be pressing against her lover. Lost in this voluptuous reverie, she tried to peer up at him through slitted eyes. As close as he was to her now, he was still only an outline against the pervasive darkness surrounding him. The breathing above her was deep, steady, exuding the excitement of assured possession. She tried to control her own heart, lest she give her game away. The hand that touched her breasts and fingered her nipples was heavy, familiar. The mouth that enveloped them, tremulous and insistent. At a deliberate pace, his head swayed back and forth, from breast to breast, teeth tugging, each time a little harder. Laurel stirred, only a sigh acknowledging this blissful invasion. The mouth lingered at a spot between her breasts, then slowly eased down toward her navel, trailing saliva as it pressured. The trickle was warm against her cool flesh. It seemed a small eternity before the mouth reached her pubes and continued its rhythmic probing. She could feel his cheeks, his chin, then his forehead as they nestled against her bush. As the mouth slipped past, Laurel opened her eyes. She was wet and had been since the first tug at her breasts. As the mouth searched her, she arched her back slowly. Suddenly she felt a stabbing pain—for the teeth had found their goal and in their greedy pursuit had gripped her hungrily.

Laurel struck out with her foot into the darkness below her. As she found her mark, a small animal growl sprang up at her from the foot of the bed. Laurel twisted to her side and threw on the overhead light. She started screaming even before the man stood up—for it was not David she saw, but Charles Palfrey, standing there naked, his eyes shining with brilliant ferocity. The low guttural was erupting from bloodied lips, blood oozing down his chin. The mouth opened. She almost strangled on her terror—for the dead man had no tongue and part of his head seemed gouged away. Laurel leaped from the bed, snapped off the light as if she could obliterate the vision by that simple gesture, and ran into the living room, then on into the bathroom, where she locked herself in against the nightmare.

Standing with her back to the door, she saw that her body was streaked with his blood. His blood. A serpentine trail of lumpish gore twisted from her breasts down to her thighs. She screamed again and kept on screaming. When she finally stopped, she listened sharply—to silence behind the door and the fading clamor of her own alarm ringing in her ears. When she dared leave her sanctuary, she found the apartment empty. After drying herself, she dressed quickly and threw both the towel and David's bloodied dressing gown into the hallway incinerator.

She made her way down the elevator to street level and to her car, parked across from the Chatsworth's entrance. She saw the vision from hell in her mind's eye. It was no hallucination, her body still ached from its touch. She entered traffic on the Henry Hudson Parkway, determined to get to West Haven as quickly as possible. She would enter the house quietly, not disturb her boy, who would be asleep. In the morning, she would be recovered and greet her son with open arms. Only one road was left to her now—a trump card buried in the mixed deal of her life. As for David? Her heart seemed to clutch itself within her bosom. She must stay away from him until her purpose was accomplished. Her tears flowed, and she was racked with a despair that could find no easy assuagement.

PART THREE

January 1982

Cardinal Nunzio, middle-aged, short, and blunt of manner, seemed completely unsettled by what Bishop Laughton had just disclosed. The cardinal's customary paleness darkened.

"When did you see this woman?" he demanded sharply.

"Only yesterday, Your Eminence." At six feet, Bishop Laughton hovered over his diminutive superior ensconced in an antique chair of Gothic design. The bishop, a gentle soul approaching his fifty-eighth year, had waited till they had finished the excellent espresso before bringing up the subject of Laurel Hunt and her unusual request. A deadly pall descended over the room, spoiling the celebratory dinner the cardinal's cook had prepared in honor of the bishop's strategic transfer from his diocese in New Haven to the Vatican.

"As I explained, the lady considers her husband possessed by some diabolic force. She trembled and appeared quite frightened as she told her story. I listened and said I would contact her before the week was out." The bishop rose and strode about the room in his agitation.

The cardinal's eyes brightened. "Very clever of you, Bishop, since by the end of the week, you will already be in Rome."

"Thanks to Your Eminence's intercession and influence, I am realizing a lifelong ambition." Laughton regarded his cardinal with due reverence.

"Even if there's any truth in what she said, which I doubt, you didn't intend to pass it off onto me—did you?" Nunzio's eyes squinted suspiciously.

"Hardly, Eminence," Laughton said peevishly. "Only she is the daughter of . . ."

"You don't have to remind me of McGraw." Nunzio sighed heavily. "Have you any idea what is entailed in sanctioning an exorcism? Endless channels must be pursued within the hierarchy, for one thing."

"I have never been tested by the darker powers, Eminence. I remain singularly unprepared as to what to think or do in this instance," Laughton said in all innocence. "And I certainly had no intention of foisting such a burden onto your shoulders. You know I am incapable of such deception."

"Yes, yes, I know." Nunzio's pudgy fingers waved a dismissal of his tactless accusation. "I was involved in an exorcism years ago." He leaned back in his chair, causing his feet to dangle inches above the parquet floor.

Laughton noticed this, although he was all tense attention.

"It happened ten years ago to be exact," Nunzio continued bitterly. "The woman exorcised died as a result. Had a heart attack. The assumption made, of course, was that the devil had prevailed. It was considered a defeat for our Mother Church."

"Oh?" was all that Laughton could manage.

"There were several such calamities during that time, and accordingly Rome's position on exorcism has been going through drastic revision since." Nunzio looked up at the bishop. "Politically it would be unwise for you to arrive in Rome trailing vestiges of such a delicate issue."

"Then what am I to do, Eminence?" The bishop knelt beside the cardinal's chair. "Advise me."

"You will do nothing—you will go, just go," Nunzio said sternly. "I know the woman you speak of. I have seen her occasionally—a rich, spoiled example of her kind. Struck me as a born hysteric."

"Nothing? Nothing at all?" the bishop admonished.

"I don't wish to tangle with McGraw, or anyone involved with him—is that clear?" The cardinal looked ferocious and rose out of his chair. The bishop was crestfallen at this response and rose slowly. "Alright, if you insist. Drop her a note, but mention nothing further about her request." The cardinal turned and extended his hand. The bishop knelt once more and kissed the cardinal's ring in submission.

Later, in his private chambers, the bishop knelt in silent prayer, asking for His understanding and forgiveness. Despite the cardinal's advice, he felt remiss in his duty toward one of the "spiritual daughters" in his diocese. But what was he to do at this decisive moment in his ascendancy to spiritual prominence? At his age, such an opportunity would not occur again. For this possible lapse of faith, he would impose a penance on himself, the nature of which he would determine through further prayer and meditation.

When the telephone rang, David leaped for it immediately. He was in midsession with Leslie Mundy, a particularly querulous patient. To excuse himself for a mere phone call was tantamount to desertion in her eyes. David knew if he kept this up, his patient's forbearance would soon turn to rebellion. That night, he had come home to find Laurel gone—and no word of explanation since. Sam had remained trembling beside him all night, and there were traces of blood everywhere. Weeks had gone by, and he had been unable to reach her, nor had she answered his messages.

"Hello," David literally gulped as he picked up the receiver.

"Hello." A man's voice. Damnation. "Davie. Peter here."

"Peter." David was temporarily disoriented.

"I did some more exploratory work on that Kunma question," Peter said. "What I found was very interesting."

David could hear Leslie Mundy pacing in the next room. *Stealer of souls, steal Mundy's—right now, please.*

"Peter, could you make it quick? My patient—"

"We're talking eternities and you want to make it quick— shah," Peter said with mild annoyance.

David relented, while mumbling in his head, *Fuck you, Miss Mundy*. "So tell me, Peter, tell."

"Well, it seems in Tibetan history that, just as Buddhism was taking hold, any renegade fighting the new religion suffered death by fire."

The stench in the hospital. There it flared again. David covered his mouth for a moment.

"Does any of this mean anything to you?" Peter asked in his best *Lost Horizon* manner.

"Peter, I can't talk now. We've got to meet. Can we do it tonight?" David spoke hurriedly.

"Not tonight, I'm afraid," Peter apologized. "I'm off to buy a collection from a dealer in Providence. There's no need to get into a panic over this, is there? Still, it's highly interesting. I'll call as soon as I get back. Be well." And he hung up.

David took a moment before returning to his consultation room. Leslie Mundy had gone, leaving a check and a note of termination. David sighed, feeling fortunate at least in this loss. He picked up the phone and called Laurel again. No answer.

He was staring down at the patterns decorating the carpet in front of him. He was so close to it that he had to be on his knees. The carpet was thick, of oriental design. Persian? His finger traced one of the yellow lines zigzagging through its surface. Every foot or so it contorted on itself, arresting small groups of blue and pink dots within its benign stranglehold. The yellow line dominated the huge carpet, like a coiled lizard. A pale sunlight suffused the room. Somewhere he sensed the presence of two or three other people. He tried to look up from his kneeling position, but something told him he mustn't do that. Instead he tried to catch the drift of their conversation.

David awakened. This was the second time he had dreamed of that room. He had never had a recurring dream before—never mind one with escalating details. He knew the dream had been triggered as far back as his visit to Bridgeport. Where was this room he saw? And why was he on his knees, afraid to look up? And could he be sure it was himself? He had the strange sensation he was interloping in someone else's dream.

The Jew in him took yet another tack—by raising the shade of the Holocaust. Were the legendary 6 million victims making a historical claim on his soul—demanding their ghostly pound of flesh? Several Passovers ago, which he sometimes dutifully observed, he remembered his father, who had died soon thereafter, confiding to his son that he'd been disturbed of late by dreams of burning children—faceless, unidentified except for the yellow star that glowed in the coals of his mind. When David had explained away the buried survivor's guilt, the old man had embraced him with a desperate tenderness and tears in his eyes. How lucky they were to be here—his own children, alive and well. It had constituted one of the rare intimate contacts between the two men and had concluded with the admonition "to say nothing to your mother. I wouldn't want her disturbed on such a high holy day." But wasn't that what the day was about? Yes, but it was Baltimore. History was all water under the bridge. Guilt was, at least in America, to be atoned at leisure, or else the other North American Jews would all go mad.

David was clearly in something now he could not easily explain away—something that shook him to the core of his being.

The two interns hovered over the inert form below them.

"He's been in that position since this morning. Is he asleep—or look at his face."

"He's always twitching like that, asleep or awake."

"Not that I've noticed."

"How long have you been on this ward?"

"Two weeks."

"Take my word for it."

"Well, I think he's having one of his seizures."

"How would you know?"

"I read his charts."

"That makes you an authority? His breathing is still regular. Look."

"Have any of the MDs been in to check him this morning?"

"That's not my department."

"Well, if he's up by suppertime, then I'd say you're right."

"I still say he's resting is all."

"Ten dollars says he's not."

"It's your money, my friend."

"They're shipping him out of here."

"How do you know that?"

"Take my word for it."

Laurel had anxiously waited out the week after her consultation with Bishop Laughton. She had resisted the temptation of calling him again in the interim. Now in her hand was the briefest of notes from the bishopric in New Haven. Rome—the Vatican—short phrases exculpating him from pursuing his duty as her spiritual adviser. Disappointed beyond endurance, she dialed his office number in the hopes that he might, by some miracle, still be there. A woman's harsh, Irish-accented voice responded after an eternity of rings. She identified herself as a cleaning lady, busy with the burdens of cleaning the private chambers of a lifetime of living by a less than fastidious priest.

The contrast between the woman's voice and her language surprised Laurel, but she brazened on and asked after the cardinal.

"Oh, that one," came the response, "he's off to Boston to consult with some visiting dignitaries."

"Then he did go to Rome?" Laurel asked in a shocked voice.

"Ma'am, I said His Eminence is off to gossip in Boston."

"No, I meant Bishop Laughton." Laurel's voice tightened.

"Oh, the other one. He's been gone alright, and for always it seems. Good riddance, I say."

Laurel hung up peremptorily, tore the bishop's letter into tiny bits, and took an unaccustomed brandy to loosen the knot of tension gathered in her neck before she determined her next step.

"My dear Mrs. Hunt, we have done everything humanly possible to help your husband." Dr. Runnicels, Immaculate's chief of staff, literally dripped Southern courtesy.

"But I'm only asking for a little bit of time. Surely you can't deny me."

"Time for what, may I ask?"

"I'm—I'm seeking another specialist to examine Hugh."

"That can be done anywhere at any time, Mrs. Hunt. But for Immaculate, this is a pressing issue. His bed is needed for the kind of cases we are capable of handlin'."

"I understand your need, Doctor. Nevertheless—"

"Your husband is being transferred to another situation more suitable to his condition." His pink baby face exuded sympathy.

"Transferred? Where? And on whose authority are you—?"

Runnicels gently pushed the letter across the desk toward her. She immediately recognized her father's letterhead. "But it isn't legal. He can't do this. What right has he—why, he doesn't know what my husband's condition is."

"Perhaps, Mrs. Hunt, but there is no other recourse." A line of worry wrecked the cherubic face. Runnicels at least looked penitent. Laurel suppressed her anger and looked away, suddenly reminded that her father indeed had the right. In the first year of their marriage, Hugh had given her father power of attorney should anything dire happen to him. Even as early as that, Hugh had shown he didn't totally trust her.

"Immaculate is a small hospital, ma'am, with very limited facilities to deal with Mr. Hunt's disorder. As you know, he only just came through another one of his seizures." His tiny fingers rustled some official documents.

"When?"

"Why, several days ago, of course."

Laurel's hand went up to her throat.

"Is there anything wrong, ma'am?" Runnicels purred.

Laurel had come to ask for his intercession with the church whose name his hospital bore. Looking at the rosy-complexioned, soft-spoken administrator behind his desk, she realized how outlandish such a request would be to him. Without another word, Laurel rose and left in defeat. Her eye caught the edge of a check accompanying her father's letter. The bastard.

David looked around his kitchen and saw how he was living. He had not had the apartment cleaned since Laurel's disappearance. He felt dull, listless, alive only as long as his patients were with him. While bolstering their needs, their sense of conservation, he had lost all energy for his own. He was rapidly edging himself into a major depression. He had been skipping meals and smoking too much. And this morning on awakening, he had felt himself hyperventilating, followed by the gradual sinking feeling that threatened to become paralyzing torpor if he'd allow it. He needed exercise, distraction. He needed to make hard physical love. And calls to Mendoza had remained unanswered. He had said Sunday and today was Sunday.

During the daylight hours, if David slept, he didn't dream. Only at night did "the room" appear and draw him into it. He was beginning to show hollows under his eyes, and it didn't take much to know his patients were noticing his condition. If things kept up as they were, pretty soon the doctor would need a doctor. He was contemplating taking a shower when his telephone rang. It was almost eight-thirty. He watched it ring. Absently he picked up and the next tightening of the circle commenced.

"David."

At last. "Did I wake you up?"

"No, I was working," he lied, and bit his lip. *It's Sunday for God's sake.*

"Do you want me to call you back?"

"No." And he scrambled around looking for a cigarette.

"David, I need your help." She said it so simply.

He smiled, otherwise he might scream or make some other foolish noise.

"Did you hear me?" She now sounded harried.

"I heard you." He hadn't for months, of course, and now it was as if nothing had happened. He lit his cigarette and inhaled so deeply, he coughed.

"Well?" was all he could manage.

"Are you alright?"

"No, all wrong," David said curtly. The familiar sound of her voice was warming him nonetheless.

"I need you, David. Now more than ever."

"Need? Me? Or theoretic me? The good doctor me? Which one is it?" Was that the rate of exchange all along? His love—alright, his desire—bartered for services rendered?

"Please, David, I'll explain when I see you."

"What makes you think it's convenient?"

"Oh, I'm sorry. I didn't realize." She fumbled at cross-purposes while he hated himself for the gratuitous put-on.

"There's nobody here—that is, right now." Natural pride massaging itself. "How about you? Getting any lately?"

"David, don't."

"Why not? All's fair in—dare I say it?"

"I'm not calling about—about us."

"Oh, are you recommending someone, perhaps?" And he flicked ashes onto the kitchen floor. Sam walked quietly out the door to his litter box.

"David, if—please don't turn away from me now." Every corny line according to the time-honored scenario, and yet his heart skipped a beat.

"What's wrong?"

"Hugh came to see Chris last night."

"He's back home?" David ground out his cigarette into the dregs in his coffee cup.

"That's just it. He's not. He was committed to Lawson House sanitarium. Papa made all the arrangements."

"Then—I don't understand."

"That's what scares me."

"I don't understand many things, of course," he flared. "By the way, did you and Sam have a tussle?"

"David, what are you talking about?"

"Well, what about the blood then? Cats have sharp claws. Cats of all denominations and species" was his final put-down.

"David! I said I'll explain what happened."

Selfish prick, he remonstrated hastily. *She's obviously in trouble.*

"This morning at breakfast, Chris told me that during the night—don't you see how impossible it is? Yet Chris maintains it's true. Last night he saw his father. Here in West Haven, and Chris is not in the habit of lying."

"He's a kid. Kids will do anything to gain attention."

"Please don't use that damned professional tone on me."

"I'm sorry." He sighed; how quickly their roles had reversed again.

"I called Lawson. At first I thought he could have driven over and then back. But Mrs. Berglund assured me he'd never left the grounds."

"Is that Anita Berglund?"

"Yes, she runs the organization."

"Then you're saying he tried to escape—"

"You're not hearing me. Escape or not, Hugh never left Lawson last night."

David's torpid state was not assimilating all this rapidly enough. "What did the boy say happened?"

"They just talked. Now Chris thinks he's cured and coming back home. I don't know what to do."

"What did you tell Chris?"

"At first I suggested he'd been dreaming, but he denied that.

Then I told him I wanted him to talk to someone else about it. Will you come?"

"Do you know the train schedules?"

"There's no time for that. I'll have a limousine pick you up at your apartment in an hour—if that's convenient?"

He would have just enough time to shave, pull himself together, and have a quick breakfast.

As he shaved, he looked critically at himself. "What can I do," he said to Sam, who was lurking in the doorway. "I'm a schmuck, but I love her, Sam, I do. Can you hear me, Mama? I love her. Another shiksa."

It was a little after noon when David arrived in West Haven. The ride up in the luxurious vehicle had been smooth and silent.

The house lay twenty miles outside the city limits. The approach was impressive enough, but unexpected. Acre after acre of carefully manicured property, oriental in design. Even under family duress, the mask of serenity had artfully been maintained in the landscape. Dwarf juniper trees studded the grounds at carefully calculated distances from one another. It was with some surprise that one came upon the house itself. The first sight was of turrets spearing the sunlight. The contrast was so sharp David wondered if the driver had not taken a wrong turn. David was no expert on such matters, but from this distance he guessed the house to be a French château in design, either lifted bodily or reproduced. *Territorial imperative in excelsis goyim mundi,* David quipped irrepressibly. He could never understand how people could feel comfortable living in such ostentation.

A truculent maid led David hastily through the house to the upper reaches. Inside, the house resembled a tastefully managed mausoleum, a mix of Louis XVI and oriental finery in a studied and artificial balance. The place existed to be photographed.

The boy's room, occupying one of the turrets on the west wing of the house, was a rustic oasis amidst artifice: simple, solid-oak paneling with high crossbeams and windows on three sides, overlooking the various vistas available to the site. The room—still too large for so small an occupant—was scaled down by its many colored pennants and posters, sports equipment, and other youthful bric-a-brac.

David saw Laurel immediately, and she almost took his breath away. She sat on a bed in one corner of the room looking at her son seated beside her. The sunlight drenching the room gave the tableau a quality of timelessness that David was loath to disturb. Laurel looked up at him, and a dazzling smile canceled the furrow on her brow. She rose and greeted him as if it were the most natural thing in the world. David could not take his eyes off her as she asked the maid to have dinner served at an early hour and inquired if David could do with refreshment. She took his hand and led him toward the boy. She was informally dressed in a light blue cardigan that matched David's own dark blue jacket and yellow sport shirt. A white, pleated shirt gave her a schoolgirl's appearance, accentuated by brown loafers with their tassels—a style David associated with the country life of the rich. She could not conceal the blush that warmed her otherwise forlorn expression. Her golden hair was down round her shoulders.

Chris was an attractive mixture of his parents. His present hangdog look rivaled his mother's in seriousness.

KUNMA

"I told you, darling. David's a close friend of Mother's and he's driven a long way to hear your story, so please, Chris." She touched his shoulder.

"But why must I tell it again, Mother?" he responded with a covert look in David's direction.

"Laurel . . ." The immediate sound of her name on David's lips brought another blush to her cheeks. The boy was looking intently at both of them now. The flickering shadow that darted in and out of the boy's eyes reminded David of the boy's father, and David blinked rapidly at the memory.

"Laurel, why don't you let me speak to Chris alone?"

The boy looked away from David's attempt at familiarity. "We've hardly become acquainted yet."

"As you will. Can I get you something? Would you, Chris?" She smiled encouragingly.

"A Coke would be alright," the boy said, then lightly kicked at the rug.

"Make that two." David moved toward Laurel and immediately the boy's head turned, his eyes harpooning David's hand on his mother's arm.

Protective hostility, David thought as Laurel left the room. Look at him, David thought, the light in his mother's eye. Otherwise he was only a youngster wearing the official costume of his generation: blue jeans, sneakers and a white T-shirt with a decal: *Windsurfer* embossed under a sloop tacking sternward.

Chris took the initiative. "Mom says you're a doctor. Are you?"

"Yes." David nodded.

"Are you one of those taking care of my dad?" Chris's look was direct, but troubled.

"Not exactly." David sat on an old sea trunk.

"Well, then what do you do?"

"I'm a therapist. Do you know what a therapist is?"

"You're a shrink." The boy sounded disappointed.

"You got it."

"We have one at school. Only he's a she." Chris picked up a hockey stick and swung it.

"Have you ever had occasion to talk to her about anything?"

"Why should I talk to her? I'm not sick." He took another swing.

"Nobody says you are. But occasionally problems arise and—"

"Any problems I have I discuss with my mom or my dad." Goal.

"Naturally. It must be terribly one-sided these days. I mean with your dad not around."

"Where is he now? Do you know?" Chris looked at him, measuring the distance between them.

"Well, maybe you know more about that than I do. After all, it seems he was here with you last night." David, still on the trunk, was clearly intended to be either the goalie or a victim of Chris's imaginary practice.

"I told Mother not to tell anyone. She promised." The boy stood, his back stiff with resentment, ready to swing again.

The moment was rescued by the arrival of the maid with the soft drinks. Chris took two sharp swipes in David's direction, then silence prevailed while the maid set the tray down on the boy's desk. David started to amble over to it, but Chris dropped the hockey stick and made a quick move. He was there first. He drank thirstily, making little-boy sounds of pleasure. David sipped slowly.

"Chris, your mother had a very special reason for telling me."

"Did she?" It was almost a challenge.

"Do you mind if I smoke?" David countered amiably.

Chris shrugged. "No, sir." He sat back on his bed and started picking on his sneakers between mouthfuls of Coke. Suddenly he seemed his age again, feeling a bit cowed by his attack on an elder—a breach in his training, no doubt.

"Your mother and I are good friends."

"You already said that, sir." He was now unlacing his Keds.

"Please, call me David." He squinted at the boy through the smoke.

"And how come then, David, sir, I haven't ever seen you till now?"

"We haven't been friends that long."

"Then you're not very good friends." The laces of one sneaker came loose.

"We're not going to get very far if we keep this up, are we?" David rose, looking for an ashtray.

"Does my dad know you're here?"

"Are we?" David lifted a small can with a few peanuts left. "May I?"

The boy hesitated under the stern sound in David's voice.

Chris nodded. "I'm sorry, sir. David." And he threw the sneaker to the ground.

"Now then, when was it that you saw him? Your father?"

The boy grimaced resignedly and momentarily shut his eyes. "Last night."

"Where?" David resumed his place on the trunk.

"I was out taking a walk in the garden."

"When?"

"I was supposed to be in bed, but I just couldn't sleep. So I decided to put on my robe and stroll around a bit."

"And was he there waiting for you?"

"Not exactly. I was about to sit down on the stone bench when he called my name and came up to me. Oh, I was so happy to see him finally." The boy's voice cracked, and he looked at the pennants on the wall above his bed.

"Finally?" David crossed his arms.

"I'd rather not talk about all that, David, sir." The boy kicked the sneaker on the ground lightly.

"Well, was he happy to see you?"

"I think so, I mean, I think so."

"How did he look to you?"

"The way he always does. Maybe a little thinner, but that was the moonlight making him look that way."

"Which way?"

"Like I said, thinner."

"How was he dressed?"

"The way he usually is. I don't know what you mean." Chris stopped kicking, but did not look up at David.

"Never mind. Would you care to tell me what you both talked about?"

"Well, he told me about his accident."

"What about it?"

"His car accident. That's why he's been away. But he said he was almost recovered and would be back home. I guess that must be the reason?"

"Reason? For what?"

"Why he looked thinner? The car accident?" A pause during which the boy picked up and finished his soda, his eyes cloudy with memory.

"Was there anything else you talked about? Your schoolwork? Your—"

"The most important thing, see, is that I must talk to my mother about the summer."

"What about it? What did he say about the summer?"

"He asked if I wanted to go to New Mexico this coming August and I said I did. Very much."

"And then?"

"He said it was up to me to persuade Mom to go out there or else for her to let me go alone and stay with Papa Champ."

"And have you told her this?"

"I did. Yes, I did. But she's still angry at Papa. They fight all the time when they're together. She keeps saying Grandpa doesn't understand her and that he's always criticizing everything she does, and she gets—sort of hysterical sometimes."

"Why couldn't he have asked her himself?"

"Oh, that's easy. He wanted us to keep our talk a little secret and I was to ask her on my own." Chris suddenly laughed sweetly and sucked up the end of his soda.

"Do you and your father often share secrets with one another?"

Chris nodded. *Truth or wish fulfillment?*

"Did he say he would be out in New Mexico, too?"

Chris nodded again, more affirmatively.

"Did he actually say he would be?"

"He asked me if I remembered the big condor he shot the last time we were there. He said he wanted to take me into the mountains again. My father's a crack shot." Chris stood up and smiled, revealing perfect, small, white teeth.

"Is he?"

"Huh-huh. Then I asked him to come to my room for a while, but he said he couldn't. He had to get back and, well, he just left."

"Just like that?"

"Oh, he walked down the terrace steps and I watched him go."

"Did he have a car? I mean, did you hear him drive away?"

Chris cocked his ear, as if he were listening for the sound.

"Did you hear or see anything?"

"I don't know, sir. I just ran back to my room then and I went to bed."

"What else did he say before he left?"

The boy's cheeks flushed, his lips pursed. "Oh, some mushy stuff, I guess."

"How mushy?"

Chris looked at David softly. Suddenly, David was included. "How much he missed me and, oh, you know, mush like that."

"You've missed him very much, haven't you?"

Two quick nods of the head.

"Is that why you told your mother about his visit?"

"How did you guess that?" And he pursed his lips, attempting to scowl.

"Well, I make it my business figuring such things out."

"I just was so glad to see him. I couldn't help myself. I wanted Mom to feel happy, too, I guess." Chris looked at David beseechingly. "My dad wanted me to keep his visit out to us this summer as a surprise. Sir, you won't—"

"Don't worry. I'll keep your little secret. We'll just keep it amongst ourselves, we three. No one else will know."

"Oh, thank you, sir—David."

When Laurel and David were alone together later that night, the full impact of her enforced seclusion in the past weeks hit her with stunning impact. The nighttime visitation held her in its insidious embrace. She had found a measure of peace being with her son again, attentive to him in her love and supervision of his life. That reentry into Chris's life provided its own protection, even denial of the evil that lurked in her life. The impact of her continued infidelity shamed her suddenly, and she resisted David's touch, moving away from it, even wary of the naked man in her bed. She switched on the lamp by her bedside and looked down at him, as if to identify him as the man who had brought love back into her life. Not the monster. She fell to her knees and gagged against the fresh, crisp sheets—trying to smother if not obliterate her fears. David waited until she was finally quiet, then gently lifted her into the bed beside him.

Their lovemaking was at first awkward, then, in their desperate need for one another, turned violent, almost punishing in its intensity. Later, exhausted, the rejoined lovers lay side by side—perennial babes in an ever-darkening wood—and listened to one another's horrors. David spoke of Mendoza and his revelations concerning the Kunma.

"Is it possible that what I saw that night could be this—Kunma," she asked, clinging to him, "and that it's connected to Hugh's visit here in some way?"

"Possibly," David conjectured. "The how and why of it are

still shadowy. The Kunma is of Tibetan origin. The mysteries surrounding it are unknown to me. Peter is trying to help me understand. I'm afraid I'm a reluctant student, somehow, and don't ask me why." Why? Why? He knew some part of that why: Laurel's husband in a hospital ward while he, David, coveted that unfortunate's wife. If a monster had erupted from this corruptive liaison of sorts, who was that monster? Wasn't his own behavior commensurate to its now threatening presence in their lives? This—monster? Could it be himself? Laurel's next words only corroborated his misgivings.

"David, I'm frightened out of my wits." She sat up in bed, her hand touching her breasts and belly. That fateful night she had arrived here in West Haven and spent an hour in the shower, scrubbing her body with brush and lotions to eradicate the dried traces of the gore still imprinted on her flesh. David placed his hand over hers and stilled its frantic search. He kissed her breasts and then the rest of her in an almost courtly adoration of her presence. They listened to the silence of the countryside outside the house. Now lying peacefully side by side, they contemplated the ghost now locked implacably in their lives.

"What does that monster want of me?" she asked solemnly.

"I don't know," David murmured, "but without it, we might never have been drawn together." And he was amazed at the simplicity of that fact.

Laurel turned slowly to face him and they regarded one another, accepting the impossible with mutual awe.

Later, David left Laurel's side and made his way to his bedroom at the other end of the corridor to pick up his raincoat. A limousine was awaiting his return back to the city. As he passed the stairway, something white shone in the darkness on the upper landing. The grandfather clock in the library intoned a rusty three times, followed by the faintest of sighs. Whatever was up there was now standing still, as if hesitant to approach.

"Chris? Is that you?" David ventured. The mass moved forward again and it appeared at the bottom of the stairs. He put out his arms and mumbled, "Mom, Mom," in a low, disoriented voice. Cautiously David took the boy in hand, knocked on Laurel's door, and automatically entered. Laurel saw them in the mirror of her dressing table. She put down her hairbrush and rushed to kneel beside her child. In the light his face was flushed and his pajamas soaked with perspiration.

"Oh, baby," she muttered, and held him close to ease him.

"Have you a thermometer, any aspirin?" David prompted.

"In my cabinet." She gestured with her shoulder toward the bathroom.

"Did you throw up?" Laurel picked the boy up and carried him to her bed. Chris shook his head slightly. She didn't like the veiled look that had stolen into his eyes. Carefully she tucked him into bed, drawing the quilt up under his chin.

"It's probably nothing but a twenty-four-hour flu." David was standing beside them. "It's going around, you know. I couldn't find the aspirin."

"I'll look." She left the boy's side hastily as David took her place.

"Chris, Chris. Open your mouth and rest this under your tongue," David instructed gently. The boy's head lolled away from the thermometer.

"Chris. Please do what I ask you."

"Chris, please do what David asks," Laurel called from the

bathroom as she rummaged around, looking for aspirin. She caught sight of herself in the mirror. She knew Chris's present dilemma had surely been provoked by Hugh's visit last night. She found the St. Joseph's bottle hidden behind the Band-Aid box and returned immediately to the bedside. David rose to make room for her and caught the look in her eyes. He had already mulled over similar apprehensions.

"Can you remember the last time you were sick, Chrissy? I can't." Laurel sat there, holding Chris's hand. Then she removed the thermometer and handed it to David.

"Chew and swallow." Laurel gently massaged Chris's neck as he slowly masticated the pink pills. "You're just a naturally healthy boy and nothing can hold you down for long." The boy was staring at her, but appeared not to be seeing her.

Behind his fixed stare, Chris was watching something else. He saw himself awakening from sleep. It was pitch-dark, except for some wavering lights a long way off. Something was clashing or clanging. He felt a stirring somewhere just beyond the shadows surrounding his bed and wondered if it could be one of the giant guardian cats who had wandered in.

"David, look! What's wrong with him? Why is he staring like that?"

"There we are. One hundred three point three. Not so bad," David said. Laurel went rigid, and David's touch on her shoulder became firmer. Chris sighed and closed his eyes.

In the hallway, Laurel held on to David desperately.

"It's only a fever," he cautioned. "Nothing else, I'm sure." The back of her neck was as cold as ice. Only a short time before, they had been intertwined where now the sick child lay burning in the already steamy sheets of their coupling. They looked at one another, cognizant of that.

"Mom . . . The boy's thin call could barely be heard.

"Go to him," David said. "Let him sleep as long as he needs to. If the fever comes back in the morning, call a doctor and then call me." They kissed furtively and parted.

Chris fell asleep almost immediately thereafter. Laurel noticed he had tucked a corner of the sheet in his mouth, something he hadn't done since he was three years old. She turned out the lamp by the bed and sat a while longer, listening to the boy's breathing. She lay down on the nearby chaise and covered herself with a blanket. Staring into the darkness, she prayed against the darkness gathering in her soul. She was being punished, again, she knew it, but it had been forever so, and her eyes closed against the thought.

Next morning Laurel woke to find Chris gone. She looked at the clock: 9:02. She immediately rang downstairs to the kitchen.

"Edna?"

"Yes, Mrs. Hunt?"

"Did you see Chris this morning?"

"Yes, Mrs. Hunt."

"Was he alright?"

"Oh, yes, ma'am. He ate a very hearty breakfast and went off to school as usual."

"Thank you. Don't bother sending breakfast up. I'll have it in the dining room."

"As you wish, ma'am."

Twenty-four-hour flu. David was right. Thank you, God, and she prepared to meet the day.

During his lunch hour, Chris placed a long-distance call to Papa Champ. He sat in one of the booths outside the school's main entrance, awaiting his connection. He was determined to get out to Taos this summer. Grandpa wanted it—he'd told him so. His father wanted it, too. And of course he wanted it. It was only his mother who objected. Why? Because she had been arguing with Papa about something he could not quite make out. He had heard only bits and pieces. It was time he asserted himself in this situation. His dad had used that word. *Assert!* He wanted Papa Champ to help in making the necessary arrangements. Just in case. It would be the first time he had contradicted his mother's desires. That couldn't be helped. Yes, she had other fish to fry. But it would be New Mexico this summer nonetheless. As for the man, the shrink called David, he felt great uneasiness in his presence. His mother had sought his "advice," sure, but what had he been doing leaving the house so late at night?

April 1982

In Toledos, Padre Dominguez stood outside his little Church of the Holy Intercession and watched the Land Rover taking Papa Champ back to his ranch house. A short, stubby Sancho Panza of a man, Dominguez was dressed in a brown soutane only shades darker than the earth that supported his sturdy figure. He lifted the hem of it and wiped his face. It was only past noon and the temperature had risen sharply, threatening to become fierce within hours. The dust in the wake of Papa Champ's car settled around him, and he returned to the cooler reaches of his sacred sanctuary. He'd been Papa's friend and confessor for fifteen years and as such had brought a carefully judged forbearance and absolution in spiritual matters affecting the old man. Having just learned about the tragic illness of Hugh Hunt and Papa's surveillance of Hugh's cause, the padre sat in the last pew of his church and reviewed the matter.

"As long as that boy needs my help, he'll get it, Padre," Papa Champ had blustered. Thank God they had been alone in the church as the old man fulminated.

"And as long as he remains at Lawson House, no one, not even my daughter, is to go near him without my say-so." His large frame shifted nervously in the small confessional.

"But, Papa, she is his wife. Certainly she deserves consideration."

"What I said goes—and if you think that's wrong, Padre, I will accept chastisement, but it will not alter my decision."

The padre often marveled at the old man's words, marveled and sometimes trembled. He seemed unusually fired up by his son-in-law's situation, and the padre was disturbed by the smell of whiskey that soured Papa Champ's breath. This signaled trouble ahead. There was no cajoling Papa in such a mood, and however irrational his viewpoint, the padre knew Papa had the wherewithal to implement his decisions. The rules of living, including those of Mother Church, were usually created by men of similar force and power. For them special dispensation should be allowed to contain their energies.

The padre looked up at the Christ on the altar and crossed himself. The Zuni part of Dominguez often strained against the Christian teachings of that unearthly figure on the cross, but ultimately he found balance in His agony. This was the meaning of salvation. One must arrive at that crucial point of understanding at all cost in the journey called life. He wiped his face again and rose to shut the church doors, trusting to trap the cool morning air for as long as possible.

That night, the room and the carpet were the same and the figures were becoming more distinct. David could see that they were sitting on a platform, addressing someone in front of them. The candles were still burning and the smell seemed to be emanating from them—rancid, fetid, and growing increasingly familiar to the dreaming man.

David opened his eyes, and for a fleeting moment he felt the weight of a long robe covering him from neck to ankles. Yet he was standing naked in the middle of his bedroom, arms extended, hands locked together at the wrists with the palms facing out. He examined his stance, trying to remember what exercise this reminded him of. Many required the arms be extended, but none with the palms facing out. Even more confounding was the fear his wrists were locked together—as if manacled in some way. The police station? No. He remained in that position, as if expecting something to happen. Finally he spoke the word—"Yamantaka"—and dropped his arms.

"You were the only one who needed to be saved. Rajneesh kept repeating that, over and over. How could you forget such a thing?" Peter Mendoza, wearing faded corduroys and some hippie shirt with a black pentagram imprinted on its gray surface, sat across from David, dressed in tan slacks and a casual blue shirt. They were in a booth, sharing a meal at a little kosher restaurant not far from Spectra.

"I haven't forgotten," David said over a spoonful of chicken broth. "Only the Raj never specified what it was I needed to be saved from." Feeling a wave of insecurity, David attempted to swallow a whole matzo ball.

"Don't slosh it around. Chew, Davie, chew," Mr. Chang commanded.

In between following orders, David attempted to jolly his companion. "You remember Rajneesh would not eat kishke— but loved matzo ball soup?"

"I remember, but don't change the subject." Mendoza took small spoonfuls of soup.

"Nothing—a note of levity in the midst of gravity for my spirit's sake." David swallowed immediately. "Besides, why get started on that old stuff?"

"There's not a note of levity in what you've just told me, Davie. Frankly, it all sounds like one of the novels on my shelves. Incidentally, do you know I tried writing one of those once—about the Spanish Inquisition, but after six rejections I put the manuscript away." Mendoza sulked and speared a cucumber in his salad.

"What was wrong with it?" David asked with real concern.

"Not enough romance. I didn't have a heroine, just a bunch of monks—which brings up this Mrs. Hunt woman. I'm worried, Davie, really worried, in fact." Mendoza caught another cucumber.

"You're worried?" David stopped eating.

"I'm quite serious. I can feel your inclinations toward this high-brow shiksa, but—"

"—never get married," they intoned together.

"Never let it come to that ever," Mendoza emphasized.

"Peter, she's Catholic. Catholics as a rule avoid divorce—

unless one of them dies." David stared steadfastly at Mendoza. The kindly old comrade had become a welcome father figure since the demise of his own parent.

"Rajneesh felt that your karma was filled with dangerous elements still unfocused. That's why he wanted you to become one of his inner circle—to go under his protection. Why didn't you?" Peter demanded.

"I've already told you." David sounded querulous.

"I like hearing it." Peter pushed his salad plate away and nodded. "I love reviewing the old days."

"The Raj had me dressed in a ceremonial outfit, which I had paid dearly to have custom-made. On the appointed day I was to prostrate myself on the ground before him in a public ceremony—and then I would be his forever. *Rajneesh*—Indian for 'god.' " David sighed heavily. "I just decided I couldn't— and wouldn't—do it. That's all," David concluded abruptly, and picked at the chicken left on his plate.

"I don't believe that's all." Peter leaned over his salad and engaged David's eyes. "That's why I asked you to tell it again."

"What's not to believe?" David answered, somewhat taken aback. Peter's eyes were boring into him. "Okay, I've never told you this." David closed his eyes, bringing the event back. Strangely, he found himself stumbling over his words.

"I—I was waiting my turn at the ceremony. It was so hot that day and crowded with worshipers, I simply dozed off. I was sitting leaning against one of those pillars in the courtyard and I had this . . . daydream." He paused momentarily. "In the dream a tall, darkly dressed man was standing near me. His long, heavy beard hovered over me—like a blessing. I couldn't see his face, but he felt familiar." Another pause. "Anyway, I heard him say—very distinctly—'You shall not bow down before any other God.' I woke up, left the garden, packed my bags, and left India." David sat there staring into his soup dish.

"Ah, so. Thanks for the note you left us," Peter said, now satisfied. " 'Good-bye,' you wrote, 'see you around,' but no explanation. Thank God you paid your part of the hotel bill." Peter leaned forward to address his salad again.

"That was over nine—ten years ago," David rankled. "Why are we talking about it now?"

"Because you didn't follow your dream's advice—not really," Peter said curtly.

"I haven't been a good Jew. If that's what you're intimating? Peter?"

"Well, you're the therapist, you tell me." Peter's eyes were now piercing, the ancient judge in evidence. "Was the figure you saw Jewish or not?" Peter asked sternly.

"I'm—I'm not sure," David worried. "He was most likely—after all, the people one sees in one's dreams are always part of oneself, but . . ."

"Not always," Mendoza chided. "To answer your question—no, you're not a real Jew—in the old sense—you're a dabbler. Sure you observe when it suits you—high holy days with your relations. Would you be eating here now if I hadn't taken you? Alright, now and then you eat deli—and you ponder the Jewish problem."

"How did we get here? We were talking Spectra talk—occult novels, occult appearances—"

"Listen, Davie, being a Jew is occult enough—but you're right. This is no time for such discussion." Mendoza attacked his salad with fervor. "Later, down along the line."

"What down the line? What are you implying?" David's hackles were rising.

"You said this Mrs. Hunt saw the ghost, right?" Peter kept talking and eating.

"Yes, incredible as it may seem, she did. And I believe her."

"And I believe you." Mendoza chewed. "We live with so many of them, it's a relief when one actually takes shape—in whatever form. The one that appeared to Mrs. Hunt obviously lacked the strength to do the mischief it intended. Why? Well, that remains to be seen."

"He spoke in some other tongue," David said in a feigned matter-of-fact manner.

"Who did?" Peter paused in his zealous mastication.

"The figure in my dream," David pressed dryly, "the bearded man. It wasn't Hebrew."

"In what tongue then?" Peter leaned forward again, a piece of lettuce at the side of his mouth.

"I'm not sure, but . . ."

"But?"

"I understood him."

"And you're sure it wasn't Hebrew?"

David shook his head. "When he finally spoke, I noticed that he had no beard, none whatsoever."

"A dream Jew converts? Unbelievable." Peter looked askance. "It tells you, you can't always rely on dreams. Tell me more about him." Mendoza was positively being a detective, savoring the information as he had his meal.

David responded after a long pause and could hardly believe

what he was saying. "The man in my dream . . . he knows the Kunma."

"Why not?" Peter relished. "Come back with me. I have more books for you to take home."

David picked up the phone. "Yes?"

"David, are you free now?" Laurel sounded tight again.

"What's the matter? Is it Chris?"

"No, you were right. He had a touch of the flu, but he's fine now."

"Why are you speaking so quietly?"

"David, I'm afraid I'm being watched."

"Watched? By whom?"

"Who else?"

"Your father? For what reason?"

"To place a check on his errant daughter." Her bitterness was awash with melancholy.

"You're perfectly entitled to your own life now that—"

"Yes. You and I know that. But tell it to Papa. I told you about my mother. He's still gunning for her through me. Although I don't know what he hopes to accomplish. He's my father and I love him, but he's an unmitigated son of a bitch."

"So what are you saying?"

"That we'd better be careful about seeing one another."

"We are grown people, Laurel."

"I know that. You know that."

"How long has this been going on?"

"All my life."

"No, I meant—"

"I'm not sure how long I've been followed, and I'm not being paranoid. I went into New Haven this morning to do some shopping. A car had been following me ever since I left home. And after I left the department store, I drove over to a new art gallery. On the way back here I saw the same car following me. There was no mistaking it. It turned off Guernsey Lane, which is the last turnoff before getting here."

"Laurel—"

"There are only one or two rather derelict farmhouses down Guernsey Lane, and this was the same red Impala I saw back in town, with the same driver."

"What are you going to do?"

"What can I do? Except we mustn't see each other this weekend."

"Laurel, I'm not very good about such things. I begin to imagine—"

"Just not this weekend."

"Then when?" he almost yelled.

"At least until I'm absolutely sure . . ."

"Of what?"

"That he hasn't set somebody after you."

"Why me?"

"I'm a married woman." A moment of silence between them. "Someone obviously alerted him about us."

"Who, then?"

"David." A long pause followed. "I inadvertently walked into the kitchen this afternoon and found Chris talking long distance. A call had come for him."

"Grandpa."

"Exactly. And he hung up shortly after I arrived as if he

didn't want me to hear any part of his conversation. God, David, I think he's got Chris spying on us."

"Laurel, it's not because—You're not feeling guilty about us?"

"Of course I'm feeling—David, what's the use and what difference does it make now?"

David's mouth felt sour for this recrimination. "It's true then—you're not pretending—about your father. Forgive me, I'm sorry. It's just—" At precisely that moment, David heard the click of an extension being picked up in another part of the house.

"So I'm afraid I'm not up for cocktails on Friday next. I probably will be out of town. But let me call you when I'm certain. Okay? Bye!" And the line went dead—as did the extension after a long beat. David still held the phone against his ear, longing for the sound of her voice to continue. Despite their short-lived reconciliation, his ache for her now insisted she had not been with him at all and it, too, had been a chimera.

Hunt lay there in his hospital bed, staring upward. The force inside him stretched itself and coursed lavalike through his being, taking possession of every passage. The heat generated turned Hunt into a living dynamo, pulsing out excruciating yet exquisite tendrils of pain. As the force devoured and consumed, Hunt stewed in a subcutaneous hell. Prostrate, Hugh Hunt screamed against the invasion, but no sound came—the mouth was again all rictus. He alone heard its echo ricocheting through the chambers of his brain till the mind's eye contemplated nothing but the scorched, jellied mass of his own ruin.

PART **FOUR**

On Tuesday, May 14, three days away, Dr. Anita Berglund would have been running Lawson House for exactly ten years. The event would be celebrated with a cocktail party and dinner given by its board of directors.

Even before a proper introduction, one could deduce that Anita Berglund, née Griswold, was a daughter of old money from Philadelphia. Brown, questioning eyes set in a pale-skin, oval face took one's measure while retaining an air of friendliness. Now fifty-four, she combined two enviable traits in her elected profession—a tough mind ruling an optimistic spirit.

One of the brightest stars of the New York Psychiatric Institute, she had approached the isolation of Lawson House with much trepidation. Upon arrival in Bethany, Massachusetts, she saw immediately that this sylvan haven corresponded to the one hungered for in her imagination. Within a year she had fallen for a local artist with a Swedish surname and married him, while revising the entire working staff at Lawson House. The sanitarium continued to be one of the exclusive rest homes on the Eastern coast, though financial troubles still existed, and Anita its first female leader, an enormous distinction for a former graduate of the Bryn Mawr Academy.

Accompanied by a male nurse, Anita made her way toward Entry C. Bright sunshine drenched the grounds, which up to a few days ago had been soggy with late-spring rains. Anita sighed a huge sigh of relief, thanking the powers that be for the days of sunlight ahead. Now the strictures of winter's discipline could be relaxed and the surrounding lawns and countryside made available to the patients. Her eyes took in the manifold pleasures of her domain. A more suitable situation for Hugh Hunt to be treated in could not be imagined.

Anita looked at the package under her arm and quickened her pace. In all her years at Lawson, she could not recall a case as unique as Hugh Caswell Hunt's. On arrival, he was physically just this side of turning comatose. Yet within a four-week period, he seemed on the road to a remarkable recovery.

Yet there was a strangeness about Hunt . . . she couldn't quite put her expert finger on it. It was epitomized by the manner in which he usually greeted her: a sustained snakelike hiss followed by his protruding tongue. She was accustomed to eccentricities among patients, and although the nurses and attendants joked about it, there was something unnervingly lascivious about it, even hypnotic. It shook her considerably. She immediately thought of her husband, Carl, to whom she was devoted.

Needless to say, in her regimen, improvement and health reigned paramount. Toward that end, Anita had made herself personally responsible for Hugh's prognosis. Of course, the presence of Hunt's father-in-law, Faolain McGraw, in the background had forced her hand, but then her qualifications in the case were indubitably distinctive. A knowledge of art, an accretion attended to by her painter husband, permitted her to mix therapy with shop talk—a balance Anita managed with ease and dexterity. The reward for weeks of work was carefully wrapped in tissue inside the box she was carrying. The white silk scarf was Hugh Hunt's first actual request since his arrival at Lawson. Initially Anita had hesitated to comply. For Hugh Hunt, the man of the world, such a luxury item was par for the course in his life. For Hugh Hunt, the patient, the object could prove potentially dangerous. But Anita's thought was an academic consideration merely. If Hunt had wanted to do away with himself, there were certainly other means at his disposal—his oriental robe and sash came to her mind—even the very bed linens. The scarf was short—the chance was worth taking and there was sufficient vigilance over the patients to assuage her anxiety.

Advising the nurse to wait for her in the garden nearby, she took the back entrance and climbed the wooden staircase to Hunt's second-floor apartment. Slightly out of breath, she knocked on his door and found Hunt dressed in his expensive oriental gown. She saw at once he was naked under it. He was holding a small, black leather book in his hand. His tongue did its usual routine, which, under the circumstances, became uncomfortably suggestive. Anita frowned, realizing how the weight he'd put on caused his basic handsomeness to shine. His kind was reminiscent of the prototype so long sought after in the social whirl of her youth.

"I think this is what you wanted." She placed the package containing the scarf on a small table by the door. "I picked it out myself in Burlington yesterday. I hope you like it." In her mind's eye, she saw him wearing it at the end-of-the-month dance for the patients. Who knew, he might even ask her to be his partner. Hugh put down the book and with great deliberation unwrapped the package.

Hugh looked at Anita and his eyes danced briefly as he smiled.

"Well, how do you like it?"

Hugh dangled the scarf between his fingers and audibly sucked in his breath as he felt the material. "Hattas," he said. "I'm in your debt." He bowed in a gallant manner.

"I beg your pardon," Anita queried, and receiving no answer, simply said, "Well, I hope to see it on you soon."

Hugh looked at her directly, a puzzled expression on his face, but then he smiled again and nodded.

"I can't stay. I have to make my rounds, and Carl will be waiting his lunch."

"Has he completed it?"

"Completed? Oh, you mean the landscape? No, I think another week or so ought to do it. I know he'll be honored to have you see it when it's done."

"Yes, I'd like that." Hugh picked up the black book again.

Golden pages . . . a prayer book? "Well, don't pray too hard," Anita said foolishly.

As Hunt opened the door, his gown loosened and exposed his bare flesh further. Anita was forced to look away and met his eyes instead. They were turned inward—completely unaware of her female dilemma. Anita descended and met the attendant nurse with a bright smile. "He's doing just fine."

KUNMA

When Anita left, Hugh took the scarf and squatted down in the center of his living room. It was devoid of all furniture except throw pillows scattered over the bare floor. A bed with a single coverlet dominated a small alcove next to the bathroom. The walls were bare and still shone from a recent coat of white paint. The high windows had no bars and through them he could see the blue sky beyond. He suddenly shuddered, remembering. He placed the black book next to the scarf and began rocking back and forth.

"Yamantaka! Yamantaka! Yamantaka!" The imprecation awakened David at five in the morning. The sound repeated three times, kept resounding round his brain and on his tongue as Sam appeared in the kitchen, surprised at seeing his master up so early. David looked down at the cat and repeated the word. It was obviously not of Siamese origin for Sam's eyes registered no comprehension.

David waited till seven to rouse Peter. Ever an early riser, Mr. Chang was his affable self. David shouted the word *yamantaka* three times.

"Well, yes, I'm here," Peter said in response, and chuckled.

"Is that what the word means?"

"Oh—it's one of many such commands that appear in the *Malorum* under 'Summonings.' "

"I heard it last night in my dreams, and I woke up with it on my tongue."

"Well, it's usually used to invoke gods of wrath to appear. Not one myself, however. Still, how can I help?" Peter was beaming by this time.

"And do they appear?" David was looking down at Sam, whose head moved from side to questioning side.

"It was used by the priesthood and shamans of various Asiatic countries, and there exists documentation that the word— or rather, the command—had its effect. Let me call you back after breakfast, if I may. My bath is ready." Peter signed off.

"Yamantaka," David repeated softly to Sam. The Siamese yawned and put his paws up on David's bathrobe. The cat had taken the word to signify some new treat. Feeding time.

Anita did not arrive at her office on Monday until after eleven. As she sorted through the mail, she spotted the large envelope marked Patelson's Music, New York. She had placed an order for copies of the four-hand music of Schubert, and here they were: one copy for her and one for Father Fundy, the only other person in Bethany who matched her abilities, which were average. Playing four-hand Schubert was a bold step, beyond four-hand Mozart. She was scanning through the score rapidly and estimating its difficulties when the telephone rang.

"Anita."

"Oh, speak of the devil. They're here. They've just come."

"I beg your pardon?"

"The Schubert. It's arrived."

"Oh!" A long pause.

"Erik Fundy, you're not going to fizzle out on me?"

"Heavens no! I'm not calling about Thursday."

"Is there something wrong?"

"Well, actually, I'm afraid there is, and I don't think it's something we can discuss over the phone."

"Where are you?"

"I'm at my office at St. Mary's." His voice was actually shaking. "I've someone waiting in the rectory. Frankly, I think you should talk to her."

"Who is it?"

"Well, it's that patient of yours—Hugh Hunt. His wife is here."

"His wife?"

"She flew up from New Haven this morning. Came directly to the rectory and waited till I arrived."

"Why you?" Anita's jaw tightened.

"You won't believe this, Anita. I hardly do myself. But she's come here to see about . . . about arranging for an exorcism."

"A what?"

"For her husband. I don't know what to make of her story. She said she had attempted arranging for one just before her husband was transferred to Lawson House, but—" His own voice actually broke.

"Is she there now?"

"Yes. As I said, she's waiting in the rectory. There's no trouble. I mean, she's quite calm about it all—considering. I know this is not exactly your sort of business."

"I'll be there in fifteen minutes."

"Thank you. I'm relieved. You don't know how relieved I am."

When Anita arrived at the rectory of St. Mary's Church, Father Fundy and Laurel Hunt had already been joined by two other men. The door to the back entrance nearly slammed into Anita's face as she approached it. She stepped back as two men pushed forward with their burden. The lady in question was screaming objections against being manhandled. One of the men actually turned back toward Anita and nodded in some show of apology. Father Fundy appeared at the bottom of the steps.

"They just came in without saying a word and forced her to leave with them. There was nothing I could do and ..." He gestured helplessly toward the group now maneuvering themselves into a Cadillac convertible.

The short, wizened older priest stood next to Anita as Mrs. Hunt was forcibly eased into the backseat. She called back for Father Fundy's help, but Anita touched his shoulder, restraining him. He looked at her in great confusion. Anita nodded and said, "Later." They watched the car ease down the drive and then gun forward.

"They shouldn't be driving like that on these country lanes. They could cause a terrible accident."

"They're experts."

"Who are they?" He was forced to sit on the bottom step at the entrance. He breathed heavily, his chronic heart palpitations aggravated by this unwelcome encounter.

How to tell the gentle priest about Faolain McGraw? And these men who had shown up out of the blue at his command? The fierce power of money had demonstrated itself in the guise of Faolain McGraw, whom Anita secretly characterized as the "The Gangster Philanthropist." Spreading his influence throughout world institutions for the betterment of mankind, McGraw figured prominently on the board of Lawson House. In absentia, he had sent a lawyer with an imperative agenda in hand: namely that Hugh Hunt, McGraw's son-in-law, be transferred to Lawson's facilities to undergo treatment for a "nervous breakdown." In consideration, the lawyer had been authorized to present the board with a sizable check, along with the requisite legal documents, proving McGraw's power of attorney in the matter. The check would erase Lawson's running deficit of three years. This "contribution" would be continued provided that a certain condition was met: there was to be no access of any kind to Hugh Hunt without McGraw's express approval. Any and all attempts to see or contact Hunt were to be directly reported to him. His continued goodwill toward Lawson House would depend on the carrying out of said mandate. Anita and her board, plagued with fiscal woes, found themselves powerless before such fulsome persuasion.

Laurel knew where they were headed even before they got there. It was the inevitable conclusion to Papa Champ's surveillance of her life. It had been foolish of her to have tried contacting the priest under the circumstances, but it was a necessary last-ditch effort. When the car arrived at the Burlington airport, a private Learjet waited to whisk her to Taos and Papa's further judgment. Laurel knew Chris would be waiting on board for her, all smiles, anticipating the long-sought-after holiday . . . ostensibly Papa Champ's idea, but monitored at a longer distance by Hugh Hunt or the demon that pursued him. No one saw her cross herself as she moved through the swinging door toward the shining expanse of metal and chrome.

June 1982

The small Tibetan museum located on Staten Island had only just begun its summer schedule. Otherwise the treasures were visible through appointment only. Miss Penelope Waddell, general director for the museum, was at home having an early lunch when she received the alarming news. Someone had broken into the museum the night before and stolen one of the holy relics. Just five feet in height, she lifted her shoulders in an expression of great pique, threw a light shawl round her, and marched out to her garage in her sensible shoes. Ten minutes later she was driving up the steep hillside that led to the museum.

Mr. August Darnelle, entrusted with opening the museum during the coming summer season, was sitting on a broken beach chair just inside the entranceway. His sweat-stained white shirt stretched over an unbecoming potbelly, and he was fanning himself with an old newspaper. At the sight of Miss Waddell's accusing eyes, he froze in alarm.

"What in God's name has happened here, Darnelle?" Miss Waddell said in a most truculent manner. Darnelle, in his forties, looking fifty, rose laboriously from the chair and loomed over the diminutive executrix. Without saying a word, he pointed a pudgy finger at the entranceway. Darnelle finally found his voice. "Miss Waddell," he whined, "I have been caretaker here for seven years now. How could anyone have done such a thing?"

"Show me," Miss Waddell said abruptly.

He walked directly to the central room on the left side of the shed and pointed toward the glass case containing the various Prenba. Different kinds of prayer beads were on display: the yellow, wooden ones of the Gelugpa sect, the white conch shell of the Charasi, the red sandalwood of Tamdin, the human skull beads, and the snake spine and ordinary layman's set. Miss Waddell, not expected to be an expert in such matters, merely looked at Darnelle in puzzlement.

"Don't you see?" he bleated. "The raksa is gone. And look there." He pointed the same pudgy finger toward a replica of Gyal-Po-Suk-Den, the malevolent, brown-faced god, seated astride his white elephant. At its base were remnants of ashes. A thin residue of incense still lingered in the air around the base of the statue. Miss Waddell could not quite place the smell, but she realized the import of what was before her.

"Who could have done such a thing?" she demanded. "It amounts to a desecration."

Darnelle looked away in agony. "I'm sick, Miss Waddell, sick." The man seemed on the verge of tears.

Miss Waddell pulled her shawl tighter round her bony shoulders and began pacing. Who would covet such an object? And what was its value in dollars and cents?

"We'll have to report this, of course. What do you estimate the value of the—stolen beads?"

"Value? None."

"None?"

"They are only large brown seeds of the *Eleocarpus janitrus*. They are common in Tibet and we have the only set available in this country."

"I mean, from a collector's point of view?" Miss Waddell challenged.

Darnelle shrugged dismissively. "I wouldn't know."

"Is there any sign of a break-in?"

"None. I made sure to lock up as tightly as usual, I swear to you, Miss Waddell."

"Alright, Darnelle, I believe you." She looked at all the tarnished gold about her, dulled by age, though its basic richness lay undiminished.

"On second thought, why would anyone break in to steal a set of useless prayer beads? And why those? Why those, Darnelle?"

"The red beads were used by the Hindus and were adopted by the priests of the Bon Po sect. They helped in their intervention with demon gods."

"Oh, then I suppose that explains—" Miss Waddell turned to Gyal-Po-Suk-Den.

"Yes, Miss Waddell, but who would know about such things?" the poor man bleated.

"Well, you do for one."

"But as a guide, it is my business. It will take forever to replace them. Our agents are so slow about such things," he lamented.

Miss Waddell had been forming a theory about the motorcycle gangs—pouring in from all parts of the country. They had set up headquarters at a pub three miles down the road. Since they had begun streaming in—around late March—a synagogue in the vicinity had been sacked and looted. Arbitrary vandalism. And now in her territory. Disgusting.

"But there is absolutely no sign of any break-in, Miss Waddell."

"Are you sure?"

"Positive. Look yourself if—"

"I'll take your word, but I'd prefer a more expert opinion. I'm sure there's an explanation, even proof somewhere. After all, that's what the police are for—to see things that elude the ordinary eye."

Miss Waddell was first and foremost a pragmatist. Her primary concern was to relieve herself of all responsibility to her board and establish tangible proof of break-in and theft. Losing no more time, she marched toward the front office and the only telephone connecting the Tibetan museum with civilization.

Laurel was awake, sitting up in bed listening. Some sixth sense had been touched and she had automatically responded. Something was wrong. At first she heard nothing. She rose and put on her wrapper against the chill mountain air. When she stepped out into the corridor, she heard it—a low purring sound, like fear slowly edging its way through the darkness. Momentarily the wisp of a sound held her captive. What was it? Where was it coming from? Time seemed to stop as she remained in a fixed pose, her breathing hardly discernible in the stillness. The cry came again after an interminable pause. It was emanating from down the hallway. Near Chris's room. Mastering her panic, she moved determinedly toward it.

"Where are you?"

"New Mexico."

"I knew it. Are you alright?"

"Barely. I miss you, David. How are you, my darling?" Laurel looked furtively behind her.

"I'm a mess. It's been two weeks and not a word from you. No, I take it back, I'm not a mess. I'm a zombie. And you're right. Your old man is a bastard."

"I wish I could hate him, but I can't." She lowered her voice. "He's a miserable old man for all his money, but this is the only way he knows how to show his love."

"By kidnapping you?"

"He calls it protecting me." Her voice fell a notch further.

"Where are you calling from?" David strained to hear the doorbell for his next patient's arrival.

"You wouldn't believe this, but right now I'm looking out the door at a goat feeding in the backyard." Laurel covered the phone with her hand.

"Where's that? Laurel, I can hardly hear you." David grabbed a cigarette.

"In the rectory of a little church not far from the ranch. I told Father Dominguez here I needed to talk to Chris."

"Is he there with you?"

"He's at the ranch. Papa got his way after all and that's why I'm calling."

"Laurel, there wasn't another visitation?"

"No, thank God, but remember my mentioning the last time we spoke about Chris being sick?"

"Yes!"

"Well, it happened again last night. I went to Chris's room," Laurel spoke hurriedly, "and when I stepped in, Chris was sitting up in bed and staring into the darkness. I started to call out his name and something stopped me. Chris raised his hands out in front of him and he started to whimper. 'Don't let him come near me,' he said out loud, 'the cats must stop him.'"

"Cats—what cats?"

"I don't know. There are none on the farm I know of."

"Was there anyone else in the room?"

"No—and he kept on. 'Who are you?' he asked, still looking out. 'You cannot approach—the Holy One. Go back.' Those were his actual words."

"Holy One? But who could he mean?"

"Even worse, his little body went rigid and he screamed, 'No, Father! No!' and made rapid gestures in the air—grunting in absolute terror."

"What did you do then?"

"Nothing. I just stood there helpless. Hardly five feet away from him—and he fell back onto the bed. I didn't touch him, I just sat by him all the rest of the night."

"Holy One. Could he have possibly meant—oh, I don't know what I mean."

"David, I think he was talking about himself. And what could that signify?"

"The boy was dreaming. He's trying to work something out in his dreams. Fear for his father . . ."

"Of his father," Laurel countered.

"Laurel—that visitation—I've thought about it. Contrary to what we imagined, I've concluded it was another powerful dream, like this one. There's no other explanation."

"My father agreed it must have been something of the kind. In this instance, he assigned Chris some chores in the barn with Foggy, the groom. Chris threw up. Foggy thought that drinking unpasteurized milk was the reason Chris was sick. After all, Chris is still a city boy and this was his first time West in several years."

"Well, that certainly explains it." David sighed in relief.

"But I don't believe it," Laurel said with deep conviction. "What Chris saw in his bedroom was real to him, and as for the imaginary visitation—whatever it all means, I know something is about to happen. And I'm terrified."

"Laurel, don't give in to this."

"To what?"

"Laurel, please, there must be a more rational answer."

"Was Palfrey's appearance a rational occurrence? If you think that, it can only mean I was dreaming, too. I was not dreaming. Oh, David, you still don't believe me."

David remained silent, but he could distinctly hear the sound of a goat breaking the silence between them.

"Laurel, what can I do?"

"As a doctor, maybe she'll listen to you," she said quietly.

"Who will?"

"Dr. Berglund."

"Lawson House." David swallowed hard.

"He's there. It's there. You want more proof—well, go to Lawson House yourself."

"But why would Hugh Hunt want to hurt his own son?" David pleaded.

"Why?" Laurel laughed like a being in such torment as to defy description.

"Look, Laurel, Chris has undoubtedly taken on guilt for what's happened to his father. Children do such things, even make themselves responsible for it." *Jargon, nothing but jargon.* He despised himself at that moment. The situation demanded a response, not reactionary pablum. It was like adding personal insult to injury.

"What must I do?" he said, his voice shaking with self-loathing.

"By telling her everything you can convince her—as a doctor—that she must permit it."

"Permit what?" His voice cracked.

"Exorcism."

David hung his head and could not respond.

"What else is there to fight this thing with? There's a Catholic priest in Bethany. I talked to him. I tried. They're friends, he and Dr. Berglund."

"Alright, calm down, Laurel."

"I'm perfectly calm. You must believe me. I know exactly what I'm saying to you, David. The padre is knocking. He's about to hear my confession. God will forgive me if I keep your name a secret from his ears."

David could hear the knocking in the background and Laurel's raised voice in response.

"David, I'll call you when I can. Remember, it's up to you. Coming, Padre!"

And the line went dead. Dybbuk, devil, Kunma, however you looked at it, they were all the same thing. The basest of illusions, what could they be otherwise? All of it. His dreams—these happenings? He could not, must not, give in to any of this. Mendoza notwithstanding. But still, he had been caught up in its wheel—and it was spinning faster.

He heard his doorbell ring. How could he clear his mind to contend with the comparatively puny anxieties of his next patient? He put out his cigarette and went to the door.

That weekend David arrived at Lawson in a heavy downpour that continued for the rest of the afternoon. He had contacted Dr. Berglund the morning after his conversation with Laurel. He had made it clear that he needed to consult with her as a doctor on some vital new information regarding Hugh Hunt, "containing rather dangerous elements." Those were his own words. Intrigued by his statement, the recent events, and most importantly, that he had been a consultant early in the case, Anita consented to an interview the following day.

David had carefully chosen a smart English sports jacket, tan gabardines, and matching accessories to set off his putative charms. He sat opposite Anita Berglund at a small teakwood table in her office. Poker-faced and tight-lipped, Anita wore a dark ensemble jacket and trousers with a white, wide-collared shirt, which belied her subtle attractiveness. The only cosmetic concession was a pair of small opal earrings—a "family heir-loom," inherited from her doting grandmother.

Anita's brown, penetrating eyes never left David's face, except to pour cups of tea—a blend prized by the Griswold clan. David admired her sangfroid as one wild detail of his story followed another. He had included everything, even his painful felony in the eyes of the law. It was a precarious moment for David, but desperation had forced his hand.

Perhaps if Doctors Berglund and Sussman had hit it off better than they did, what was to follow might never have transpired. Perhaps it was the workings of karma—one can never be sure. Havoc had preceded this fateful meeting and hereon havoc would lead to devastation.

"Kunma," she said aloud, almost to herself. "Tibetans are Buddhists, aren't they?"

David nodded tensely.

"And the country is overrun with Communists now, isn't it?"

"Has been for years," David answered patiently. "You might say the local religion itself is an endangered species. Their leaders are putting up strong resistance to prevent extinction."

They sat in silence again, the sound of distant birds chirping at odds with the nature of this colloquy. Anita leaned back in her preferred chair, with its embroidered headrest, and her left hand lifted to support her pouting lips. "What exactly is this Kunma, then?"

"Anita, that's what I'm here to find out. First, I need to reaffirm that everything I've told you is fact. You know enough about me that, if you chose to, you could jeopardize my career and even my life."

"The police, you mean."

"Exactly. If you doubt the veracity of any part of my story, well . . ."

"That depends on what you want. It still sounds to me that, at the bottom of things, we're dealing with a high-level delusional system. Mr. Hunt's records confirm my own." She blinked slowly with self-importance. "Yet, you're implying the man is a murderer, or might be."

"Or in league with someone—or something, that is."

"This tea's cold." Anita sighed. "I'll have some fresh sent up."

"Please don't bother on my account."

"Then I'll bother on mine. I don't hear this kind of thing every day, you know."

"I'm sorry. I didn't mean to sound so preemptory. All I need is a chance to see and speak to Hunt again. I need to observe him in as close a manner as possible."

"Spend time at Lawson, you mean."

"Exactly."

"Well, I can't offer you a job."

"I don't want a job. Another arrangement, perhaps."

"Such as?"

"Consulting physician, research, anything." David shrugged. "I need to be sure what it is we're fighting."

"Dr. Sussman . . ." Anita hestitated.

"David, if you don't mind."

"Hugh Hunt was accepted here as a patient. What you're suggesting is that there is, for lack of a better word, some supernatural element in this case. As an administrator, I have the interests of my board to consider. As a good doctor, I have the interests of sound medicine at heart, not to mention the welfare of over a hundred patients. I need time to think over what you've told me."

"How long?"

Anita rose and checked her desk diary.

"Give me till Friday."

The carpet. A turquoise blue was in it he hadn't noticed before. The sunlight shone in the room from a high, oblong window to his right. The walls were covered with mythic figures in various stages of deterioration. He could make out one huge pair of hands with palms extended and fingers splayed. Candles exuding the smell of a rancid fatty substance clogged the air.

He saw a collection of books, stacked against the left wall with gold-lacquered undersides. And three figures—at the top of a small platform—wearing oddly shaped hats, their voices droning. He saw a mouse nibbling away at one of the huge books.

His wrists were bound together. He was beginning to look up, for someone had signaled.

Then the flames—and the stench.

David lay there quietly reviewing what he had contemplated

in the mind's eye of sleep. More and more pieces were being added to a growing scene—tantalizing him, forcing his intelligence into a corner.

The dream activity had increased since his visit to Lawson House. His bed table was stacked with material from Spectra, all concerning one subject: Tibet. Peter had underlined clearly the important sections.

David checked his clock: 5:07. He had had only four hours of sleep, but felt invigorated, as if he'd managed his quota of eight. He would read till nine, breakfast, pick up his mail, and start his work at ten with the first patient. He would stay in all day or until Anita called. She had said Friday. Time enough for her to have made inquiries through her institute connections. The "karma bum" would have his case reopened. If he hadn't heard from her by midafternoon, he'd contact her. He picked up the book lying by the side of the bed and switched on the lamp. He looked down at the paperback and saw the hieroglyphics that represented the word *Tibet*. His fingers moved over the symbol and sought out Mendoza's pages.

The band of light oscillated up and down the frame of Hunt's body. It moved to a rhythm other than the one governing the vibrations inside his skin. He fought against the forces as best he could. If he lost, he would be drowned. Gradually the two energies moved relentlessly toward his head and interlocked. The resulting lights were blinding and he lowered his lids against their dazzlement. The pain started behind the retinas and reached out toward the hypothalamus in the brain center. It pulsed together into a tight skullcap that burst in a downward rush. The hidden orifices of the body opened like hungry mouths to receive the heat. He moaned as the wave engulfed him. His nipples distended and he convulsed.

He lay there breathing irregularly, body drenched in perspiration. He still wore his oriental robe, now deeply stained, and it clung to him like a limp mantle.

Gradually a cooling started at his feet and edged upward—slowly. The heat was gradually encircled and lay dormant. Occasional fingers of the heat darted.

A single word shaped itself in his waking consciousness—TUMO—fire in the snow.

Anita Berglund's conclusion was swift and she believed comprehensive. She was just out of her bath and would shortly be on the way to preparing her breakfast. Carl had left early to work in the barn on his landscape. Upon further investigation, David Sussman's reputation as a flaky outsider of the psychiatric hierarchy had quickly been substantiated by his recital that would do honor to Edgar Allan Poe. Pursuing the outer fringes of psychoanalysis could only lead to folly, and his studied attempt to charm her had been thoroughly resistible. She persisted in regarding Hunt's "difficulties" in the light of her own diagnosis and the medical reports that confirmed it. She had been unusually successful over the years in her ability to assess the larger scientific picture of patients under her care. Accordingly there was no need to contact McGraw, as agreed, for approval.

Clearing her throat, she proceeded down to the kitchen to pack Carl's lunch for the day and prepare her own meal. Anita decided to treat herself this Sunday morning to a perfect country breakfast. In her green wraparound and brown Indian moccasins, she started to prepare two eggs—sunny side up—link sausage, fresh corn muffins with homemade strawberry jam, and coffee. She loved to cook and it was remarkable that a woman in her midfifties, with her appetite, could still retain a decent figure. In that respect, she resembled her mother.

She opened a fresh can of French Quarter coffee. She loved the chicory flavoring and put three tablespoons into her old blue-and-white-stained percolator. Her preserves stood, lined on three separate shelves, in a little alcove storage room off the back entrance to her kitchen. The strawberry preserves were on the top shelf along with the apple and pear. She climbed a mini-ladder and chose one of the mason jars and wiped it off on her wrapper. She placed it on the sideboard and checked the muffins, which were just about done. The sausages lay draining on a sheet of paper toweling alongside the jar of preserves. Anita picked out a small dish with a blue-and-gold border from the dishwasher. It was pure Woolworth's, but she adored cheap china. There had been too much Wedgwood in her life. Turning the gas on under the frying pan holding the eggs, she went to open her jar of strawberries. When she uncapped the jar and broke the protecting wax, the smell that rose to her nostrils almost caused her to black out. Nausea gripped her stomach and she staggered backward. She lifted the jar to look inside and simultaneously it slipped from her grasp onto the tile floor, where it smashed into a thousand pieces. The liquid spread everywhere, like tentacles from a bloated growth. Anita's floor became soaked in blood. In the middle of the wreckage, large pink objects flapped about like fish out of water—flipping back and forth through the glass slivers that cut new gashes into the frolicsome fruit. There was no mistaking what they were—not strawberries, but human tongues, pulsing like living things in a last-ditch gasp for life.

David was the sole occupant of the Cessna twin-engine plane heading north from La Guardia. High cumulus clouds were a bank of cushions, easing him along to his destination at Burlington airport. He had left hastily, left Sam in the care of a neighbor (whose dog loved Sam), and canceled his appointments for the next three days. The trip itself would take over an hour. At the airport, a taxi would be forced to double back over the Massachusetts border to Bethany, another twenty minutes at best.

On the phone, Anita's manner had been clipped, but he could tell that something had gone haywire.

"How soon can you get here?"

"I'll take the next available shuttle up."

"One thing. You're not to go to the hospital. Come to my house. We'll decide what's to be done from there."

"I understand."

"No one must know you're up here. My address is . . ."

By one-fifteen, David was on his way. He could hardly believe his sensational luck. Anita met him out front and together they made for her study. She had spruced herself down, wearing a lavender muumuu, with a pathetic beaded necklace round her neck. But she had applied some rouge to her cheeks, which only served to highlight the haunted look in her eyes. She was trying to keep herself under control as she described the events of that morning.

"Later I went to the ward personally to check on Hunt. He

was restless and complained about his burning sensations again."

David took the grisly tale with surprising stoicism, allowing for a wisp of nausea coiling at the base of his stomach. The event, he understood, was another escalating detail in a story continuing to unfold.

"How long had he been restless?" David prepared for the worst.

"The nurse in charge had reported he'd been so for the past two days." David blanched. Then this is the third day. This is it. He swallowed several times to keep his gorge from rising. For in past incidents, the third day was a cooling down of symptoms—the result of some catastrophic event having occurred while Hunt was in the throes of the burning sensation. Here was another repetition of that syndrome.

"Can I get you something?" Anita asked shakily.

"A Coke. Have you got a Coke?"

"Coca-Cola?"

"It'll settle my stomach. It's the best thing for it."

"I'll take a look."

They sat facing one another while he stirred his soft drink with a spoon.

"You should have seen me after." Anita's experience had obviously softened her. "I wish I'd known about Coke. How did I miss it?"

"I got it from an ex-junkie, but mothers use it on kids, too. The trick is to stir it and settle the carbonation."

Anita nodded, watching as David drank the "magic" elixir.

David posed what was now their mutual concern. "The question is, how do we proceed?"

"Ah, yes, the third day . . ." Anita put her hand to her forehead in disbelief. David reached out and took her hands, which were visibly shaking. His first gesture of intimacy with the formidable high priestess of Lawson House.

"I need to be by his bedside for as long as possible. As I explained, the third day has always been the crucial one—I know something will take place. With him. Around him. Even within him. Some special manifestation that must follow these incidents. But I must be there to see."

"Why do so many things happen in threes? Schubert's divine triplets, so they say, Christ the Savior getting out of his mess on the third day, and three strikes, you're out." Anita paused and looked at him blankly. "Oh, God, do you realize what kind of risk I'm taking doing this?"

Anita sighed and cleared her throat. "The next check on Hunt will be at five o'clock. There's no one else in emergency right now, so you're lucky. Another check will be at eight, and a final one at eleven, then nothing till morning."

"Is there a phone in the ward? Some way I can reach you—just in case?"

"I'll be here with Carl all evening. It's fifteen minutes away from the hospital and there's a pay phone right outside the exit. Whatever you do, don't use the hospital phone. The switchboard would have to connect you. I don't want anyone to know you're there." She had no intention of apprising McGraw of her decision. She had to risk it.

"And what did you do with . . . them?"

She stared at David and swallowed.

"Where are they?"

"When they stopped twitching, I—I cleaned up the floor. Cleaned the whole mess up."

"And what did you do with . . . them?"

"I wrapped them in newspaper, dug a hole in the garden, a big hole, and burned them. I used some kerosene."

"What made you decide to do that?"

"My grandmother always told us that evil things had to be burned and buried in the ground—then a prayer said over them."

"I never heard that one."

"Beats Coca-Cola, doesn't it?"

David had not let go of her hands all the while. He kissed her on the cheek and she blushed.

"I couldn't remember the words of a prayer, so I just thought *prayer* and tried to make my mind a blank as I watched them burning from the porch. The smell was unbelievably awful. What I was really thinking was, there goes almost a hundred years of psychoanalysis up in smoke."

" 'There are more things in heaven and earth, Horatio, than are dreamt of in our philosophy.' "

"Hamlet?" she responded tonelessly. "As I recall, he couldn't make up his mind about most things.

"Still, there's one thing you can safely say about Shakespeare—he was a better writer than Freud."

Eight o'clock had come and gone by the time David reached the emergency ward. Before him, row after row of white beds—a collection of shrouds—with Hugh Hunt in the middle as their scabrous pendant. David had not seen Hugh since his visit to

Immaculate. He felt a rising frisson as he contemplated the man lying there preternaturally still, the tips of his front teeth glinting through slightly opened lips. A small bedside lamp glowed duskily, keeping half of the body in shadow. The effect was to make the man's inner division almost palpable. A tube stuck out from his right arm, held firmly in place with a bandage and adhesive, leading up toward a bottle of glucose solution suspended from an apparatus above his head.

The ward was situated on the extreme north end of the complex, far enough away from the main part of the grounds as to exist quite independently. No corridors or passageways connected it to the main house. Light seemed to creep dimly through two large dormer windows. The space might once have served as a meeting hall or even a ballroom during the Civil War.

David spotted a door marked Office on the right side of the ward and eased himself into a rattan chair facing Hugh Hunt's bed. David was dressed in a lightweight summer suit, which was no protection against the encroaching chill. He had promised not to smoke and assured Anita he would move about every half hour to forestall the risk of nodding off. He listened to the country sounds surrounding the building and steadied his nerves for what lay ahead. When he looked at his watch, it was a few minutes after nine. He had sat practically immobile for almost an hour while night descended over northern Massachusetts. Moonlight forced its way into the ward. The ivied panes filtered its effect over the room, and the other beds hung in pale attendance. It was now possible to believe these uniformed shapes concealed beings waiting for some command to begin their nocturnal sport. David shook his head against this disconcerting vision. He needed to keep strong guard against the fulsome prompting of his imagination. He sat back in a chair and tried to relax. He thought of doing his breathing exercises, but it might attract someone's attention passing by. The tension burrowed into the back of his neck muscles and almost lulled him into a false sleep, but he tossed it off by digging his nails into his palms.

Hugh's expression had not changed. The light was almost lambent now over his features. David realized Hugh had shifted his position in bed while he had been moving about the ward. In an effort to stay awake, he started to study Hugh's face. Within a minute, it became a blur and David's chin dropped to his chest.

Then he snapped to attention. Hugh Hunt had started to move—first imperceptibly, then the fingers clenched and his mouth went slack. David sank back into the chair and sat legs apart, leaning forward. The fingers clenched again.

And unclenched.

Clenched.

Unclenched—crablike—ever so slowly.

A minute later David caught his breath. The insidious stench was filling the chamber as Hunt's movement shifted to his hips, which thrust upward in the same slow motion action as the fingers. David felt something stirring in the atmosphere and he gripped the arms of the chair. The activity in the air was getting him light-headed. He made every effort to keep his eyes riveted to Hunt's body. His pelvis was now pushed forward and his mouth formed an oval as if something was tunneling into him. The hips lowered themselves onto the bedsheets and the mouth gradually closed. It seemed part of some graceful erotic dance.

David stared at the second hand of his watch. Its steady rhythmic pulses helped balance his own heartbeat. Suddenly his head fell apart, and he felt a growing lightness. He kept watching the second hand, which began to blur. He was losing the battle against the pressure in his head. He sank into the chair and closed his eyes.

When David opened them again, he was staring directly at the ceiling, only the ceiling was exactly two feet away from him. His heart almost leaped from his chest. He raised his right hand in protest and saw his fingers penetrate the wooden beams above. What was happening to him? More dreaming? If so, the scenario of the room with the carpet had taken a dramatic turn. Then he looked down and saw an extraordinary sight. David Sussman lay asleep in the rattan chair below him. But David Sussman was also on the ceiling. Only once before had he experienced this sensation—in Rio Porto, Mexico, when he'd been induced to chew the peyote root. The sickness following had far outstripped its reward. He looked down again. There he was sprawled out ten feet away. This must be a dream. In a moment, he'd will himself back and no doubt face another phantasmagoria. He watched his fingers and wrist disappear again into the wooden beams. He could see light, knobby notches heavily scarred—signs of termite activity. The collapse of another historical site was imminent.

He looked straight ahead. The ceiling now seemed to be retreating. He was floating backward toward the ground, toward his corporeal self. He raised his arms, almost in protest, and for a fleeting moment saw that they were encased in long, black sleeves—as if part of a robe. In a blinding flash of light behind his eyeballs, David awoke with a start in his chair and realized that Hunt was sitting up in bed. The sight was made more phenomenal because Hunt was simultaneously still asleep in bed. Two Hugh Hunts were before him, caught in different attitudes. David rose out of his chair—his legs pure jelly—the stench gaggingly sweet. The Hugh Hunt sitting up shifted his position and sat sideways by the sleeping one. The figure sitting up had a glabrous head, the skin over it dark brown with a jaundiced tint. The head hung loosely on its neck. It lolled and with effort slowly raised itself until David could see its face. It was another person. How had he gotten in and when? But David sharpened his scrutiny—the skin over the face and bared chest was furrowed, tight-mottled; the nostrils flared spasmodically. The head kept up its languid motion as if the creature supporting it were newborn—a naked thing unused to life. The gyrations stopped finally and the half-lidded eyes opened and looked directly at David. An eagle's glint shot out and David thought, *Mongol.* The eyes fluttered again and the expression changed. His demeanor suggested someone lost in satiety—gorged even. He smiled—the specter's mouth was smeared with blood—and he had no tongue.

The Kunma himself was before him.

PART **FIVE**

David closed his eyes against the sight of the bloody mouth as a profound lassitude unfurled itself from the pressure in his head. It stole along his limbs, leaving him locked in the rattan chair. From some dim corner of his being a buzzing sounded—rasping voices rising and falling. The smell of musk enveloped him as the command asserted itself—*Yamantaka! Yamantaka! Yamantaka!* The specter had appeared.

The Kunma was looking down at him—a hideous grimace on its face. It was attempting to speak. What resulted was indecipherable, yet the monotonous drone seemed to cling to David epiphytically, like another layer of skin seeking to suck through his own. Trance-bound, David slowly raised his head and looked at the wraith. Through its guttural efforts at speech, David sensed shards of hatred, while tears flowed from the distended eyes. Its mouth twisted to form a single word—*Gomchen*—followed haltingly by another—*Yongen*. Without a tongue, the monster snarled in its struggle and repeated the two words over and over. It then sank to the floor and prostrated itself before David. Shades of Rajneesh—only now he was the "god." *Gomchen—Yongen.*

David remained immobilized as the heat intensified and flooded his solar plexus, then turned to ice. He felt soft groveling moves, then a clawed hand rested on his knee. A deep silence descended over the ward. While David attended to this incomprehensible litany, a door was simultaneously opening and closing within him. The reek of musk lingered briefly, then appeared to vanish through some undisclosed aperture. The pre-chill of dawn crept in while David sank lower into himself and slept.

PART SIX

Gradually, the sun rising in the east caused pale fingers to edge their way through the deciduous trees and lightly tap at the dormer windows. The wooden interstices framing the glass cast imprints on the floor, giving the chamber a cathedral-like ambience. The early cardinals and blue jays signaled one another from their perches, and from the not-too-distant village of Bethany a motor revved and echoed incongruously in the morning air.

What seemed hours later, David woke with a start. He pushed himself into a fitful wakefulness and sat there feeling foolish and overwhelmed—at the mercy of emotions never experienced before. His hand clutched something. A white silk scarf. His fingers tormented its fold. Kunma's greeting was lying across his lap. Not far from him, Hunt slept in his bed, still wrapped in shadows. The other had come and gone. For a moment, the memory of the heat stunned and a trace of lassitude insinuated itself. He feared to approach the sleeping man, his face now turned away in the darkness. David looked at his watch: 6:17. He would have to get out of the ward before the Lawson routine began. And so it did, unmindful of the cataclysm that lay dormant at its center.

David and Anita did the best they could under the circumstances. It was seven-thirty and they were huddled together in her private den.

Anita fingered the scarf in utter disbelief. *"Gomchen?"*

"It's the Tibetan equivalent of 'rabbi' or 'priest,' " David answered. "It also means 'teacher.' "

"And this?"

"The white scarf is a traditional sign of reverence, called hattas."

"That's the word he used when I first gave it to him." Anita winced. "Well, do we contact Father Fundy?"

"Wrong church."

"Is there a Tibetan religious organization we—"

"I doubt it, up in this neck of the woods. Besides, it would take too much time." David's fingers went limp around the scarf.

"What about the police?" Anita ventured.

"And what do we tell them?"

"We must do something." Still in her morning robe, Anita looked worn, disheveled even.

"We wait."

"For what?"

"For one—the newspapers. Three days later a victim surfaces without a tongue." David twisted the hattas in his hands now. "That's the deadly result the Kunma inflicts on his victims before returning to Hunt. He returns to further enslave him."

KUNMA

The walk over to Anita's house had been only a temporary solace for David. His head was still a whirl, although, surprisingly, his heart action was normal. He placed the white scarf over the arm of his chair and drank the home-brewed tea slowly.

Anita moved to her desk, picked up her letter opener, and wrestled with its length between her palms. She simply stared at David in a penetrating manner, her challenging "doctor's" look. Finding perfect veracity written on his solemn face, Anita's cheeks reddened.

David sobbed a single sob and a piece of corn muffin fell from his mouth to the floor. His sense of dislocation was threatening to overwhelm him.

"David, look at me. Could you have dreamed this whole thing? Could the episode have triggered some form of hypnotic suggestion?"

"Were the tongues a dream?" he said quietly.

Anita shook her head, taking courage from the weird tangibility of her own experience.

"And this, what about this?" David unraveled the scarf, seething with anger. "I didn't bargain for any of this. I came seeking closure for something—something tangible, comprehensible, a runaway psychotic even. Not this—this—Frankenstein creature groveling at my feet."

"He actually called you his . . . teacher?" Anita put down the ivory letter opener.

"The word is *gomchen*," David said sardonically.

"But where? When?" Anita wheeled.

"I don't know."

"And what does he expect you to do?"

"I don't know that either." David nodded sadly in resignation.

"David, have you told me everything?" She was trying not to sound harsh. "You must keep nothing from me if I'm to help."

"I told you what happened," David whispered.

"Alright. One more thing. You said you heard some voices. What language did they speak in?"

David's eyes swam in bewilderment. A bewilderment fraught with a secret knowledge he could not articulate.

"I understood—everything—that's all."

Anita sat back in her chair. The sweet violet patterns on her headrest belied the congealed vessel of fear resting against them—fear for the thing waiting back at the hospital she headed and for this man before her, shrouded in some harrowing complicity.

David spoke haltingly, "It . . . it was as if our meeting was . . . predestined to take place. Every event I've described guided me toward this moment—and believe me, I'm the last one to believe in that sort of crap."

The sound of Carl coming down the stairs broke the spell.

"Where do we go from here?" Anita hastened, pushing her head harder against the violets.

"You've heard of doubting Thomas. I felt the Kunma's touch—there's no retreating from that any longer. Don't do anything, Anita, until I get back to you. There's someone who can help us." David started to rise from his chair. As he did so, the hattas slithered off the armrest onto the floor, where it gathered like a curled snake. "He's in New York. Trust me, and I'll take this token with me." Leaning down, David picked up the scarf and put it around his neck. The result, shorn of its danger and mystery, was debonair.

Anita started clearing the tea things as her genial bear of a husband stood stretching in the doorway, bringing present reality into sharp focus.

Peter Mendoza had spent a sleepless night. David was on his mind. He wandered around in the darkness of his little store in worn leather slippers, touching the books with their enfolded secrets ready to terrorize yet entertain. His apartment allowed access to Spectra through a side door in the alley adjacent to it. He spoke to the books as he passed them, not unlike the way his dead wife had spoken to flowers and often awakened them to life. She'd never spoken that way to him, although a daughter was somehow born in their impasse. His daughter, Amy, had disappeared seven years ago, taking his wife's jewels and a goodly sum from his safety-deposit box. He had not heard from her since. In this crisscross of karmic currents affecting him, Peter felt the awesome weight of this self-knowledge. His fortune as husband and father was deeply unassuaged. But for David's reappearance in his life, he would have continued to wither on his own branch. Beside his books, there was no one closer to him now than David—for certainly Peter Mendoza's sense of well-being had been rescued by David's karmic dilemma. He felt privileged to be part of its resolution. Contemplating David's arrival, Peter turned the sign around in his window to Closed for the day.

Hours later in his apartment, Peter removed the small ashtray and, tossing its contents away, returned it to David's side as he prepared to light up again.

"I saw the Kunma" were David's first words as he entered the apartment.

"I knew you would," Peter replied. "He has been drawing you toward him. It was only a matter of time."

"Could I have a glass of water?" David had recounted the entire event.

"I could boil up some tea?" Peter rose with alacrity to prepare it.

"No, thanks, water will do for now." The taste of Anita's home brew still nestled in David's memory of yesterday's disclosure.

Peter did as he was bidden, then sat back in his chair opposite David.

"I keep seeing the two of them—Hunt resting and the Kunma sitting up beside him. It was almost obscene—the possessor and his possessed."

"And you will see him again—the possessor—even in other guises," Peter ventured.

"Then it was the Kunma Laurel saw that night in my apartment?" David looked up at Peter.

"Yes, I believe it was," Peter said steadily. "Mrs. Hunt's nightmare visitor as one of her 'paramours,' shall I say delicately, was part of the plan to draw you to him—and partly a punishment for her . . ."

"Infidelity," David interjected.

"Precisely." Mr. Chang put his palms together. "That's why his attack was—to say the least—halfhearted."

"You mean he could have killed her," David said, terrorized at the thought.

"Except he was more interested in you than in her." Peter's

chin rested against his fingers. "While you were speaking, I kept going back to the Tolos monster—I've been trying to fit certain things together concerning its origin and evolution, and you know it's extraordinary what prescience Rajneesh had concerning the two of us—in our separate ways."

"What sort of prescience—concerning what?" David finished his glass of water.

"Don't think I wasn't prepared for our little conversation today." Peter picked up a book on the table and placed it gently in front of David. He next put on his slim, silver-edged glasses and opened the volume at a place already marked by him.

"I want you to study this picture—it's a reproduction, of course, but nevertheless . . ."

"*Estan calientes,*" David read out the caption printed under the reproduction. "That's something like 'it's hot.' "

"Exactly right," Peter said cryptically in his best *Lost Horizon* manner. "What do you make of it?"

David turned to the book's red cover. "*Goya's Caprichos,*" he said, looking at Peter. He flipped quickly through its pages.

"Do you know them?" Peter unfolded his palms and edged his chair forward.

"Of course, remarkable stuff—so tell me."

Peter swallowed slowly. "You're looking at four monks eating with rather grotesque expressions of delight on their faces—with one fellow monk rushing to join the feast. They've all obviously imbibed too much wine. But can you imagine what they might be eating?"

David bent to examine the picture more closely. "It's difficult to tell. Eggs?"

"Would it surprise you if I were to say they are ingesting parts of a human brain?"

David pushed the book away from him as if the act were taking place on his lap. "You're kidding me" was his only response.

"Hardly, Davie—I kid you not. To make matters palatably worse, there was a time when I—too . . ."

David's mouth fell open. Peter's steady eyes met David's perplexed gaze. "Goya was even more graphic about such ecclesiastical mishegoss, but the plates were seized by the Inquisition and Goya was put to torture."

"Surely they didn't . . ." David hesitated.

"No—Goya was a national treasure. He was merely 'punished' and released, then carefully watched. While the plates in this series were destroyed, *Estan Calientes* was permitted to remain in the catalog because of its ambiguity. 'Eggs,' you said. Well . . ."

David studied Peter's sadly lined face. "Are you that close to your—past life—that you can actually see it, live with it?"

"Yes, it's remarkably vivid. Rajneesh confirmed my suspicions of it, and as a judge of the Church I was witness to, and often involved with, the prisoners' fates. There were many who were tortured and even torn apart. Heads were shaven, brain matter exposed and gouged at. It was extraordinary to hear a man pleading his innocence and within seconds spouting blasphemies as part of his cortex was invaded. It made no difference if the man was actually innocent or not. His tampered brain proved how basically deceitful and inharmonious human beings were to God's higher purpose. The Inquisition reaped glory to His name, while ripping knowledge with their pincers and ingesting the human particles they purged. As such, the unacceptable contents were purified by those who partook of them. This done in imitation of Christ, who took upon himself the sins of the world, in an insane parody of that idea."

"How does this relate to our Tolos creature?" David kept examining Peter's face ever more closely. "The Tolos monster is half-demon, half-human."

"It's really the same principle." Peter replaced the Goya reproductions with one of the Tibetan demon. "The bestial part of the Tolos feeds only on the human skull."

"Surely not to purify itself." David's voice rose in contention.

"In another way. The monks ate to the greater glory of God—to become vessels of His holiness. Now regard these others." Peter turned to the pictures of Tibetan demon gods. "These are related to the Tolos. Notice the changes in their physiognomy, how they become—"

"More human," David said, exhaling in wonder.

"By imbibing the brain the creature gains the human's intelligence and slowly evolves, leaving its animal self behind. Notice how the postures of these evolving creatures changed. The heads start looking upwards—looking for their higher purpose in the universe."

"Pity the poor beast," David lamented.

"Hence the two-sided dilemma of the Kunma. A beast with no tongue who must possess a human to achieve its goal."

"What could that be? Its goal?" David sighed.

"The goal, I suppose, of any living being," Peter said sadly, then remained silent.

"To be happy," David filled the silence.

"And to be redeemed—in some way."

"Oh, God—the bandwagon of salvation."

"What about the tongue, the Kunma's missing tongue?" David answered like some prosecuting attorney on the attack.

"Hunt will become the Kunma's tongue. He will speak for it. When the process of total ingestion is accomplished."

"You mean, total takeover of Hunt's persona. But Hunt appeared to his son. How was that 'accomplished'?"

"That was not Hunt. It was an astral projection of Hunt—made by the Kunma. The boy was asleep. It appeared to the child as a very vivid dream. The boy's need for his father made it real to him. You, of all people, know of such things."

"Yes, I know. Rajneesh spoke of such manifestations, and I experienced it briefly at Lawson House."

"An intimation of some inherent power you must possess."

"How does Tibet figure in all this?" David was still prosecuting.

"The creature called you *Gomchen*, 'teacher,' and *Yongen*—in many languages, even in colloquial Hebrew—signifies 'young.' But in this configuration it is a Tibetan name—not a description," Peter said sadly.

"But why the other tongues—the ones in the jar for instance?" David rose as if addressing a jury or a witness in court.

Peter laughed. "Davie, if a child were to tell you such a Bubbamansa, how would you interpret it?"

"Well, with a child, a child demands attention and will rattle on until he gets it. In other words, of course—"

"Of course, of course," Peter remonstrated jovially. "The lady psychiatrist, she didn't believe you. The tongues appeared to her in order to command her attention."

KUNMA

David nodded slowly. There was a long silence before Peter ventured to ask his crucially planned question.

"Have you decided yet who that dark figure was that appeared in your daydream in Pune?"

It was then David opened his briefcase and pulled out the white scarf.

"I think now I'd like a drink—something stronger," David said. Peter reached up to a shelf jutting out of the wall, then filled two glasses from a half-filled bottle of brandy.

"I'll join you, and maybe when the time is ripe, you can teach me how to touch the ceiling. It would save, believe me, if I ever want to repaper the walls—*Gomchen*.

"As a former judge," Peter rambled on, "I would have looked down at such things, but at my age, there's nothing for it but to look up—and even beyond." He sipped his brandy and made a pleasant face.

David drank his down to the bottom, hoping to gain some steadiness for his jangling nerves.

Peter watched his struggle. "Whatever happens next, you can keep your eyes opened or closed—whichever—you will be forced to see." Peter touched the scarf lightly, then passed it over to David, a reminder of it as a greeting from another dimension. David took it and touched it gingerly. He exchanged a look of soulful complicity with the older man, then rose and embraced Peter, who had risen as if to salute David with the remainder of his brandy. David embraced his friend and held on.

"Take the leap, Davie, take it." Peter kissed him on the forehead.

175

David called Anita just as she had returned home from Lawson House, the afternoon spent sitting by the somnolent Hunt, asleep in his hospital annex. She had posted two nurses to watch over him until her return later that evening. She had scanned local newspapers and her editions of *The New York Times,* foolishly she thought. Whatever horror there was would manifest itself three days after David's sighting of the Kunma, so David had confirmed. That meant by tomorrow. Yet what was she to look for? She would do her best to read carefully and watch the television news. The telephone rang. She picked up, switching off the burner under the whistling kettle. She continued her tea preparations as she spoke. She hardly understood what David was saying until he mentioned something about India.

"My friend was with me when we went there to see Rajneesh."

As he continued with details of that long-ago pilgrimage, she managed to pour the water over the tea leaves and set pot and teacup down on the table without spilling the contents.

"David, would you mind? Hold on a minute—I'm having tea and I'd rather not have it here in the kitchen."

"How can you face that room?"

"I'm having the entire floor redone tomorrow. In fact, I've thrown out every single jar of preserves I have on my shelves."

David held on as Anita moved into her office. She settled her burden on her desk, poured out one cup, and picked up the extension.

"You were saying?" she said in a shaky voice.

David, running on high energy, seemed to be deluging Anita with information.

"Please," she pleaded, "slow down. And try to help an old tired WASP. What were you saying about—a what—bardo?"

"The bardo is the Buddhist's view of purgatory." David slowed down to her measure. "There is a heaven and a hell with nine steps leading from one to the other. In essence, it's not unlike Catholicism. This Kunma is someone whose spirit is trapped in hell."

"And how can *you* help him get out?" Anita said, trying to gain courage from the family brew.

"You heard what he said. He called me his teacher."

"From another life?" The tea was scalding on her tongue.

"Which implies I'm part of his karmic destiny."

"There's that word again. Honestly, I feel like I'm watching one of those films on television."

David beamed as the sluices of his absorbed knowledge opened the doors of his suppressed knowledge. "Oh, yes, I guess it doesn't sound very Freudian. But, come to think of it, it is. Very."

"How?"

"Well, take Freud's own studies in hysteria . . ."

"The word does not appear in any—"

"*And* the oedipal fixations, *and* the labyrinth of the Mino-taur . . ."

"Freud was dealing with myth, *not* living reality."

"Oh, come on, Anita. They're still contending that one."

"I still don't understand."

"In all those mythic instances, Freud was dealing with the

notion of destiny overwhelming the individual self. It's the word *destiny* that equates 'karma.' " David could almost see Anita shaking her head. "Okay, let's see. Oedipus shtups Mama—out go the eyes, and the poor, liberated bastard wanders the countryside sightless, but happier for it. Catharsis—end of tragedy."

"What does that word mean? The S-word?"

"Oedipus and his mother make out sexually, right?" David said rather cheerily.

"Ah, yes, they certainly did—unfortunately." Anita blew on her teacup.

"Exactly. But that's where the Buddhists did the Greeks one better. Because he put his eyes out and atoned for his royal screwup, he's allowed, after death, to walk through to a higher level and get reincarnated out of, say, seventh grade instead of third grade."

"And that's what reincarnation is?"

"In a nutshell. Brownie points earned during each lifetime so that you can choose an incarnation more enlightened."

"I wonder what Hunt did to deserve the Kunma."

"I don't know enough about the Kunma to offer an explanation."

"Then what becomes of Hunt in the end?"

"They will become inseparable. One will depend on the other."

"But, one is spirit. Can spirit really commit murder?"

"I told you about my experience in Mexico with mescaline. There have been thousands of others reported and written about. What in most circles is considered a faker's trick or optical illusion was second nature to some ancient and not so ancient religions. Yes, there is an astral force that can project itself beyond the human form that contains it. It even resembles the body in its fleshly solidity and can lead an existence of its own." *Oh, God, Laurel, where are you,* he thought.

"Up to a point, you said."

"True, it needs the parent body, but for how long? I don't know that one either. Freud was playing around with theories of reincarnation before he died. But his thoughts were scattered and incomplete. Actually, we're in Jung's territory."

Anita nodded in assent. Shuddering involuntarily, she asked, "And . . . the tongues? What was that all about?"

"To force you to believe my story."

"Spiritual blackmail. Incredible."

"You say Hunt hissed and stuck out his tongue at you?"

"It was positively nerve-racking." Anita put down her cup.

"It's a Tibetan's way of saying hello—it's a greeting, Anita, I think he was merely being sociable. We're on the verge of a remarkable adventure."

"Adventure or misadventure?" Anita was shaking in her boots; she had been forced to accept David's story as fact. Yet a pocket of doubt persisted in some chamber of her intelligence— a protective measure against being swamped in the supernatural that seemed to be beckoning her to shores that encroached against a lifetime of practice and experience.

The voices on the platform were harsh and spoke in unison. He felt the touch of hands on his shoulder and on either side of him; purple sleeves came into view. He rose and saw the mouse in the corner, staring in his direction, its whiskers tense with attention. His wrists were bound together by a leather thong as before in his dream. The rancid smell of butter lamps swamped him, and he shut his eyes. He and his two guards traveled the long carpet with the yellow design, and in a moment he felt the cold air of the corridor. He opened his eyes in relief and, breathing deeply, saw the two bald monks dressed in purple, walking beside him, mumbling prayers under their breath. He himself was in a black robe decorated with patches simulating those worn by Buddha. His mouth traced a sneer as he saw them duplicated on the robes of his guards. They were taking him somewhere. The corridor they were in was lined with peeling frescoes of gods, a continuation of those displayed in the chamber they had just left. Only here, most of the figures were headless while their hands continued making gestures of mercy. Birds and rainbowlike halos surrounded these mammoth figures, all in various stages of decomposition. Mercy, the abbot thought. They will show me no mercy. The hypocrites! And he spat on the cold stone in contempt.

The doors leading to the lower parts of the temple were massive. Their brass inlay formed two wreathed dragons circling a central mandala. As the doors opened, the mastiffs chained in the courtyard struggled against their fetters and barked, as if adding their sentence to the one to be passed on him by his judges. The cobblestones under his bare feet were still wet and, as always, treacherous with slime. The monastery was located in a valley so profound that the sun never penetrated its walls until midday, then shortly disappeared. The sun had not yet pierced this courtyard and the cobblestones were freshly washed on his behalf. Another augury of doom. They climbed up the ladder stairway to a still higher temple. There was one more to go before reaching the courtyard where his punishment would be pronounced and executed.

KUNMA

He paused at the bottom of the ladder, as did the two monks with him. From where he stood, he could look upward to the mountains surrounding the monastery of Dorje. There, the winds that tore at the peaks could burn a person black in minutes, if exposed to their fury. Perhaps there was more mercy in such chastisement than was to be meted out in the deceptively calm atmosphere surrounding him.

He could hear the sound of the prayer poles and their flapping flags before he entered the main courtyard. At his appearance, he was hit by a riot of sound and colors—robes in yellow, russet, maroon, orange, and white. His ears were blasted by the beating of drums and the bleat of conch horns blowing demons away. Simultaneously, the prayer wheels started to revolve, adding their grinding sound to the din. The Black Abbot had arrived to face the population of Dorje Monastery. He tried to steady himself. He stood alone, cursing them under his breath. He saw that some of his own people were part of the jeering mob. One figure, alone, remained motionless, almost a bas-relief in contrast. Yongen, staring in his direction from a nearby parapet. Their eyes met, and even from where the Black Abbot stood, he could see the boy was crying.

"You can keep your eyes opened—or you can keep them closed. Either way you will see."

David was sitting up at the side of his bed. Mendoza's words interjected themselves within the event, compelling his full attention.

What was it he was seeing or being forced to see? The dream room had been a place of incubation—obviously, now the doors had been flung completely open. The figure in his daydream back in Pune was himself—the Black Abbot—the random pieces were coalescing to create a former picture of self. Or, was his imagination capriciously railroading him toward some wholly fictitious calamity? He was being hustled toward serving some dark purpose—manhandled in the vortex of the occult. He could not hold back now. He would have to continue the plunge and risk its consequences. Yet, what had he, David, done? He was in the twentieth century and he refused to accept ancestral guilt or any part of it. And why should Yongen call him Gomchen? For that matter, who is, or was, Yongen? David rose from his bed and put on his bathrobe. He clutched at it. Yes, it was still white.

He stared at the stack of Tibetan materials strewn over his night table and on the floor and lay back in bed. All this newly acquired knowledge was only feeding the behemoth of his superconscious and spewing into his dream state. The only vestige of his tender self was his pervading loneliness for Laurel. God—Hunt's wife!

He had a premonition of a loss so complete he could hardly bear to contemplate it. He thought of her tangible self, her flesh, her scent. Where was she? What was she doing? What time was it in New Mexico? Did she still love him? And when they spoke again, what was he to tell her? He wrapped himself in the sheets that, in his imagination, threatened to become his shroud.

San Francisco Chronicle
news item

JUNE 26—The body of an unidentified man was discovered this morning in a trash

compactor in the basement of the Trans-
american Pyramid in the Bay Area. The
man had either been thrown to his death or
committed suicide. The body, lying on its
side, was pressed completely flat. His teeth
must have bitten off his tongue during the
death throes, yet the organ was otherwise
not located in the debris. The dead man's
wrist bore a wristwatch still in perfect working order. A police investigation is under
way to determine . . .

*The long ragdong trumpets had thundered through the valley,
signaling the close of the day. This was followed by the mournful
cry of the long copper and silver horns, inlaid with turquoise and
more than ten feet long—resplendent heralds of the closing day.
The sound stung the heels of the monks who scattered through the
alleyways toward private sanctuaries inside the gompa. Within a
month, the temperature would fall to forty below zero, and the
already isolated fortress would begin its long siege against the merciless season of the snows.*

*From his vantage point inside the tower on the second level,
the Black Abbot watched as one by one the others gathered for
the meeting that would decide their future. He saw the shabby,
foul-smelling monks edging their way to the clandestine room of
the Old Ones. Sheltered by the sudden blanket of twilight, they
crawled like intrepid ants against the fearless wind. Their hoods
covered their faces and their bodies were almost bent horizontally
against its force. He would have important news to divulge. The
caravan bearing the new Dalai Lama toward the capital at Lhasa*

was reportedly three days away from Dorje. Here preparations were already under way for the welcoming of the boy incarnation. The abbot, too, rejoiced, but for a completely different reason. He had come a long way from his humble beginnings as a black-smith's son—the son of a "black bone," the most despised of all people—but he had worked and fought his way until he became an abbot, the highest ranking among monastery officials. He had retained the appellation black to celebrate his preeminence, yet now his purposes were seditious. Yongen appeared, panting from his run up the winding steps, to remind him they were all awaiting his presence. Only Yongen, his acolyte and spiritual son, knew the reasons for his delight. Soon the others would know.

Together they descended to the lower passages of the gompa, leading to the darkest of the temples, where the Guardians of the Law were kept. Stuffed effigies of beasts, ancient weaponry, and moldering tapestries of demon gods lined the walls within which the old gods of the Bon Po religion lay entrapped, prisoners of the enlightened ones who ruled above, the followers of Buddha. Yongen struck a match and lit a candle waiting inside the entrance-way. He preceded the abbot down the corridor. The Tolos monster appeared in the flickering candlelight. The second entranceway had been reached. At close range, the agonized expressions of the human victims being fed upon appeared ecstatic, therefore more terrible. The suffocating smells of a hundred monks rose like a corrupt incense as they knelt before the Black Abbot. Slowly he took his place before the image of the god Mahakala, the Terrible Red One, with his projecting tusks, three eyes, and pendant of human skulls and bones. The abbot looked over the assemblage. He could feel their excitement as a palpable thing. Here silence ruled and the butter lamps burned brightly. The rude winds could not penetrate this subterranean shelter to disturb the wicks. Only a high wail could be heard from far off. Yongen touched the abbot's arm; he then removed his raksa rosary hidden within the folds of his sleeves. The red seeds of the fury worshipers were brandished from hidden pockets, and one hundred shaven heads bobbed in prayer.

One more figure hurtled out of the darkness to join them. Chagpa, of the Yellow Sect monks, had entered, late as ever, his soot-smeared face set in a foolish grin. Chagpa stuck out his tongue at Yongen and blew air gently in his direction. Yongen looked away and sat cross-legged at the abbot's feet. A few suppressed giggles were heard from supporters of Chagpa, who draped his arms over a stuffed tiger's head. He cocked his head to one side and his eyes darted between Yongen and his master. The abbot waited for complete silence.

"They call us the followers of the devil dancers and they call us cannibals." A low murmur was heard from some of the men. Shaven heads shook in response.

"We were denied our animal sacrifices. They said we sought power at the expense of the higher attainment of the soul." A ripple of mocking laughter punctuated his remark. From his perch by the tiger, Chagpa continued to grin foolishly.

"Our beliefs spring from the country of Ling. Then we were warriors. We reveled in our powers and, unlike our 'superiors,' fought victoriously against the great enemy, China. In Lhasa the Chinese are triumphant. They have the ears of the Dalai Lama. Here there are only the legends of that proud time and the reminders." He spread his arms toward the walls and ceilings. "Reminders of a time when we lived side by side with the followers of Buddha. For centuries. Then we were betrayed and outlawed in the name of that supposed god and were persecuted for our beliefs." He paused. His harshness now took on a reflective tone. "I, too, lived beside the Buddhists. No! Like them. Convinced theirs was the way. Gave up my youth to atone for my birth. 'Black bones' I was born and 'black bones' I remained, until I 'elevated' myself in their eyes. I became a recluse. I wore a white skirt hanging down to my feet with a waistcoat and shirt. My ears were pierced by large gold rings and my hair touched the ground. I prayed and fasted, a single bowl of tsamba my only sustenance. I wore their saffron robes; night and day I pursued the 'noble' twelvefold path. Right thinking, right mindfulness, right suffering, that I might end suffering altogether. I complied with such things, but I could still burn the snow beneath me with my own body heat."

A whisper of "Tumo" rippled amongst the listeners and high-decibel sounds of respect were emitted from chapped lips.

"All this to reach nirvana, a heaven so far away as to be non-existent. There is no such salvation in Bon Po—only the nurturing of the dark powers in a cruel and senseless world.

"I say, what price goodness or good works? Man fights alone in an alien universe, which chews on itself at the center and its indigestions are the cataclysm of the world. Right now the caravan transporting the Holy Child is three days from reaching us. It has paused in the village of Farsi, and, no doubt, his retinue has imposed taxes on the people there, forcing them to contribute food to the traveling hosts. Food the village can ill afford so that the child be received properly.

"Again, I say, what price tyranny that passes for religion. There is only naked power in the universe to be seized and used. In the *deepest parts of your being, you all know this to be true. I have returned from pretending to be what I am not. You have all seen me wield the whip of my office—in their names. Now it is time to regain the power which is rightfully ours: to live life, true men of the Bon Po, and use our magic powers over them to rule this country. The time we have all longed and prepared for has come."*

A general hissing spread like a wild snake uncoiling through the chamber. The abbot was forced to raise his arms to ensure silence before continuing.

"And we are not alone. Already the gompas at Pun-Gon, Gan-Ra, and Se-Dan await our victory in order to achieve theirs. The temple police are with us and the hour has arrived for the Stuffed Shirt Committee to step down and be exterminated." He took a long pause. "I said the Holy One, the boy Dalai, hastens toward us. He shall never leave Dorje alive."

A deadly silence descended as the abbot looked at their up-turned faces steadily.

"I will be responsible for the manner of his death."

An audible gasp escaped a few lips.

"Your roles will be assigned. As soon as the 'Holy One' is dispatched, we will overrun the monastery and destroy its leaders. Followers of Bon Po, not since the reign of King Me-Agston will there be such a rout of the dogs."

An image blurred out the eyes of the zealot priest. The outline of a child's head interposed itself in David's dream state. Chris's face came into focus.

"Do not approach the Holy One! Do not touch the Holy One!" Laurel had repeated the child's words. David sensed, but did not see, the stirring of young arms flailing against some unseen enemy

in the darkness. "*Do not approach the Holy One,*" *his hammering heart instructed him, while his mind reeled in its attempt to deny the evidence of his vision.*

David sat in the lotus position on a pillow. He intoned a Tibetan mantra slowly, trying to draw new resonance from the words with each repetition and help destroy the hold of his dark incarnate self. Midway round the tenth repetition, a voice ran in his head concurrently.

"*Fool, why don't you claim what's yours to claim?*"

"No," David shouted aloud. "Whoever you are—whatever you intend—never."

The voice was insidiously soft. "*Why?*"

"*I don't want that kind of power.*"

"*You do. You always have.*"

"*No. I've wanted respect.*"

"Total *respect.*"

"*Recognition.*"

"World *recognition.*"

"Stop!" *David's palms broke apart in confusion.*

"*Power. Admit it.*"

No answer.

"*You would eat the world if it were possible. Admit it.*" *The voice maintained its seductive urging.*

"*I admit it.*"

"*And yet you starve yourself. It's true. Eat.*"

Silence.

"*You'll always feel lesser for not having eaten—*"

"*Who is this? I don't know your voice.*" *David's fists were now clenched.*

"*Don't you? What of the boy—the new incarnation?*"

Something cracked and David opened his eyes. The wick of the votive candle, already low when he'd begun the mantra, had split the glass vessel containing it. Wax had spread out onto the floor. David blew out the flame, then hastily scraped the shards onto a newspaper and emptied them into the trash. He'd have to wait till the stain hardened before relieving the parquet floor of its scab. *Who had spoken in his head? Himself, of course—which self?* "Get out," he said aloud.

David's hand stopped shaking as he lit a cigarette and exhaled in relief. A puny response, but a response nonetheless. But was this really a solution? Solution or not, it was a positive directive, and David was in no position to quibble. He had to try. Anything.

It was seven-fifteen on a Sunday morning. He'd pack a small suitcase and find hotel space and there decide what to do with his patients. First, he would board Sam with his neighbor across the hall, then make his move.

In his growing paranoia about being discovered by the Kunma, David had tried to reach Anita from a drugstore ten blocks away from the Hotel Westbury, where he'd taken rooms. Three days since leaving the Chatsworth, he was still frantic about a crack appearing in the wall of his defense. From various lobbies of hotels and office buildings, he'd managed to contact all his patients. Ostensibly David was on a special mission—back to India, he'd decided—the farther away the better. He had cleverly, if a bit shamefacedly, peeled through his patients' objections and two personal attacks. He would be bound to lose one or two come September, but he'd have to risk that (if there was to be a September at all). Three days had gone by without any dreams. He'd stay at the Westbury till the end of the week—meanwhile making other plans.

He stepped into the Western Union on Third Avenue and sent off two telegrams. "Imperative. Get Chris out of Taos until further notice"—the message went to both Faolain McGraw and Laurel. He signed them "A friend" and addressed them c/o General Delivery, Taos, New Mexico. Laurel would know who had sent them. He owed it to her, to the boy—and his own conscience. Let McGraw think it a threat of kidnapping—anything, as long as it rallied his protective instincts toward his only grandson.

David stepped out into the street and in broad daylight he saw an innocent face, resting against a silken pillow, while someone, beyond the glow of candlelight, watched with hostile eyes. Pain seized his temples, and although his hotel was only blocks away, he was forced to take a cab. The vision was clear and simple. Those hostile eyes watching the child were David's own. He was the Black Abbot. He had telegraphed a warning—against himself.

David lay on his hotel bed half-asleep. As he shifted his position away from the windows, he saw Laurel by the bathroom door. She was leaning against the wall at the threshold of the john, staring at him. Her body, half lit by the yolk-yellow light from the bathroom, was breathtaking. He turned his head sideways as he lay there on his stomach. How long had she been watching him and how was this even possible? His body, however, responded, and he became instantly erect. He sobbed once and buried his head in the pillow. His body throbbed for action,

KUNMA

even as it broke into a cold sweat. He lay there unmoving—
afraid to either fully awaken or sink back into sleep again.

The hand that brushed against his neck and then his cheek
was unquestionably familiar—even the scent was there. He
reached up and met the fingers. Oh, God—it *was* she. He
turned and with a stifled cry gathered her body to his. Beyond
them both, the yellow bathroom light cut a diagonal into the
darkened bedroom. David's breath was hot with desire, and he
could hear hers responding. He felt her breath on his neck
before her face came into focus out of the murk. Two eyes were
staring steadily into his own—an eagle's glint—a slow spasm
as of a camera clicking. Then a dead milky whiteness. He tried
to turn away. The Kunma was with him again—lying by his
side. Strong arms grabbed his shoulders from behind, spun him
around, and threw him on his back. The Kunma rose above
him, his powerful arms pinioning David to the sheets. Their
eyes met, and the living and the dead lay there in deadlock.
Peter was right—it could assume other forms.

At close range the Kunma was even more formidable than
at first sight. The bare torso was young and muscular. The neck,
a distended stump, supported the glabrous head now looming
over David. White spots flecked his lips, and a thin drool was
forming at the corners. The jaws moved as if they would become prognathous as David watched. Long-taloned fingers dug
into his shoulders. Only the eyes, bare slits, betrayed the hurt
that had provoked this attack.

"Get off me!" David started to squirm against him, his voice
strong with fear and resentment. He realized he had addressed
this chimera directly for the first time. The Kunma's expression
remained steely, and David realized he was naked. The Kunma's

stomach bellowed rapidly as if trying to fan its own inner fire, and with a shock David saw the bulbous erection suspended over him like an animal in rut. In that instant the spittle spread at one corner of the Kunma's mouth and, dangling like a spider's thread, loosened to land on David. He could feel it like a tiny flame licking against his chest. The Kunma's eyes glazed hypnotically, forcing David's memory backward.

Yongen was staring at the abbot over the jeering crowd. The geylongs had resumed their dismal howling and the conch horns their braying contempt for the prisoner.

Silence fell like a thunderbolt unleashed from the hands of a demon god as the yellow doors opened at the northern end of the courtyard and one by one the twenty temple police entered. They forced their long, pleated aprons to sway in a frivolous gait as their wooden staffs clattered in unison on the flagstones. They stationed themselves on opposite sides of the courtyard, creating a phalanx between them and the platform containing the four golden chairs. Their begrimed faces were masks, frozen in the traditional snarl. Only their eyes moved, slowly from side to side, taking in the measure of the crowd. The abbot watched their arrival with cold disdain. Two days ago they were his sworn accomplices in the planned insurrection. Today they were his implacable enemies. Chagpa, the insolent member of the Yellow Sect monks, stepped out of the crowd and spat on him.

Obviously Chagpa had betrayed him, hoping, no doubt, to curry favor with the Buddhists.

He'd taken a chance and accepted Chagpa as one of his followers because of his influence among the Yellow Sect lamas and his position on the committee welcoming the new Dalai Lama. As other monks of that contentious order congratulated Chagpa, the abbot understood that Chagpa had been a plant. The abbot, in his blind zeal, had risked and lost. He looked around for signs of instruments of torture. There were none. Instead, sharp glints of light branded his eyes from the balcony over the opened doors. Four men stood there in blue gowns encrusted with elaborate jewels. Their spiked, golden crowns heralded them as members of the Dalai Lama's retinue, which had arrived yesterday. The sun had made its daily miraculous appearance in the central courtyard, and these new arrivals were its glory. In the crystal pure air, the lapidary effect was stunning.

Death at high noon, the abbot judged, all the while watching the four dignitaries sliding forward on invisible feet toward the edge of the parapet. Like a red wave, ten tonsured monks in russet robes emerged from behind it and stood at attention. Was the child going to make an appearance? It would be a cruel but apt stroke on the part of the committee. The abbot inhaled sharply through his nostrils. The child should not be made to witness what was to come. He was a mere boy. There would be time enough for such spectacles. Time enough to learn the invidious casuistry of Buddhist diplomacy. The child would inherit it all—if he survived. The eleventh incarnation had been poisoned—as was his predecessor before him. The new candidate would be the twelfth. Better to have died in sacrifice to a nobler cause than to become the potential scapegoat for political differences at Lhasa. He looked up at the balcony and saw the faces were indeed Chinese. The scum, he thought. He had meant to strangle the boy as he slept while his followers executed the boy's retainers now shimmering in their perch above him—but he had been imprisoned before he could accomplish the deed. The temple police were to have held the grand committee hostage—until the monastery was taken and

*the abbot's own justice was meted out. A low roar of voices greeted
the appearance of the committee.*

*A clash of small cymbals radiated like the sound of heat itself.
A single Chofna drum beat a steady tattoo, and as the last of the
four prelates emerged into the sunlight, the tiger thigh-bone trumpets squealed mercilessly. He cast his eyes downward, but the hems
of their brocaded silk gowns flicking dragon tails could not be
avoided. No. He would not shut his eyes against their display of
power. It would be misconstrued. Instead he raised them to the
platform and ground the approaching figures to perdition in his
imagination, even as he contemplated their awesomeness. La-Chi,
Dra Tshang, Kam Tshen, and at the center Ken Po, in their padded vests, their golden hats adorned with elaborate turquoise and
other, golden ornaments. Inch-long fingernails dangled like new-
spun stilettos from their fingers. They climbed in thick-soled boots
and sat together slowly, carving out an image in space, in a syn-
chronized study of absolute authority. Not once did either of the
four men look at the abbot. The latter studied them with a careful
scrutiny, as if to mark each in his memory for future reckoning.*

*But the abbot was beginning to feel the effect of the blazing
sun on his shaven head. Automatically, seeking a measure of comfort, he looked for Yongen again, hoping to see the boy still ensconced on the balcony above the kneeling trapas. His anchor. His
hope. Their eyes met as his sentence was pronounced.*

*"For your plot against the Holy One, you will be given one
hundred and fifty strokes of the whip in the very service you have
defamed, and then suffer death by burning. Whereafter your ashes
will be placed in a crude urn and carried to Lhasa. There to suffer
revilement by the Temple guards."*

KUNMA

They would piss him to perdition, the abbot knew. Yongen's scream tore through the abbot's numbed senses. A surge of concern for the boy so overwhelmed him that he was surprised to feel tears preparing to spring from his eyes. No, he must not cry. His tears would also be misinterpreted. They would see them as a sign of weakness and cowardice. Instead, he lifted his head, smiled with a fierce joy, pointing to the child Lama, who had finally made his resplendent appearance on the high parapet, and shouted to Yongen, "Avenge me!" He saw Yongen raise his arm in a gesture of acquiescence and then dash away as guards were ordered to follow him.

The abbot felt the first strokes of the whip against his back, but he would not bend his knees against the lashing. He could only hope Yongen would survive to honor him and their purpose against the Buddhists.

The shouts he heard counting out the strokes seemed a ghostly echo of the one still jangling in the corridors of his memory. Suddenly David was choking—a mass of whiteness was gathering within the confines of the bedroom. Invisible jets hissed. The air became putrid with the stench of burning flesh, and David was pushed into the heart of it. He stood stock-still and saw his body light up like a living copy of a Vasari diagram. Licking flames rushed throughout the canals of his system, and David became his own throbbing generator of self-destruction. He exploded into flames, his head bursting open like a fiery melon spewing crisped seeds. In continuing gradations, his flesh chunked and sizzled away from him as he suffered death in the realm of spirit where all things are stored—where all things are real.

David sat stoically while he repeated his tale of disaster to Peter Mendoza, and the old man's face had taken on an ashen pallor. David's description had recalled similar scenes in Peter's history—its details so accurate that the older man could not speak for a while.

"I was lying down on the floor of my hotel room," David said as an afterthought.

"And Yongen?" Peter finally spoke.

"The Kunma was gone." David looked around Peter's kitchen, feeling reassured by its solid reality.

"He had accomplished what he'd intended all along—to draw you to him. Now I have my answer as to why you could not become part of Rajneesh's inner circle."

David uncrossed his arms, but his hands were clenched as he stared at Mendoza.

"The karmic wheel moves continuously until the necessary conjunctions are made." Peter gazed compassionately at David.

"Where's the necessity in all this—tell me that." David's voice was truculent with tension.

"The incarnations of the ancient past are now among us," Peter answered with a sad smile.

David, aghast, stammered, "But how long has this—taken?"

"From your research," Peter countered, "when would you say Buddhism finally became the official religion in Tibet?"

David's answer came quickly. "A long period—between the twelfth and thirteenth centuries. It was a slow and painful gestation."

"Karmic rebirth links time and space in an unforeseeable

logic." Peter raised his hands and his fingers interlocked in an old judicial gesture.

David made a contemptuous sound.

"It's strange to me," Peter said, "for someone who has experienced what you have and your wisdom regarding human behavior, that you remain reluctant to fully enter and complete this task."

"I'm still not used to the idea"—David was positively threatening—"that the past, a far distant past, can so invade present reality as to dominate it, make claims on it." And he again folded his arms belligerently.

"But the past was equally then a present time," Peter responded firmly.

"Still, it's the past, Peter, and I'm walking in it even as we speak."

"You're fortunate." Peter nodded and his eyes blinked rapidly.

"How so?" David looked up at him.

"The people who figure in that backward glance are here with you—as part of your evolution—and ultimately"—Peter paused to clear his throat—"you will have living beings to occupy your life. Look, David, look at my karma—an uncaring wife dead, an uncaring daughter vanished, and myself a remnant of an ignominious past life in Spain where dissolution was a daily occurrence. Loss. Loss. Everywhere."

"Have you still heard nothing from your daughter?" David put his hand on Peter's arm, relieved to move on to another subject.

"No, not a single word. Would you believe me if I told you

I hired a detective once, seven years ago, to find her for me?" Peter blushed.

"You never told me that." David kept hold of Peter's arm.

"Of course not—I was beside myself, I still am on that score. Like Shylock in your beloved Shakespeare, I could not admit my Amy had deserted her old father. So I was covert. I gave up the search a year ago—I've given up on finding my child. Oh, goodness me." He shook his head.

"I'm sorry," David said with much feeling.

"But just think now." Peter started swaying gently back and forth in his chair. "I have become the detective, and you, Davie, the subject. I follow you." Suddenly tears sprang into the old man's eyes, and he removed an old-fashioned handkerchief from his pocket and dabbed his face. "Come, Davie, one lost child is enough. We must not permit such negligence to occur again, if you catch my meaning."

"Chris." David's face scattered in fear.

"Yes, the blond Lama child incarnate. Life is extraordinary, isn't it?"

July 1982

"The boy stays here."

Papa Champ had already consumed half a bottle of Wild Turkey and the sun was only just beginning to set. The arrival of the telegrams had broken the uneasy truce with Laurel. Unlike in Papa's own impoverished childhood, where parental abuse was the norm, Chris had fortunately been spared the fireworks between father and daughter. Papa's ranch hands, Tomito and Raul, had taken Chris into Toledos for an afternoon showing of *Superman*. Papa was now convinced his daughter needed to be locked up in her room till suppertime—in fact, until he changed his mind, this would remain a mandate for the rest of the summer.

" 'A friend,' huh. A friend sent these telegrams." He had confronted his unruly daughter. "As if I didn't know."

Faolain McGraw, known to his family and friends as Papa Champ, had taken refuge in his glass-enclosed trophy room. Evening was about to fall, and the display over the near distant Sierras promised to be spectacular. He had come back from a long trip in Thailand—back to New Mexico, the only place he'd called home since he'd settled outside of Taos, over thirty years ago. He sat now, uncomfortable in his gray suit. Deep creases along the crotch and inseam indicated that he had not bothered to change for days. He was barefoot, a big man—a football player in his college days, who had turned to big-game hunting in his middle years. Suspenders held his messy yellow polo shirt in place. He had been handsome, but his present sagging jowls and liquor belly disguised that. Now he was balding; wisps of yellow hair hung lankly across his pate.

At seventy-two, he had expected, God willing, to glean the fruits of his labors both temporal and spiritual. His vast financial holdings, which had commenced with copper tubing in Minnesota, now extended into copra, tungsten, and sundry by-products in the Far East. That part of his expectations lay secure, but none of that ever fully assuaged the deep bitterness that had spread like an oil slick on the main waters of his life. His young wife, after six years of marriage, had run off with an insurance man. He would never trust another woman the way he had Marianne.

There remained his child, Laurel, the only constant in his

life, and with her own marriage, he felt all his efforts in her behalf had succeeded. Then came the summer of their "little talks" and his greatest fear was laid bare. Laurel was indeed her mother's daughter. Now Hugh, his handsome, resourceful son-in-law, had suffered a mental collapse. Papa's old blood vengeance roared inside him. He took another shot of whiskey to break its spiraling hold.

What was he to make of his daughter's sad, disjointed story? The medical reports had stated the case squarely, if not clearly, to his unlearned head. Shortly after his arrival at the ranch, he had arranged for Hugh's transfer to Lawson House in Massachusetts—on whose board of directors he figured prominently. Hugh had been correct in assigning power of attorney to him. He had colluded against his wife—and wisely so. Papa had been his subtle adviser. Clearly it had been necessary to get Chris here to Ranch House to restore some order in the boy's life.

"He stays here. Chris remains here," he roared again to the empty room. The last rays of the sun were beginning to set behind the range, and the glass doors overlooking the vista caught this in a reflection tinted with a violet, rosy hue. Distantly he could hear the station wagon pulling up to Ranch House, bringing Chris back where he belonged.

The boy looked a bit "peaked" to Papa, and when he asked for his mother, Papa nodded to Tomito, who left the room and unlocked Laurel's door. The boy and Papa enjoyed a long conversation during which Papa identified the various locations where his trophies had been "bagged." Like one younger than his years, Chris never tired of hearing Papa's safari tales. Laurel appeared, ending his reminiscences as they prepared to have supper together. Laurel did not take her eyes off Chris and hardly touched her food. She was worried by how frail he was looking.

The next day, Chris had been assigned some late-afternoon chores in the barn and missed the next round of fireworks, which took place outside on a side veranda of the house.

"All boys his age go through something like that. It's all that television. And considering the guff his mother adds onto it, I'm surprised it's not even worse."

"But it's happened three times, Papa—the last one only two nights ago. You recall when he had his fever? Back East? Well, Papa, that was the first time. And now here—you see how pale he's looking."

"Give him a few days riding round the ranch, and you'll see the difference."

"That means you don't believe me."

"Among other things, Chris never mentioned anything about what happened a couple of nights ago. And there is nothing— and I mean nothing—of importance that happens here that I am not aware of."

"No, of course not."

"Do you find anything wrong in that, Daughter?"

"You know I appreciate everything you do for Chris. He didn't say anything to you—well, because he doesn't want to appear vulnerable in your eyes."

"That may be, but the case of the nighttime heebie-jeebies is closed. I'd know in a second if there was anything really the matter with the boy. If he's inherited your overactive imagination, more's the pity."

"Thanks." Laurel bit her lower lip.

"Oh, it can be attended to in time."

"But, don't you see, he doesn't remember."

"How's that?"

"Thank God for it—he doesn't remember the day after the dreams occur."

"Well, that's what a nightmare's all about, I guess."

"Your guess measures very poorly against my fear for him. Chris only knows he's been sick—without knowing the reason—and he doesn't like to be sick."

"Well, tough, Daughter. Tough. Because you're going to have to live with it. I repeat, Chris stays here and all the conniving kidnappers in the world, provided there were any in the first place, won't get within an eyelash of that boy. Not if they value their lives."

"You're so powerful, aren't you? So very powerful."

"That's the first truthful statement you've made in a long time."

"Why won't you even try to believe me?"

"I know the smell of truth when it's spoken. God damn it, woman, it was the milk that upset him—not all the rest of . . ." He sighed heavily. "Right now, you're just raving, so I suggest a long shower to cool off."

Taking a deep swig at his bottle for the day, he slammed the screened-off door in her face, signaling an end to their conversation. In a short time, he would make himself purposefully drunk and incoherent, but her own guarded animosity toward him was at a dangerous breaking point. Laurel remained on the back patio, certain of her feelings, but uncertain of her next move. As usual, Papa had isolated himself in his trophy room—a part of the house she ordinarily avoided like the plague. Laurel hated her father's sanctuary with its fake air of death turned triumphant. As usual, giving in to impulse, she pursued him there and knocked. When there was no answer, she tried the doorknob and, to her surprise, found it unlocked. As she entered, Papa's huge frame was slouched in his favorite leather armchair. He had not heard her enter. He looked up, stared at her, then picked up a cigar.

"How did you get in?" he sneered.

"You forgot to lock it. Tell me, what is it that makes you persist in this irrational attitude toward me?"

"You've got that the wrong way round, little girl." He lit his cigar.

"I'd like *you* to tell me the truth for once—I want to hear the words—without any evasion."

A long trajectory of smoke was his only response. His arrogant expression caused a red splotch to break out on her neck.

"I've told you to cool down and I meant it." He squinted at her through his next puff. "Do we have to go through all this— bull—every day? Spare me."

"Stop it! Stop punishing me. I'm not my mother. I am not responsible for what she did."

At this unexpected turn, the old man stiffened in his chair and the skull beneath his skin showed through with glacial sharpness.

He's going to die, she thought. Her intuition was clear and certain. But even this appalling insight could not diminish her outrage. She had gripped the back of an armchair opposite his, and the leather still burning from the sun's destructive work aggravated her discontent. Papa made a dismissive gesture and turned in his chair, causing the whiskey bottle to topple over;

tentacles of the sour mash crept over the parquet floor.

"You pathetic, drunken old man," Laurel said in abject disgust.

Papa picked up the ashtray on the table beside his chair and flung it wildly in her direction. It missed Laurel by several feet, thumped against the snout of a stuffed grizzly, and smashed to pieces on the stone floor.

He's going to die. He hates me and he's going to die soon, she thought, numb with her premonition. She watched as he salvaged the remaining third of the bottle and pulled at it like a wizened child seeking succor. The image was made further grotesque by the old man's Adam's apple, bobbing convulsively in its sagging turkey folds. Whiskey dripped all over his denim ensemble and yellow boots. The giant Papa of her childhood seemed desperately diminished and suddenly even fragile. She almost ran to him in a surge of pity, but held her ground, knowing it was too late to appease him now on any level. He wiped the whiskey from his chin and forced himself to focus on Laurel, standing by the doorway. His eyes played a lopsided but malicious game with her.

"So tell me. Was it after confession that you did it? You ducked out on Tomito—I'll have his hide—and made your telephone call to your Jew."

"Tomito is a perfect watchdog—and I repeat, I had nothing to do with the sending of the telegrams."

"No! No, of course you didn't. What do you take me for? A cretin?"

"To hell with you!" She turned to go.

" 'A friend' indeed. Indeedy. What are you two trying to cook up?"

Laurel turned and sat, prepared to finish what she had started.

The old man shook his head. "You've no shame. If you could involve your own son in this tawdry little affair of yours, you've no shame."

"I have none when it involves people I love."

"What could you both have to gain?"

"Why don't you answer that, big Papa Champ?" He looked at her perplexed, the tables unaccustomedly turned. "What do you hope to gain in keeping me and my son prisoners in your house?"

"Answer my question and don't give me any more of your bullshit."

"You want an answer. Alright. Here it is. I love David Sussman. I want to be his wife."

"Never," he answered quietly.

"I want him to be Chris's father."

"Love!" the old man snarled back in parody. "We already know, don't we, about your kind of love?" And he shambled away.

"I've made my mistakes. So what."

"You're a married woman and you're talking blasphemy." He finally picked up his bottle, now completely empty.

"Oh, you pious old hypocrite. A woman left you years ago and you've retreated into your ivory tower, where only a Madonna would pass muster."

"Shut your sacrilegious mouth." He held the bottle as if it were a potential weapon.

"How many Madonnas appear on your American Express card?"

"I'm warning you . . ."

"Have you ever faced the possibility that she might have had good reasons for leaving you? Your wife. My mother." Laurel approached and saw her father's trousers stained with whiskey.

"I won't hear another word about that whore."

"Of course. What else can she be? What else can any of us be?"

"The second truthful statement of the day," he retaliated with drunken gusto.

"At first I thought you were right, but now I know she was right. I only hope wherever she is—alive or dead—she found a little of what she was missing." Laurel sat, desolate at the memory of a woman she could hardly recall.

"Well, then, you just go right ahead and try it." His mouth hung slack, making him appear clownlike.

For a moment Laurel, lost in her sense of release, was confused. "What are you trying to say?"

"Run off with your Jew doctor. See how far you'll get. This time . . ." He paused, his eyes clouding over some secret intent.

"Say it! This time you'll catch up with me and get your revenge. That's it exactly. The sins of the mother will be finally paid—in full—by the daughter. And what do you think you've been doing to me all these years?" She moved toward him. "I run back here, like an idiot, time after time, seeking your love and understanding, but getting punishment instead. And I've taken it like the silly convent girl I am, not knowing the difference between the two."

"You're an ungrateful wretch."

"*Bitch* is what you mean. All that's left for you or your dirty henchman to do is to kill the bitch and the slate will be clean.

Go on if you have the nerve." The fight was going out of her and she shook her head, closing her eyes.

"I will block any attempt you make to leave your husband."

"I've already left him."

"I'll have you declared an incompetent mother and you will lose your son."

"To whom? To a madman? To you? He'd only hate you for it later. Poor Chris. If there's any hope in this miserable household, it's in him."

"He loves his father. He'll despise you when he finds out what you've done to him."

"And how about what his father's done to me?"

A long silence fell over the room while Laurel suppressed a sob. This was worse than anything they had experienced before. It was useless to go on, and now that it was over, she wished it had never happened. She knew she'd lost Papa forever. The waning light of day emphasized his fragility, and the fangs and claws surrounding him made a mockery of his manhood.

"Papa. If I said I was sorry, would you believe me?"

"No."

"Papa."

"If you wish to leave, you may. Chris, however, stays here with me."

"You know I won't go without him. I'd never see him again. You'd see to that."

"If you choose to remain under my roof, it will be according to the house rules. Think it over."

"Papa, please."

"I want your decision in the morning."

When Papa passed her on his way out, his face was bloated,

but the eyes were curiously serene. He saw her now ever so clearly. Every inch her mother—once his Marianne. He sighed and grabbed the wall for support against his daughter's beauty and his remembrance of its source.

"And don't try anything foolish—like trying to sneak yourself and Chris out of the house without my knowing. We are very well guarded here at Ranch House. The Lord rewards the righteous. Besides, you wouldn't get very far."

Laurel lowered her head in resignation. As usual, he had turned the tide in his favor.

"Papa." Laurel's voice was that of a twelve-year-old girl. The sound stirred memories in Papa's ears. But, always on the alert, he turned instantly deaf.

"I think I'll need a little replenishment," he said, his back to her, and lifted his empty bottle up to the light.

Laurel broke into tears and rushed past him out of the room.

Back in his own apartment, David opened his eyes and found himself staring at a shoe. He shut them again and waited a decent interval before taking another look. The shoe was still there. He reached out and touched it. He picked it up and rose from the floor of his bedroom. The other shoe lay in the closet beside his small brown suitcase. He sat on the edge of the bed and dropped the shoes at his feet. There they were—a pair of blue canvas shoes with four holes for laces. He had purchased them at Bloomingdale's at the beginning of the summer, along with the blue, knit stretch socks he was wearing. He stood up and stepped into the bathroom. He turned on the light and looked into the mirror above the sink. There he was—David

Sussman—shirtless with only socks and trousers on. He was alone and badly in need of a shave.

What time was it? Where was his wristwatch? He walked back into the bedroom and saw its face glowing on his bedside table. The moment he picked it up, he knew it had stopped. A gift from Denise. Next, he raised the shade at the window. Outside shown a bright blue sky and he saw the smoldering flames in the courtyard and the faces of the jeering trapas. He lowered the shade with a snap that almost pulled it from its fixture. He stepped into the john again and began to shave. He looked down at his arms. Hastily he threw off his trousers and shorts to examine his body. He was intact. Yet he had seen himself destroyed. How many times had he repeated this self-examination since leaving the hotel? He looked at his body again, then shaved quickly before stepping into the shower.

He dried himself thoroughly and dressed in a fresh set of clothes, then threw up the shade on both windows, but did not look out through the panes. Would he continue seeing the same vista from his own windows? The feeling of the robe against his skin persisted as he lit his morning cigarette. Only three were left in his pack. He inhaled deeply, savoring the bitter comfort on his tongue. He would go to the corner for a hamburger before picking up Sam. What he thought next so terrified him that he could only contemplate it with a frozen calm. Would the Kunma try to kill Chris? Was that what he would be forced to witness next? "Avenge me," the abbot had cried, pointing to the child on the parapet. Could cruelty of such magnitude—madness of such proportions—be the end game of universal justice? And what of that long-ago youth—

Yongen—now the avenging devil bent on cruel redemption? He looked around his apartment and thought of Yongen. It now seemed such a natural thing to do. He placed four candles on the corners of his carpet, sat in the middle, and allowed the Black Abbot to reveal the knowledge, wrapped in his memory.

When the abbot first found Yongen, he was no more than deyong— a slave—stoking the kitchen fires with yak dung so that the meals were properly prepared for the monastery. His body was covered with burns from the roaring fires that blackened the cauldrons. He had been eight years old when put into this service—and at fifteen he was the oldest of the boys. A tall, lean, dark-haired, black-eyed youth who, during those early years, had often thought of ending his life by falling into one of the cauldrons. He had nothing to live for—no one to love—no one loved him. His parents were nomads and his father a brigand who raided passing caravans and terrorized villages. The boy was born near Phari— the dirtiest village in the Himalayas—where the garbage piled up for decades and the inhabitants were never free from its stink. He had two sisters who had died in the water test. When placed by custom in the icy stream as an infant to test his endurance, he, too, became mortally sick. He was about to be abandoned as unfit to survive the nomads' life, but he rallied and lived. When he was about eight, his father heard in his travels of the vision that had appeared in the sacred lake of Lhamoi Latso. In it, the priests at Lhasa saw the place of the incarnation for the next Dalai Lama, and sensing his opportunity, Yongen's father raced his wife and the boy to the designated area near the Dorje Monastery.

There he sought out the local nukhwas, or medicine man. First he bribed him and then threatened his life if he did not properly prepare his son as a contender for the holy seat. The nukhwas was a clairvoyant who could read one's past in the way one spoke. Ultimately tempted by the money and the promise of an important position at court, he gave up his scruples and undertook to instruct Yongen. His father let it be known in Dorje that his son was subject to visions. In such, he was visited by the dead Lama, who described how he had been poisoned by his ministers and how Yongen was to be the successor. News was sent back to Lhasa, and within three months a delegation departed the Potala to investigate this claim. Eight men arrived, wearing simple peasant clothes. One of them came forward with two drums in his hands, asking if Yongen recognized them. The oracle had drilled the boy to choose the most humble of the objects proffered for recognition, but he was only a boy, used to a mean existence, and when the drums were laid at his feet, he reached for the large, decorated one. It was the wrong choice. The other drum had belonged to the sacred predecessor.

Almost immediately the delegates packed their belongings and prepared for the long journey back. Yongen's father's claim was found false and the nukhwas was discredited. The boy was made into an object of ridicule, and since he was his father's son, they called him Kunma—thief—thief of the soul. One of those who attempt to steal a higher identity for gain. Both the nukhwas and his father beat Yongen severely for having failed the test—thus preventing them their chance at a greater glory. The boy remembered little thereafter. His mother left him at the gate of the temple at Dorje, for otherwise his father would surely have killed him in his disappointment and rage. This was his mother's solution for her son's life. Yongen was dressed in a fur cap and a padded

cotton jacket when he was found. On the day he first set foot in
Dorje, a woman who had given birth to twins was being buried
alive with her devil's spawn, outside the monastery's compound.
A dire beginning to a new life.

Inside those walls, he feigned stupidity and lived at the most
servile level with the temple toughs as his only friends. And the
boy missed sleeping with the dogs on top of him on chilly nights.

Then the abbot came to Dorje and Yongen was assigned to him
as a servant. When the abbot asked if Yongen could read, he hung
his head in shame. No one had ever addressed him in a kindly
manner before. The boy blushed when the abbot said he would
undertake his instruction and wept for the first time since he was
a young child. The abbot became his mentor, his spiritual father,
and was responsible for having his head shaved and the cutting
of his pigtail—keeping it as parents would have if they were with
him. The abbot became both his mother and father. In return,
the boy, at the time of the abbot's sentence and death, promised
the abbot that he, Yongen, would avenge his master's death. And
then vowed, "Even as you die—so will I, in exchange, love for
love." All this finally coalesced and the abbot—David—lowered
his head and wept. His body taut with pain, he hugged himself,
accepting the sinuous, yet insidious, traces of his lives and this
boy's part in it.

McGraw woke up and found himself in a puddle of Wild Turkey. His denims had soaked up the 100-proof bourbon like a
blotter, and the yellow cowhide boots were scarred. He raised
himself to his elbows and found he was in the attic. Daylight
etched itself over the battered trunk under the eaves. The slatted
streaks created haphazard patterns through the broken lattice-

work. He had passed out and accidentally smashed the bottle as he fell against some old mining equipment piled up around the trunk. The whiskey label, embedded in a jagged frame of brown glass, was draped over the edge of a corroded steel wheelbarrow like a treacherous bracelet. He'd come up here to look for something. What was it—and how long had he been here? The opened jar on the barrel gave him his clue and he rose clumsily to it.

He grabbed the jar and spilled the contents onto the floor. As he squatted down beside the mess, preparing to rummage, his secretary startled him. Ralph Gough was a combination bodyguard and manservant. He stood in the doorway, surveying his boss and the rubbish he'd strewn all over the floor.

"What is it? I told you—"

Ralph held out a batch of phone messages. As McGraw advanced toward him, the reek of the sopped-up whiskey intensified the smell of decaying furniture. Both assaulted Ralph's nostrils like a razor cut. McGraw rifled through the messages. Life's treacheries were becoming too much to bear.

Hunt's pulse had slowed down again and Nurse Emma Joe had faithfully recorded the event. As she left the ward, the Kunma raised himself out of his hospital bed and quietly wandered down the hall. He stopped just short of the staircase and raised his head to catch the nearest vibration of activity. His thoughts then turned to the Black Abbot—and their last encounter before his death. Following the abbot's immolation, Yongen had been captured by the palace guards, led by Chagpa. Before Yongen's tongue was torn from his mouth for his complicity in the plot against the young Dalai Lama, Chagpa had forced the boy to perform several sexual acts with him, then left him to the perverse pleasure of the guards, who, one by one, thrust into his body from behind. Before they tore out his tongue, he repeated his abbot's final command to him. "You will be avenged," he said faintly.

In the bardo he had emerged as the Kunma. Within it he'd suffered the punishment meted out to those who die in anger—the state called shedang. His body had been torn to pieces, then rejoined and split apart over and over. Still unrepentant, he had been spewed out into the world, an avenging demon. In this guise, he had first sought out the incarnations of those who had inflicted lethal punishment upon his mentor and himself. Tongues torn out and brains gouged were the tokens of his savage ignorance. He found great pleasure in destroying the incarnation of the nukhwas—the medicine man his father had inflicted on him. In this lifetime he appeared in the body of a false psychic with an Armenian name, and of Chagpa, who had violated him, in the person of an English art dealer who had designs on his now living chyrsalis—Hugh Hunt. There had been others. All of the abbot's judges at Dorje had been located and exterminated. He had invaded Hunt cunningly until the symbiosis was now complete. The child Lama had escaped the abbot's attempt on his life, but the present incarnation of the "Holy One" would in time compensate for that dereliction. The Kunma had chosen his living disguise with a sense of irony that as a boy in Tibet he could hardly imagine of himself. Hugh Hunt was the father of the Lama's incarnation and as such he was time's victim. In serving his purpose, the Kunma's revenge would include his own unthinking and uncaring father and would be emblematic of all men who abandon their own flesh and blood. All would suffer, save one—his beloved abbot, to whose purpose he had emerged from the bardo to fulfill. The time of the ordeal had arrived after centuries of waiting, and the abbot would be present to witness it. How amusing it would be to flaunt Hunt's mask in this dimension. Engine of destruction and then torch of sanctifying grace. It would be up to the abbot to decide what would follow in the aftermath. He was still his son, his Yongen, but love could so conveniently turn to hate if thwarted—that, too, was a form of loving he understood so well. He would continue to obey his master out of the old love for him. If denied his destiny, the Kunma would not hesitate to destroy him or any in his way—so savage was his need to fulfill his darkest longings.

It was almost noon and the ward was now empty when Hugh Hunt raised himself out of the hospital bed and automatically made his way to his private quarters by the back stairway. The Lawson House staff members were at their midday meal. Without haste, he changed from his hospital whites into one of his summer suits. Here the weather was still balmy, but the suit chosen would be even more appropriate in his next destination. It was remarkable how well he felt—a fact confirmed by the mirror above his dresser. The distress lines had gone from round his mouth and forehead, and he realized suddenly how long his eyelashes were—adding a touch of manly beauty to his appearance. In his hands he held his wallet. It had followed him here to Lawson House. It had been kept as part of his personal effects and obviously been left for him in his room, awaiting his return. Just before he left his rooms, he saw the black prayer book. He fingered it momentarily and said, "I won't need this anymore." The rapture of his newfound health coursed throughout his being and he itched to follow its fierce urgings.

A few latecomers moved hastily toward the dining hall. Hugh Hunt left his apartment and walked casually away in the opposite direction. He did not increase his pace as he approached the hedges that would lead him away from Lawson House to the outside world. It was as easy as that. His fingers pressed on the raksa beads in his pocket.

Laurel sat listening to the phone ringing below the stairs. It was 7 A.M. Automatically, she tried her door, hoping to find it opened as the first sign of her longed-for reprieve. Such, of course, was not the case. She thought today she might tie her bed sheets together and slip down over the second-floor balustrade. She hadn't attempted that yet. To her chagrin, as she looked over her balcony, she discovered a young Mexican farmhand already on guard. He looked up at her from his chair and grinned a gold-toothed smile. He was drinking from a large coffee mug—probably his morning whiskey. Feigning to take some air, she went through an elaborate display of stretching and yawning. The man stood still and watched. She suddenly realized she was dressed only in a thin negligee and rushed back into the room, slamming the French doors. The phone had stopped ringing.

"Are you traveling for business or pleasure, sir?" the airline hostess inquired winningly.

"Both." Hugh's smile answered hers. "Just one way to La Guardia, with a connection to Albuquerque, New Mexico, if that is possible."

"Certainly, sir. There is a plane leaving La Guardia twenty minutes after your landing. Now isn't that fortunate?" she said, her eyes almost twinkling with delight.

Within ten minutes after arriving at the Burlington airport, Hugh Hunt boarded a twin-engine Cessna that would lead to his landing in New Mexico. It would be best to arrive in Albuquerque before sundown. He needed to gather the clothes and equipment commensurate to the task. He would probably need to stay overnight at a hotel before moving on to Toledos and Ranch House beyond in the morning.

There were only two passengers besides himself—a young man who worked on business charts of some sort and a portly, middle-aged gentleman who within ten minutes in the air fell promptly asleep while reading a paperback romance. Watching the cumulus clouds float by, Hunt thought of his son, Chris, and the trip he was planning for them. He could hardly wait to see his boy again. He had been away too long. He smiled, thinking of him.

Some signal went off in David's head and he awakened. His mouth stung with nicotine and he sat up vibrating with nerves. Automatically he called Anita and got her answering machine. Two follow-up calls to her office met with a busy signal. He reached her on the third attempt.

"Anita?"

"He's gone, David, gone!" Her voice was audibly trembling.

"What are saying? Hunt's dead? What?"

"Where have you been? I've been trying to reach you for days. I left messages with your service—" Choking sobs. "He'd been behaving so normally. I couldn't believe how well he was doing and now—" Why had she not been able to anticipate this cruel twist of chance? Instead of keeping Hunt under constant surveillance, she had still preferred to think of him as a textbook schizophrenic. She had not listened to the deep promptings of her fear, or, if truth be known, she had allowed her fear to cloud her customarily sound judgment. Wittingly or unwittingly, she had double-crossed herself and David.

"Anita, try to calm down, please."

She remembered her mother's admonition to keep a good face on things no matter what—a sore point of contention in their relationship, but a veritable lifesaver at this moment.

"There's no explanation for it. After lunch I went to the ward to invite him to see Carl's finished painting. His bed was empty. There was no trace of him. I had the entire grounds searched quietly, I was afraid to send out any further alarm. David—David—there will be hell to pay."

"You mean Hunt has literally left Lawson House?"

"Nobody saw anything—or anyone. His room was as neat as a pin. His robe was casually draped over a chair. He'd obviously changed into one of his suits. All of his books were stacked. And worse—all his personal effects, including his wallet, were missing. How did he manage that?"

David answered quietly, "It wasn't Hunt who managed that." He heard her groan. "Did you call McGraw?"

"Over and over—I haven't even been able to get through to him, never mind know what to say to him when I do."

"Don't try contacting him any longer."

"Then who? The police? What do I say to them—look out for a living dead man?"

"There's nothing further you can do, Anita. I suggest you

quiet down your staff and hold tight till you hear from me again."

"Tell me—tell me something so I can stop shaking. Is this part of your karma business? I feel like some child who's closed her eyes against the bogeyman, hoping it would go away—and it did."

"I think I know what he's up to and where he's headed." David pulled her back from self-recrimination.

"Where?" she said like a lost child.

"I'll call you when I get there. Trust me. Meanwhile, not a word of Hunt's disappearance must leak out. Find any excuse to explain it—you hear me?"

Just as leisurely as his own nemesis, David showered and shaved, changed his clothes, and reviewed his proposed plan of action. It was first necessary to go over it with Mendoza before booking a flight.

"Of course you're going to follow him?" Peter said rather cheerily over the phone.

"The only thing is, what will I do when I catch up with him?" David said.

"The struggle will be monumental, Davie, no doubt, but you'll know what to do. Let the abbot guide you."

"I've already asked." For some reason, David was sitting on the floor while talking to Peter.

"And what does he say?" Peter's cheeriness continued.

"The almighty, good old-fashioned panacea. 'Trust in the moment—you're capable of many things.'" David leaned back against an armchair in his living room.

"And while you're at it, pack a gun, Davie—like you used to."

"Pune." For a moment David was back in his bug-infested hotel room in India.

"Yes. Ara and I didn't know what to do without you. At night, returning from the ashram to the Blue Note was a fearsome journey in itself."

"I was good, wasn't I?" David realized with a dash of pride.

"We'd hold the flashlights while you held the gun. It was a long, dark walk back to that hotel. Your skill was unbelievable—I'd forgotten how many snakes you'd pop off on a given night." Peter smiled with pleasure.

"God, I haven't shot a gun since the Kennedy project and I haven't seen my roommate who taught me how since. What happens to ex-marines?"

"From my limited knowledge, I think they marry and bring up other marines just like them. Besides, shooting a gun is like swimming, I'm told. You don't forget the hang of it."

"What good will a gun do?" David's excitement was suddenly reined in.

"There are several factors here, Davie, you must keep clearly in mind. The Kunma is Hunt—and Hunt is flesh. Now, he has, I trust, automatically assumed you will be following him to witness . . . whatever his plans are in relation to the child. You are, therefore, part of that plan."

"Only to the extent of my preventing him from carrying it out," David answered with asperity.

"Which is in direct conflict with your bargain with him to carry out your vengeance on the Holy Child."

"How can we be sure it's not a trick, and I'm not being drawn to my own death?"

"If he'd intended to dispose of you, he would have done so long before this. Besides, he is doing this for you—remember, he professed his love. It is the fundamental truth behind his design."

"You said there were two things," David reminded Peter, and grabbed a cigarette while shifting to the couch.

"The second thing is a bit more complex." Peter flipped a page on a calendar on his wall and abruptly it was August. "The Kunma will be single-minded. He will have no mind for anything else, knowing you are with him in the coming action," Peter said gravely. "And yet . . ." The thought had just occurred to him.

"Yet, what, Peter, for God's sake?"

"Precisely for God's sake." Peter sighed. "And for his sake, I wish I really knew what the balance in Hunt is."

"There is no balance, Peter. Hunt is a complete cipher. He's only a pawn. Why are you taking this tack now?"

"But flesh is flesh—and perhaps if there is one trace left, it might prove the Kunma's weakness."

"Peter, I can't follow you."

"The point is, perhaps there is still life in Hunt. Some vestige alive of his own persona. If so, you might find a way to get through to him."

"Sure, I can drag my couch out with me and ask the Kunma to do a little session," David mocked.

"Hugh Hunt is the boy's father. As his father, there must still be some measure of resonance for his son's safety. An unexpected glitch, a momentary lapse. As a father myself, I under-stand such things, and someday, hopefully, you will, too," Peter rhapsodized.

"I follow you in theory, but how can one be sure? We're dealing with a monster, a demon," David underlined his terror.

"Yes, but even demons aspire to paradise," Peter answered, resuming his cheery manner.

"Only after the fact, not before or during. Otherwise, it would lose its status."

"You can laugh all you like, Davie," Peter chuckled.

"Besides, I might not be able to reach Hunt on any level," David pursued relentlessly.

"You'll have to keep a very sharp eye for such a possibility then." Peter rose from his chair and stretched one arm at a time.

"In other words, Mr. Chang, it's too late for the porters." David put out his cigarette.

"Much too late—on that subject you'll find a gun is easier to purchase the further west you go." Peter saw he needed to clean his breakfast plates before leaving.

"What about yourself? Don't you fear the Kunma after all?" David said hesitantly.

"No, I'm not part of his karma in any way." Peter chuckled again. "Have no fear, David."

"You certainly seem to be enjoying yourself, enjoying this farrago."

"Oh, Davie, not at your expense. Goodness, no, but I'm about to do a little traveling myself."

"Not another book collection." David rose impatiently and Sam sidled up to him.

"Better than that. I received a letter from Amy this morning—I couldn't believe it. She's been gone seven years and then a letter." Peter looked at it as he spoke. "She's married. Or was. She has a child. They are living in Michigan of all places. And I'm going out to spend the rest of the summer with them," he said beaming. "Should you need me, leave a message at this number. I will check it every day."

David smiled ruefully. "God bless you, Peter—for everything. And give Amy my regards—even if I've never met her."

"Oh, we've all met somewhere along the line, David, never forget that. So shalom, Abbot."

"Tripp? Is that you?"

"Hey, Chris, how be you?"

"I'm doin' fine." Chris was seated in his grandfather's chair in the trophy room.

"Where are you?"

"At my grandfather's ranch, like I told you I'd be."

"When are you coming home? I got a neat new set of golf clubs. My dad got them for my birthday." Tripp was eating his peanut butter and jelly sandwich for lunch.

"Great. Anyway, I called on the chance you might like to come out and stay at the ranch." Chris threw his legs proprietarily over the armchair.

"Have you got your own horse?" Tripp said, chewing heavily.

"Wait'll you see her. She's a palomino."

"I don't think I know what that is."

"Well, if you come out, you'd have one, too. The place is crawling with horses."

"Hey, neat-o, Chris."

"Is it a deal?"

"But, see, my mom's got this dumb trip to Europe all mapped out and my dad's coming along." Tripp hesitated, taking his next bite.

"Why don't you let them go and you come out?"

"Well, this is supposed to bring the family together again, you know."

"You mean, they're not going to be separated anymore?" Chris crossed his legs and leaned deeper into the leather.

"We're leaving next week. How about your folks?"

"What about 'em?"

"Are they still going separated?"

"Hell, no, my dad is comin' out here real soon."

"Is he better?"

"Lots. He's promised to spend August with us. We're going hunting with a real rifle. A thirty-aught-six Browning Bret—with a range-finding scope—like last time."

"I don't know anything about guns, but I appreciate you inviting me and all that."

"Well, okay, tashi-shag!" Chris sat straight up, his feet dangling over the armchair.

"What?"

"What, what?"

"You just said something." Tripp swallowed the last of his lunch.

"I said see you."

"Is that some Western talk?"

"I don't know what you mean."

"Okay, whatever it is you said, the same yourself."

"Okay, Tripp. Take it easy."

"See you, too, pal." Tripp finished his milk, sad not to be able to join his pal, but happy at the prospect of vacationing with his reconciled parents.

Chris leaned forward in his grandfather's chair. He hated not being able yet to touch the floor with his boots. He loved the smell of warm leather and old cigars that permeated the room. He looked up and contemplated the stuffed condor's head and pantomimed shooting it with an invisible rifle. Too bad about Tripp. He could hardly wait till his father came and they would go into the mountains together. The calendar already read August 7. He aimed his imaginary trusty rifle at the malevolent eyes again and fired.

PART **SEVEN**

Except for Easter and Christmas, Padre Domin-
guez rarely set foot in Ranch House. This morning he was
tempted to drive up and discover for himself what had prevented McGraw from attending yesterday's service and supper.
The old man had never missed morning mass while back in
New Mexico.

Padre Dominguez had tried calling several times, but Ralph
Gough, McGraw's overseer and secretary, had indicated his boss
was not available to come to the phone. The surly man would
offer no explanation, and his customary condescension toward
the priest was now so exacerbated as to make another phone
call impossible.

It had not rained for over a month, and the padre's little
garden behind his three-room apartment was suffering its
yearly drought. He had so few pleasures and taking care of his
little plot was his main joy outside the Church. He had just
finished watering the agave when he heard the sound of a car
stopping outside. Who could be wandering around Toledos at

this hour and in this heat? He anticipated the knock before it came. He put down his watering can, wiped his hands on his soutane, and once inside his apartment, removed the broad-brimmed hat that protected him against the sun. He waited for the knock again, to be sure, before opening his front door. When he did so, he came face-to-face with a young man wearing a pair of blue slacks that matched the color of his eyes. He was holding on to a black leather suitcase; behind him stood a taxi with its meter still running. The name of a Taos firm was emblazoned in black on its blue doors. The two men looked at one another. The man dropped his suitcase and smiled winningly.

"Padre Dominguez? My name is David Sussman. I'm from New York and I think I'm going to need your help."

Ralph Gough watched the speck on the horizon approaching Ranch House with a feigned indifference. From where he sat on the back patio, it would be ten minutes before he could determine what kind of vehicle it was and another three or four minutes until it came up the driveway. The thing looked like some maddened desert insect or lizard scuttling across the arid countryside, throwing off sand in its wake. He'd wait till it arrived before checking up on the old man. He'd been in the attic for almost two days now, and it was about time he came down.

Ralph Gough, at forty-one, was as mean-spirited as he looked. Lanky, tall, with squinting black eyes and thick lips firmly lecturing the world that it owed him a living and the world was not to forget it. Barrel-chested, he wore his "cowboy" outfit like an official badge of some high command. He raised his denimed legs up to the railing surrounding the patio and lowered his Stetson against the glare as he watched the car in the distance taking shape.

Chris was in the billiard room in the back part of the house when the car came up the drive. He was alone and bored. Tomito and Raul were taking their siestas somewhere and his mother was upstairs asleep. She spent so much time by herself now. The same was true of Papa Champ. Chris's anticipated vacation out West had proved a mixed blessing. He turned on the television set in the game room and just as quickly turned it off. Inexplicably, Papa had disconnected all the sets, deciding, after all these years, that they were anathema to life at Ranch House. Chris should have gone into Taos this morning and waited for the matinee of *Superman*. He'd seen it once, but twice was even better. He picked up the cue stick and shot the six ball toward an uninteresting combination on the table. He watched it break up in a series of mad clickings that culminated in the sinking of the eight ball in the far right pocket from where he stood. He'd defeated himself, so there was no point going on. Damn siesta time. Here he was in his neat denim pants, his favorite cotton, plaid shirt, and yellow cowhide boots (like Papa's) with nothing to do. More and more, he found himself alone. He passed the trophy room and looked inside. It was empty—only the familiar smell was comforting. He saw the stuffed condor and thought of his father. Each morning he'd awakened with the thrilling thought that today would be the day. Now, seven days later, it was as it had always been— promises fading into emptiness. He'd decided not to hope for anything in that direction. If he arrived, well and good. If not, it would take very little adjustment to fall back into the norm.

By this time, Chris was outside the door leading up to the attic. A tray of food was at the base of it. He could tell it had been lying there for some time by the curdled look of the gravy over the pork chops. Also, the coffee was dead cold. After investigating these things, he listened at the door. Not a sound. He tried the door. It was locked. But then it was always locked.

"Papa Champ," Chris called tentatively. Then he gave a good, lusty yell: "Grandpa!"

There was no answer. Wanting to get out of the house, he descended toward the large living room with its chintzy curtains and stuffy lamps and pictures. His least favorite room. He opened the front door and stepped out into the driveway.

A maroon 1980 Seville station wagon was shining in the bright sunlight. Chris ran to it and sat down next to the driver's seat. Whose was it? He closed his eyes as melancholy overtook him for an instant then stepped out of the car.

"Hell, there he is." Chris looked up at the window and saw Ralph's stubbled face smiling down at him. "We've been looking everywhere for you, boy." Ralph turned and shouted back into the house, "He's out here!"

"Whose car is this?" Chris asked suspiciously, unused to Ralph's display of goodwill.

"You'll never guess, boy. You'll never guess."

Coming toward him from out of the house was his father, dressed in his old hunting outfit. Chris's heart practically leaped into his throat and his face reddened as he ran to meet him.

"Dad. Daddy." He grabbed his father round the waist and held on tightly. *Please don't let me cry,* he begged inside himself, but it was useless.

"Daddy. Oh, Daddy!"

"You didn't think I'd break my promise, did you?" Chris looked up at his smiling face. "Did you?" The smile widened. His handsome father was looking down at him, looking the way he did before the accident, and he'd kept his promise. He'd kept it.

"You're all better," Chris said with amazement.

"All better," Hugh echoed.

"Have you seen Mom? Have you—"

Hugh raised a finger to his lips, and a cunning expression lit up his face. "Later. Let's make it a surprise."

"A surprise?" Chris whispered uncomprehendingly. It was then Chris noticed Ralph coming from the house. He was carrying Chris's hunting pack and bore a rifle in each hand.

Chris looked at his father, his face still wreathed in a blissful smile. "A surprise," he repeated affirmatively, and nodded his head.

"He's there. I knew it." David opened his eyes, bloodshot with effort.

"How can you be sure?"

"I can see him."

"See him?" Padre Dominguez turned toward his riding companion.

"Don't slow up, Padre, and for God's sake, look where you're going."

"I know these roads like the back of my hand, señor."

"Can't we go any faster?"

"No, señor." The padre shrugged apologetically.

"Why not?"

"I've never tried." He shrugged again.

The speedometer registered a prehistoric 45 mph. David looked at his watch. It had been twenty minutes since they'd left Toledos.

"But you say you saw him? How?" the padre persisted.

"Besides being a good Catholic priest, my guess is you are part Indian. Am I correct?"

"Sí, my mother was a Zuni."

"Didn't she tell you—well—any bedtime stories?"

"Many, but what are you trying to say?"

"How much more time before we get there?"

"Twenty minutes, señor."

"Well, I'll do my best in that time." Since leaving Taos, he'd picked up a .38 revolver in an alarmingly easy transaction (American Express) in a store dealing in camping equipment. He'd projected the gun out the car window, sighting rock formations at varying distances, and began warming to his former skills. It took barely a mile before the ping of connections reassured him that it was indeed like swimming. He had not entirely lost his knack. The padre suffered the impromptu gun practice with a baffled patience. David finally leaned back, patted the weapon, and placed it in his single piece of luggage.

"Señor, you were about to tell me a bedtime story."

Ten minutes later, Laurel woke up in her bedroom feeling groggy and unrefreshed. The sleeping pill had not completely worn off. She'd fallen into the habit of taking a siesta to catch up with her sleep. Nighttime brought on her watch over Chris and the dreams that now plagued him habitually. Chris had been moved to a bedroom directly below hers, and Raul had been instructed to allow the boy's mother to attend him should there arise the need. Each night over the past two weeks, Raul had escorted her down to her son's bedroom and then back. Laurel, facing another torpid day, sat on her bed, unable, unwilling, to move.

Padre Dominguez had not once taken his eyes off the road during David's "bedtime" tale. Out in the open, the giant cacti with their increasingly grotesque formations seemed a fitting background for what had quietly been coming at him from his passenger.

"Do you mind if I smoke, Padre?" David asked, signaling an end to his recitation.

"Please, señor, while I do not smoke myself, I still enjoy the smell." The road was becoming bumpy and David had to wait for the right moment to light up.

"So, what do you think, Padre?" David leaned back. "Not being a Catholic, I don't know if what I said makes any sense—to use the wrong word."

"Señor, in the seminary I was taught many things to help me realize my vocation as a priest, but it was all—what is the word?—an over . . . over—it did not change for me what my mother had taught me first—about the spirits."

"I thought as much, and I think the word you're looking for is *overlay.*"

"Ah, that one, I rarely use it—but that is it, precisely. Thank you, señor."

David smiled and blew smoke out the window.

"You have ten minutes before we arrive. Should you like to resume your practicing."

As Laurel finally rose to cross to the bathroom, she heard the sound of footsteps rapidly approaching her door. Someone was yelling something in the local Mexican patois outside her window. She could make out only the word *patrón.* Then the knocking started on her door, which turned into insistent pounding.

"Ma'am, get up, ma'am." It was Ralph Gough outside. In a moment he would turn the key in the lock and enter. She ran to fetch her dressing gown.

The front door was wide open when David and Padre Dominguez arrived. The heat of the afternoon was pouring its lacerations into the reception hall, mitigating the effects of the air-conditioning. A rustic chalet born of the forties, David assessed instantly: moose-antlered and pine-knotted with a gigantic fireplace yawning blackly in the middle of the room. As they entered, they saw Tomito, the mestizo bodyguard, dressed in khaki trousers and a gray, sweat-stained shirt. He sat staring at the sofa flanking the fireplace. Padre Dominguez rattled off something in Spanish and the Mexican looked up, his beady eyes unaccustomedly soft and dazed. He pointed to the sofa and muttered, *"Muerto."* The padre gasped and moved toward where Tomito pointed. A body possessed the entire length of the couch. Stockinged feet poked out of an old Indian blanket that covered the rest of the head and body. When Dominguez pulled back the blanket, a strange wail erupted from the back of his throat and he fell to his knees, his lips quivering in prayer.

David had never seen Papa Champ in the flesh—only a photograph in Laurel's bedroom in West Haven and occasionally in magazines and newspapers. The eyes popped out from their lids like two burning lamps. His mouth, set in a parody of a smile, was clamped down over the protruding tongue hanging out like a comic's tie—only bloated and engorged. A Halloween mask made truly sinister by the livid rope burns circling the old man's neck. *"El patrón está muerto,"* repeated Tomito like a child. The padre continued mumbling, and for a moment he looked at David. David read the inquiry in those eyes.

The smell of alcohol and piss leapt up from the blanket and David shook his head, turning to Tomito.

"Do you understand English?"

The Mexican nodded abstractly.

"Where is the other patrón?"

Tomito looked up in confusion.

"El Señor Hunt. Where is he?"

Tomito made no answer, he merely blinked.

"Was the Señor Hunt here when . . ." David pointed to the body.

This time Tomito shook his head and made a vague gesture with his hands. Padre Dominguez intervened and exploded in rapid patois. Tomito, faced by the stern-looking priest, stammered a reply.

"What did he say?" David asked.

"He heard Señor Gough tell la señora that the old man left a note saying he couldn't find it and that's why he had to do it."

"Find what?"

Padre interrogated Tomito once more.

"No sé, Padre, no sé."

"La señora Hunt, where is she?"

Tomito turned to David and pointed toward the staircase.

"Shall I come up with you, señor?" Dominguez asked.

"No, Padre, you stay here."

Both men automatically looked back at the corpse. Ordinarily, David would have closed the sightless eyes glaring up at him, but they were so distended, it would have been grotesque to try. Instead, he covered the face with the blanket and raced up the stairway, calling for Laurel. The sound of moaning through an opened doorway on the landing drew him toward it. He ran into the room and found Laurel prostrate on the floor by the bed, making helpless, childlike noises. She was partly clothed, as if grief had overtaken her while dressing. David leaned over and swooped her into his arms. Even distraught, David marveled at her pale beauty, so long out of sight, but forever lodged in his mind and body.

"I knew he was going to die. I could see it—and could do nothing to stop it." She sucked in air with a long-drawn-out shudder. David covered her mouth with his hand, raised her from the ground, and replaced his fingers with hungry kisses. Laurel responded immediately. Tears of relief broke the dam of terror and restored a measure of sanity. David took her face in his hands. Poor Laurel, she looked wan and disheveled, but here she was—his adorable shiksa. All he could do was repeat her name over and over.

"David, he couldn't find it," she cried onto his shoulder. "What do you suppose my daddy couldn't find? What?"

"Hush." David patted her back gently. "Later, later." He let her tears flow. "Now I need you to listen to me and do what I ask you to."

"Don't go. Oh, please, don't go."

"I want you to finish dressing as quickly as you can. Slacks and a pair of boots."

"Why?"

"Because I love you—and I'll explain the rest downstairs." There, he'd said it, and with a simple finality. Her terror shattered at his admission. She stood there, her eyes still swimming.

"Don't go."

"If I don't, you won't get dressed."

She nodded sweetly and kissed his face and neck, still unable to believe his miraculous presence.

The human condition was never-endingly ridiculous, David agonized. Here they were encircled in cataclysm and he was getting aroused. Oh, idiot state. He backed away from her.

"Laurel, hurry, it's very important."

A merry glimmer gave a lie to her tears, and she kissed the tips of her fingers and placed them on his mouth.

"Dress," he said sharply, and like an obedient child, she did as she was told.

He would wait till she was altogether before revealing his plan, but first the body had to be removed.

David was at the top of the stairs when Ralph Gough shambled in, followed by two Mexican ranch hands. Padre Dominguez, by this time consoling Tomito, rose from his seat beside him. The priest and Gough had never hit it off. Gough had no use for religion of any sort.

"What in hell are you doing here?" Gough barked at the priest. "And who told you to come nosin' around?" The two ranch hands hesitated in picking up the corpse.

"What happened, Señor Gough? I can make no sense from Tomito here."

"It's none of your damned business anyway." Gough slammed his hat on a chair and yelled at the Mexicans, "*Vaya, muchachos. I said vaya,* God damn it."

"As el patrón's confessor, I have a right to know," Dominguez insisted.

"Well, maybe as his confessor, you might be able to tell me what happened," Gough blustered. But the grief under it was genuine.

"It was suicide? No?"

"It was suicide. Yes. I found him swinging up there in the attic."

Wild fear passed through the Mexicans like a wind of ill omen. The padre crossed himself. If only he'd had an inkling. He would have risked breaking the silence of the confessional to intercede. But there had been no warning, no indication even. Now the old patrón's eternal soul was doomed. May God grant him mercy.

"What was it he was looking for?" The padre asked with a forlorn sigh.

"The attic's littered with junk. Whatever it was, he didn't find it."

"What could be so important that he—"

"You'd better keep your mouth shut, whatever it was, if you know what's good for you, Padre."

The priest flushed and blocked Gough's passage toward the doorway. "Where are you taking him?"

"I've made arrangements with Forbishers in town. We've got to get the old man looking right. Otherwise people might start having ideas. You wouldn't want that to happen. I mean, the

newspaper and magazine people pokin' around?" Gough signaled the men out and suddenly his voice softened. "Anyway,
he was drunk. I don't know what was eatin' at him, but he was
drunk. You know, like he sometimes gets without knowing why
himself. Forbishers will take care of everything. Make him
right."

Yes, Padre thought, *perhaps this was the least they could do
for him under the circumstances.* In their own separate ways they
loved the old man. As they looked at one another, they understood this tie—the only junction at which they met.

"Where's my hat?" Gough grumbled, and turned to where
he'd left it. He saw David standing at the bottom of the stairs
watching him. Gough's chin jutted out. "I don't think I know
you, mister."

Almost immediately Laurel's voice was heard from the top
of the landing. "He's a friend of mine, Dr. Sussman. David, this
is Ralph Gough. He runs Ranch House for . . ." David nodded
curtly and Ralph glowered. The name of the Jewish doctor was
all too familiar to him.

"We came together," the padre affirmed defensively.

Ralph said nothing, thinking as he watched Laurel descend
the stairs. By a grim quirk of fate, he realized she was his boss
now and would remain so until she fired him. A strong possibility.

"Ralph, where is . . . where is Papa?"

"I called Forbishers in Taos, like I told you I would, ma'am.
They're all ready to go to work on him."

"Of course. Yes, you must. When Chris comes back from the
movies, we'll be going into Toledos to spend the night there."

She turned to the padre. "We'll be flying back East after the funeral." David admired her show of strength and smiled. Gough misinterpreted it and scowled.

"Ma'am, Chris is not in town to the movies."

"He's not here? He didn't—"

"No, ma'am. He didn't." Ralph looked at David now with positive hatred. Yes, he thought, a woman is nothing but a whore. The old man was right, as he tended to be most of the time.

"Chris is with his father," David spoke softly. "Isn't that so, Mr. Gough?"

"Chris . . . with his—" Laurel turned pale.

"Well, if it wasn't his father," Gough smirked, "it sure was somebody who looked like him."

Laurel grabbed on to David's hand for support.

"His father," she repeated, and couldn't go on.

"You were asleep, ma'am. He wanted to—" Gough looked directly at David. "He wanted to surprise you later, ma'am."

Laurel turned to David. "David, did he—Papa—did he . . . ?" Her nails dug into David's palm.

"No, I don't think this time. He had no reason to. Besides, that was not why he came here."

"Where did he take Chris?" Laurel said numbly, then turned to Ralph and repeated her question.

"Huntin'," Ralph answered laconically. Gough was uneasy, uncertain what was going on.

"Where? Where?" Laurel practically screamed.

"Never mind, Mr. Gough," David spoke in his best professional manner. "You go ahead with your arrangements. I'll take care of Mrs. Hunt."

A mean smile played across Gough's lips. "You do that, Mr. Sussman. Too bad Mr. McGraw wasn't here to welcome you personally. I'm sure he would have enjoyed the honor." Gough was doing this for the old man and would risk the daughter's wrath. He wiped the inside of the brim of his hat and started again for the door.

"Mr. Gough." David's voice stopped him at the threshold. "How long was it since Mr. Hunt took his son hunting?"

Gough turned. "You mean you don't know the answer to that one, too? Why don't you ask Mr. Hunt yourself?" And he left, slamming the door behind him.

"Señora, I'm so sorry." Padre Dominguez was standing by Laurel's side.

"David," she said, disregarding the priest, "how did you know?" She was breathing heavily, swallowing in fear.

David turned coolly toward her. "Would you be able to find the spot you told me about?" Time was holding them in a curious bind. Although the events had moved precipitously forward, everything now seemed to be in slow motion. Was it the heat? The shock of the old man's suicide?

"Spot?" Laurel repeated.

"In the mountains."

"What spot?"

"Where the vultures gather," David said firmly.

"Hugh took Chris there?"

"The Kunma took him there." And he sighed with the full weight of the past weeks. "Is there a car available?" David asked Laurel, but her face was buried in her hands. He turned toward Tomito, who was still sitting by the fireplace. "Tomito, is there a car outside we could use?" David spoke with exaggerated deliberation.

The Mexican shook his head. "Señor Gough, he take the station wagon now with el patrón. The pickup go into town this morning, not yet back."

"Padre." David turned to face him. "Forgive the further imposition, but . . ." Dominguez acquiesced immediately. "I thank you, but I need to make a condition," David said apologetically.

"And what is that, señor?"

"That I drive. Do you think your Chevy can take it?"

The priest shrugged. "Well, it will be a novelty for her."

"It's too late." Laurel looked up. The old superstitious self had repossessed her. "I can feel it. It's too late."

"No." David stepped in front of her, forcing her to look up at him. "If I miss my guess, it's not too late." And he started toward the door, hoping against hope that he was right.

"Dad, why are we coming here?"

The shiny Seville was edging its way through the canyon toward the high mesa. Chris had not passed through these mountains since that traumatic episode many years ago.

"You remember this place, don't you?" Hugh's face was concentrated as he drove. They had left the last semblance of a road behind over a mile ago and the terrain was beginning to tax the sleek vehicle. Hunt had requested a Land Rover, but none were available. Heat waves rippled in front of him like a mirage beckoning him ever forward to the topland. Packets of dirt kicked up and spread like bird droppings over his windshield. Hugh turned on the wipers, but the splotches kept reappearing.

"Dad?" Chris repeated cautiously, waiting for an answer to his question.

"Not now." Hugh spoke harshly for the first time. "It will be alright, you'll see." He leaned across to pat Chris's shoulders. "You can open the box of ammunition and load up as I showed you. Would you like that?"

Chris had looked forward to this moment, but the sight of the mesa in the distance took some joy out of it. He peered through the blistered windshield and wondered if they were coming here as a test. He knew what was up ahead, and what he'd see when he got there. They were coming so Chris could prove his mettle. His first shot would be at one of them. Like when you fall off your horse, you'd better climb right back on, if you don't want to be afraid of horses all your life. It was going to be like that. Only it had happened so long ago. His elation at vindicating himself prevented the bad part of his feelings from nabbing him. Mentally he went over the whole process of loading, sighting, and tempering the recoil. He'd been practicing all summer and was sure to surprise his father with his acquired skill. He turned to the backseat for the box of shells and saw the condor's hell eye looking at him. He started to sweat. His imagination and the heat. He must wipe his palms before touching the shells. Surreptitiously, he rubbed them on the sides of the seat. The car was beginning to bounce and Hugh slowed down. The ribbon of a pass was cluttered with jagged stones, fallen from the surrounding peaks. The fragments jutted haphazardly, making all passage forward perilous. As the car careened, Chris was suddenly lifted out of his seat and knocked against the window.

"Put your seat belt on," commanded Hugh, and Chris reached under to grasp the end of the straps.

"I guess no one must come here much," Chris volunteered while searching. He held the two ends of the safety belt in each hand and the car settled down. Chris peered again through the silt-coated windows and wondered how his father managed to keep his course in these conditions. It was a mystery.

"I guess maybe I won't need this now," Chris chirped in an effort to lighten things, but he'd spoken prematurely. The car was lifted into the air and listed badly to one side. The straps slid out of Chris's hands and he collided against his father's body. The next minute the car righted itself on its axis, throwing Chris across to his side with a jolt.

"Whew," he said, his fear laced with admiration for his father's skill. Suddenly he laughed. "That was neat."

"I thought I told you to put your seat belt on."

"Yes, sir." Chris scrambled to follow the order. The bad part was beginning to sneak back up on him. He would wait until things were easier before saying or doing another thing.

Suddenly, the Seville scraped the side of a huge boulder and came to a grinding halt. Both occupants in the car were shaken about, and Chris had once more fallen against his father's shoulder. Hunt, moving with lightning speed, turned off the ignition and left the automobile to investigate the extent of the damage. Chris looked up from where he lay sprawled out across the driver's seat and almost immediately slid back to his side. Hugh was standing in the doorway, blotting out the patch of blue sky behind him.

"Are you all right?" Hunt said. Chris noticed a small trickle of blood moving slowly down his father's left nostril. He must have banged his face against the steering wheel, Chris figured.

"Your nose is bleeding." Chris watched with surprise as Hunt's tongue darted out and caught the zigzag line of blood in a single swipe. Like an iguana, Chris thought, goggle-eyed.

"We'll have to walk the rest of the way. It's not far." Hugh moved back into the driver's seat and turned the engine over. Hugh gently eased it into life after several gasps and began artfully dislodging the Seville from the rock. "We're lucky the damage isn't worse," Hugh muttered as he continued in reverse. The blood started oozing down his nostril again and the tongue repeated its deft business. The car hit a smaller impediment behind it, and instinctively he took his foot off the pedal and switched off.

When Chris tried to leave the car, he found his door jammed—stuck—and he was forced to ease himself out from his father's side. Momentarily blinded by the sunlight, Chris tripped over some stones as he stumbled out. Just like the last time, he lamented, and scrambling to his feet, he checked his legs and arms for damage. Hastily, he dusted himself off with a bandanna from his back pocket. He didn't dare look at his father. Clumsy, he was just clumsy, that was all. But he'd make up for it. His shirt was torn at the elbows. Scratches, but no blood. From the corner of his eye, he saw his father standing several yards away. His body was rigid as he stared through the glare toward the mesa. His arms suddenly shot upward and descended, making a wide arc as if to contain the area within their circumference. The boy heard a chilling snarl and for the first time was aware of how sound echoed in the mountain pass. Far off past the mesa, cumulus clouds slumbered together. That would mean bad weather in the offing in that distant place. Papa Champ had instructed him about that. Around him, everything looked parched and covered with a burnt orange, lemony tint. He wished that he'd brought his new hat for the occasion. He'd picked it out in Taos himself and paid for it out of his allowance. The thought he'd been suppressing jumped out at him, demanding his attention. How could that sound he'd heard have come from his father? It wasn't human. Hugh turned slowly and walked toward him. He hesitated midway and his wrists began to flop aimlessly.

"Dad, are you okay?" His boy's treble echoing came back at him.

"Get your gun and let's go." His father's voice, soft and caressing, carried easily over the distance between them. His green eyes, catching glints of the sun, sparkled almost merrily.

As if solemnizing the occasion, Chris answered, "Yes, sir," rather gravely and returned to the car. He passed one of the shotguns to his father, who stood behind him, then grabbed the other for himself. He turned off the air-conditioning and forcibly slammed the door shut.

The good feeling resurfaced and Chris became almost jubilant. The whole disastrous trip up here was going to be worth it after all.

David did not dare close his eyes. The road was beginning to be narrow and promised some thorny problems for the Chevy. The padre was pale enough now with his car doing seventy on this treacherous thread of a road. Laurel was riding in back with the padre's rosary in her hands. As David navigated the distressed vehicle, he wondered how much the Kunma knew. He could so easily facilitate catastrophe to his pursuers if he suspected their purpose. Yet he appeared unknowing. Or un-caring. Was that nearer the truth? Was he so bent on complet-ing his mission that he could not see or sense their encroachment on that design? That was Mendoza's take on the monster's disposition. Or, was their pursuit part of the Kunma's now inscrutable plan? Time was still on David's side—unless something unforeseen occurred to stall them. If there was any true justice prevailing in that ever-shifting duplicity called the universe, all concerned around him and on the mesa were in for the revelation of their lives.

The stench of sweet rot was so overpowering that Chris almost slid down the side of the mesa. His father had already neatly scaled the forty feet to the top. He'd carried the two rifles up with him—making a trail for Chris to follow. The boy, full of purpose and youth, managed the ascent with some dexterity, but made the mistake of pausing to look back.

"Chris. Keep coming." Chris could see his father's face and shoulders hanging over the edge. His arms beckoned, urging him upward. Against the blue sky, Hugh's flapping limbs moved like those of the creatures behind him. Haunted by that image, Chris hung back. Where was he to go? His father had the guns, and to lose his nerve so prematurely would forever cancel his father's respect for him. He reached forward, his heart pumping madly in his chest. He saw his father's arms groping toward him. They were less than three feet from one another. His father's fingers stretched and clamped round his wrists. When the reek of death slapped him, Chris leaned back and almost pulled away, but his father's strength prevailed and now Chris lay splayed out on the top ground, panting in fear

and revulsion. The odor was even more gagging than he recalled. The only new detail was the smell of salt. He hadn't
remembered that. Not more than fifteen yards away, the source
of the profound stench squatted like a band of demon judges.
Their diamond-small eyes were brightly alert with malevolent
prescience. There were hundreds of them—vultures of all sizes,
gathered together as at some predestined trial in high summer.
A few were still floating down from their rookery above. They
glided on outsized wings, the matted feathers choked with fecal
matter, molting even as they closed like mantles round their
hideous bodies. Their necks craned in serpentine thrusts and
their gabbled speech rivaled their smell.

Stunned, squatting on the top of the mesa, Chris saw his
father bowing to them, his forehead almost touching the
ground as the monsters hopped and fluttered together, croaking
in a kind of anticipation and distorted joy. Chris watched his
father's back and, beyond him, the evil shifting of the pack.
Some of them came forward to smell out the small intruder—
their red wattles distending in surprise.

Hunt looked up from his squatting position and the memory
of a summer past presented itself and alerted his senses. What
was he doing here? Instinctively, he turned and looked at his
son, then back to the gathering birds. Stung by this moment
of recall, he turned back to his boy and shouted, "Run! Chris!
Run!" Chris looked at his father with apprehension and bewilderment.

"Son! Run! Run! Now!"

Something coalesced in the boy, and numbly heeding his
father's command, Chris slid back toward the mesa's edge.
Keeping an eye on his father, Chris grabbed his rifle and slipped

over the edge. Using his boot heels like brakes, he kicked his way and rolled over backward down the last ten feet, his eye searching, even as he tumbled, for a possible hiding place.

Minutes later, the Chevy hit the first of the major roadblocks. They had already tried sealing themselves in against the spurting dust and sand, but the padre's car, besides being of a venerable age (vintage '61), lacked air-conditioning. They had cracked open the windows halfway, but still the padre was holding a white handkerchief to his mouth, with David and Laurel pressing Kleenex tissues to theirs. The absence of seat belts forced the occupants to grip the bottom of their seats for ballast—except for David, who was compelled to absorb the shocks with stoic determination. Laurel eventually gave up and slid in between the front and backseat, to make a resting place for her head on the worn brown leather upholstery. The car had barely traveled a half mile in this battleground before a loud explosion on the left back wheel signaled a flat tire. They hobbled twenty feet farther before David braked to a halt.

"Padre, have you a spare?"

The old man nodded, still holding the handkerchief to his nose.

"And a jack?"

Again the nod.

"Can I help? Please let me help," piped up Laurel.

"Rest outside in the car's shadow. Come on, Padre. Wipe off the windshield, I'll do the rest!"

The hoarse chorus of the scavengers had reached fearsome proportions. Groups of the creatures were sliding around Hunt—

their wattles shaking spasmodically until a thousand death heads preened for his attention. He turned and saw the cause of their complaint. Chris had obeyed him and disappeared. Even as his heart beat in relief, he was cursing himself in the old tongue. He moved to the rim of the mesa. There was no sign of the boy anywhere. He saw the rifle upended in the gravel below. He straightened himself as if yanked from within by a powerful force, and his brain dimmed in submission to it. The Kunma scanned the horizon for the missing boy. Where could he have gone? Back to the car? Unlikely. He was there, some- where in the surrounding mountains. They were full of clefts big enough to swallow a little boy. If he was lucky, he might have stumbled on a cave. So be it, boy. This lapse would not occur again. He was not going to be denied his ultimate sat- isfaction on this plane.

That the boy would have the audacity to undermine his plan raised his ire, and he shouted his displeasure to the skies for this momentary crack in his command. His figure became phosphorescent until his shimmer merged with the lemony bleakness of the landscape. The birds took instant flight and their gibberings rose in counterpoint. The combined echoes shivered up the canyon and became a single sound. The ner- vous dung droppings of the birds splattered his now less than trim hunting jacket and boots. The Kunma stood there, reveling in his defilement, and smiled.

He would search for the boy and bring him back to the mesa. By then the craven clan would be reassembled and prepared for what he would offer them. The tender parts of a young boy would be their feast. *Ai-yah! Ai-yah!* Come and feast. Long used to the wayward fare of dead rattlers, stray coyotes, and other small wanderers of this plateau, the sight and smell of human flesh that lingered in their ancestral memories, and even occasionally gratified in this barren hole, would be sure to precipitate a vicious fight within the carrion hosts. The ritual sacrifice would commence with cutting open the boy's chest with his knife and ripping out his heart. He would offer it to the King Vulture, who was hovering on the rocks surrounding him—ready to assert his supremacy among the pack. Then the body would be hacked into strips and given to the other birds. After they had eaten, the bones would be pulverized with a stone, and the powder would be the final offering. This, too, they would eat until there was nothing left. Thus the ritual murder of the Dalai Lama incarnation—planned by the Black Abbot—would finally see its completion and part of his karmic debt to the abbot would be realized. He could sense the abbot's approach. He could smell him in the atmosphere. How proud the abbot would be of this accomplishment. And achieving it, he could gratify another of his pleasures. Only after the last rib had been pulverized and ingested would he reveal the Kunma to his airborne flock. Death would know death and rejoice in the knowing.

David was deeply worried. He felt shaky in the knees. Changing the tire in the blistering heat had made a sopping mess of him. All he needed now was to suffer dehydration and he'd had it. The padre was still out of breath and dizzy from just cleaning the windshield. His white handkerchief had turned into a golden blob, and he'd tossed it as soon as they'd taken off again. To compensate, Laurel had passed several wads of tissue to him. They would have to stop to clean the windshield every few miles or so. The wipers were not strong enough to counteract the grit spewing up from the road. Laurel had now withdrawn back into herself and had stopped praying. He checked his watch. It was almost four. The sun's rays would start losing their potency shortly, and that would ease their burden considerably, but make it harder to track down his prey. "Hold on, everybody," David yelled as he pressed down on the pedal and the car braved forward.

The cave was cool and dry, but Chris was dying of thirst. His tongue felt thick in his mouth and it was becoming hard to swallow. He could see the entrance from where he squatted. The shadow on the limestone wall had slanted perceptibly since he'd been here, a sure sign the sun was setting. He'd run as fast as his legs could carry him, anxious to put distance between himself and the nightmare on the mesa. Twice he'd been tempted to take cover: once inside a series of boulders forming a natural lair, and secondly within a narrow cleft partially hidden by some petrified mesquite. The first would have been a dead end if he was cornered (besides it stank powerfully of coyote). The second was wide enough for a boy to manage. Both, however, were too close to the mesa.

Instead, he had struck a zigzag course over the rocks, thankful not to be crossing dirt, where the telltale marks of his boots would reveal him. He avoided any semblance of a path for that very reason. He'd seen enough television to be wary of such traps. It was tougher loping about the treacherous rock waste, but it spelled safety. He'd spotted the remains of what was once a horse—its bones picked clean by the ever-vigilant buzzards and polished to a high calcified whiteness by the wind and weather. He had seen several of the nemesis birds swirling down to perch on nearby crags—scouts always on the lookout for the insatiable needs of the pack. Ducking from their sight, he'd slid down a short incline of loose stones and run smack into the entry to the cave. Too tired and frightened to search further, he dimly sensed the hand of providence and accepted the shelter gratefully.

Once he'd stopped running, he surprised himself at the anger welling up inside him. The small cave contained no animal smells, so nothing was bound to come back to reclaim its own. Still, he needed to be on the lookout for scorpions that infested these parts and the coral snake that Tomito cautioned could strike without warning. He'd wait until it was dark before venturing out. It would be cool then, and he would just keep walking until—well, someone would be bound to find him.

Please, God, don't let it be my father. But his father had said, "Run! Run!" Why had his father brought him to that place, then? The fear that had always complemented his love for the man was now preempting that love. What was he doing in front of those horrors? Was he actually kneeling? Why? His anger swelled. He'd foolishly thought the trip was to be some rite of passage. If only he'd managed to keep his gun, but he'd been too scared after dropping it during his descent from the mesa. His boyish frenzy mounted, but warily he caught himself and listened for any telltale signs of approach. The only sound he heard was a long, sustained booming. In the depths of his heart, he understood his karma was powerless to interfere with it. He grew quiet, embracing this knowledge, and his fingers stopped their agitated dance against his body.

The booming echoed again, and he placed his hands against

the walls of the cave, allowing the coolness of the stones to penetrate his body. Finally, he breathed a deep sigh of relief, then sat down and crossed his legs under him. He placed his arms in his lap and felt waves of peace rising within. He would wait for dusk in this position. Fleetingly he thought of his mother and grandfather. A surge of love rose to quell his anger. He wet his lips with his tongue and the sense of peace pulsed forward slowly.

The obscenely crenellated head cocked in wonderment while the loose red folds jiggled like a mad earring from its neck. Below, the smell of its own kind rose to its nostrils. Yet the odor was deceptive and even puzzling to the stalking creature. It emanated from a source foreign to it—a source conceivably meant to feed its hunger. A carcass for potential feeding was lodged in the shade made by an overlapping rock formation. It was a place usually commanded by a furry, four-footed beast—a scavenger in its own right, but equally rife for eating. The thing resembled the two-footed ones that occasionally prowled the countryside and intruded on their territory. It was sitting on its haunches, upright and unmoving. Strapped across its back was a steel object known to spit an ominous fire. The smell of decay hung about it like a cloud. In some dim corridor of its mind, the smell registered and the beast recognized it for what it was: dried waste droppings from its own entrails. Its powerful shoulders rippled and the wings unfurled in a menacing benediction. It glided forward with an offsetting grace to land within a yard of the other presence. The unmoving thing was either resting or its life was ebbing away into the ground from some unseen wound. The eyes were wide open and the vulture examined them for signs of life. For an instant, the alien eyes were interlocked. The vulture blinked and fluttered away to a stone promontory above the silent one's head. The bird was puzzled. The thing was neither dead nor fully alive. The gray, feathered neck pumped like a small bellows in its agitation. It was clumsy in many ways, but it was a delicate master in matters of death. It hopped gingerly to the side, repeating its ancient servile dance of expectation as it waited. It would be sure there was nothing to fear before making a move. By small gradations it would insinuate itself nearer the carcass. Once certain of its demise, the bird would pick out the eyes first, before returning to the pack to report his find.

The old Chevy was taking its brutal punishment with incredible fortitude. David could see the padre smiling behind his Kleenex. The old man had every reason to be proud of his possession. Another triumph of yesterday's crafts over modern expediency. Their routine was paying off. Cleaning the windshield every five miles or so made it easier for David to judge himself tactically. He hadn't driven a car since last summer, when he and Denise had rented one for a weekend in the Adirondacks. Laurel lay stretched out across the backseat, letting her body absorb the motion of the car as it pitched forward. She, too, was lost in memory. Chris would be thirteen in December.

Please, God.

The Kunma spotted the skeleton of the dead horse at about the time the Chevy entered the canyon where the battered Seville stood deserted. His eyes had pierced the terrain for a radius of five miles—closing in in ever-tightening circles. No immediate sign of his quarry, but an accelerating excitement told him he was close. The boy would either go into shock at the sight or attempt to run away again. If shock, he might have to carry him on his back up the mesa.

The craven creatures smelled blood, and with one false move, they would tear the boy to pieces. It was chancy enough with Hunt's body hidden in the shelter while he searched for the boy. If any real danger were to threaten his ligature, he would know. As fast as thought, he'd be back to defend the vulnerable automaton. But time was wasting, and the shadows were lengthening on the land below. He drifted down next to the horse's skull, which palely reflected the burnt orange penumbra blanketing the region.

Stillness. Layers of it. Bright and numb at the center. Chris remained in his cross-legged adoration of it. He was here in this limestone womb of a cave and not here. Whatever happened, he would now accept it as part of the continuum. Fear had long since drained out of his body and he'd forgotten his thirst. He'd been partially aware of things crawling over him, then crawling off. He could be another stone for all the invertebrates knew. A dull sound drifted into the cave. The dying fall of some disturbance echoing in a numberless countdown.

The boy's bent head lifted slowly. His lidded eyes focused on the entrance to the cave, and the air suddenly seemed to tighten. He heard loose stones falling over themselves like a shaman's warning rattle. He saw the shadow filtering onto the entrance to the cave. It rose out of the low, horizontal one that traced the sun's daily legend. The outlines of a crouching figure stood frozen against the deep orange stone. The shadows doubled over for a moment before the substance entered the cave. It smiled. The boy recognized the smile and yet could not be sure he did. Whatever it was, it stood naked before him— human and inhuman at the same time. Chris looked at the taloned hands.

"Do not touch the Holy One," the boy said simply in a tongue familiar to both. The Kunma smiled obscenely. The boy could see there was no tongue in its mouth.

The light continued to fade and the landscape was splitting in half, one part a doelike beige, the other a maze of blue-black triangles. The shadows accentuated the embrace of the canyon on either side of the Chevy. David could still see the bright mountaintops, innocent of their inevitable eclipse. Exhausted, Padre Dominguez had been lulled into a fitful sleep. The ever-narrowing road had stopped spitting up at the intruders, and the steady purr of the engine suddenly seemed a comforting reminder of civilization in this lunar place. Laurel watched the mountainside sliding by her window with a hypnotic regularity. She shifted her gaze and saw the maroon Seville in the distance, roasting in a patch of sunlight.

David felt Laurel's hand on his shoulder.

"Look," she said, but he'd already caught sight of the car. He also saw that it was surrounded on the driver's side by the preying birds. Laurel's hand tightened. David drove on less than a hundred feet and came to a stop. As if disturbed by the lack of motion, the Padre awakened and looked about bewildered. He saw that David was standing in the burning road.

"Señor David," he called. Laurel was hunched forward over

the driver's seat, her eyes glued on David. Dominguez rubbed at his slightly rheumy eyes and saw the flash of silver in the sunlight. David, pistol in hand, was advancing on the beleaguered car. Padre removed his glasses from the pocket of his soutane (he was useless without them) and smelled his own sweat still clinging to him. He saw the baleful sight up ahead and crossed himself. David was halfway between the two cars when his gun went off, scaring the gibbous creatures into the sky.

Even with his eyes wide open, everything was a brilliant blur. It was unbelievable. Or was he hallucinating? He was in the clutches of a frightening creature, ostensibly a man, who had stumbled upon him in a cave.

Another door opened and he knew this episode was linked with others he'd experienced during the nighttime. Soon his mother would appear again and make everything right. Yet deep within him he could see the bed, feel the silken sheets glowing in the steady light from the butter lamps while his sleepy eyes tried to penetrate the cordon of light to where something rustled in the darkness beyond.

"Do not touch the Holy One," he had chided. The next word that came to mind was impossible and he rejected the nightmare thought.

"Mother! Mother! Come!"

He felt the heat now seizing him and realized he'd lost his hat somewhere. He looked around and found himself level with one of the vultures. Its eyes were fixed on him with the expressionless gaze of a dead fish. Automatically, Chris looked about for his gun. Instead he saw his captor moving among a flock of the carrion, pushing them away from a rock shelter at the base of the mountainside. The man seemed to be trying to shift their focus from something hidden in the covey. His bald skull rose over the other evil heads as a sustained hissing escaped their locked beaks. Making a noisy retreat, they were giving way before the naked biped. The smell of dry blood hung thickly in the air and Chris coughed. Fleetingly, he remembered swallowing a penny as a child. The smell turned to that copper taste in his mouth, only now doubled and quadrupled in potency. He coughed again and, disregarding the malevolent sentinel, ran toward the rock formation.

Hugh Hunt's body was as the Kunma had left it—sitting up like a drunk who'd fallen in his stupor. The eyes were still opened and their opacity reminded the boy of all the other alien eyes around him. It was his father, squatting there, looking helpless and smelling awful.

The boy forgot everything that had happened up to this point. Instinctively, he grabbed the gun strapped round his father's shoulder, pulled it over his head, and swung round to face the Kunma, whose back was to Chris as he continued to intimidate the birds. Chris cocked the gun. Any minute now the strange man would turn and see him. Chris felt his father's body slouching against the side of his left leg. He had toppled over during the removal of the gun.

The Kunma, satisfied that the birds were far enough away for him to reenter Hunt's body without risking an attack, started backing away from them. He had arrived in time to save the body from being hacked to pieces. More and more birds were being drawn to the spot, and the uneasy pack, in closed rank, were beginning to stomp and peck fiercely about, drawing blood from within the fold. His first impression when he turned was that Chris was standing guard over the defenseless body. He advanced slowly, his smile frozen, as Chris raised the gun. *What price bravery?* he thought.

"What did you do to my father?" Chris yelled defiantly, his body tense with purpose. "Who are you?" The Kunma kept advancing.

"You'd better answer me." Chris cocked the gun higher, recalling as he did the creature had no tongue.

The smile vanished from the Kunma's face and became a pitying smirk. This mere slip of a boy was Hunt's son and ostensibly was now his.

"Don't come any closer! I'm warning you."

At this precise moment, David's gun went off farther down the canyon pass. The birds rose in a whoosh, and Chris waited till its echo faded, then fired into the air in response. He prayed the shot he'd heard signaled a friend nearby. The gun's recoil had cobbled his unsteady knees and it knocked him to the ground. When he sat up, he saw the Kunma standing above him, holding the gun in his hands. Above his head, the angry and disconcerted birds formed an ever-shifting corona around the naked man's head. The connection between this man and his father hit him so forcefully that he began backing away from him on the ground. His face flushed in preparation of the unwanted tears of confusion and anger that stung his eyelids. In their first gush, he saw the naked man hover in the air above his father's body and lift himself down into him. He saw his father rise. In his hand was the gun. He approached Chris, smiled his fabulous smile, and spoke, "*Day Moo Rha Lita Rin-*

poche." His tongue emerged and hissed his mocking welcome. Chris thought of the word he'd been trying to forget. "Father," he said, and blacked out.

David watched the squalling beasts rising round him like an airborne carpet. Some of the creatures, were shedding as they took off.

"Night's swift dragons cut the clouds full fast"—a midsummer night's dream, indeed, David thought, mentally finishing Puck's speech.

"Damned spirits all, that in crossways and floods have burial, already to their wormy beds are gone." The Seville was empty. No bodies, whole or in segments, begrimed the shiny tan upholstery. He was actually grinning when the sound of Chris's shot scudded above his head. Did echoes boomerang endlessly in this godforsaken place? He had fired twice in succession. Moments later came a single reverberation that, from its density, indicated a heavier weapon. Unless he was mistaken, it had originated from behind the eastern ridge to his right. As he watched the vultures in their flight, he saw they were gyring round and heading in that same direction. He turned and waved frantically toward the Chevy. He kept on waving till the two figures emerged and started toward him. The gun was still hot against his palm. He checked his watch: 5:08.

Chris's father was kneeling beside him, stroking his hair. From where he lay on the ground, he could see his father's foul-smelling hunting jacket, bunched in a discarded heap. The pearl gray lining, with its designer label, was exposed. His second thought was that his father had done away with the naked creature, thereby rescuing both of them. But the other image slid into place, as scary to the boy as the sight of the actual sliding into place. The fingers caressing his hair might be those of whatever it was masquerading as his father. Chris cautioned himself to remain inert. He must not move—not until his heart stopped pounding and he could figure what to do. His slitted eyes focused on a large rock within arm's length. The man's fingers kept caressing and kneading the young neck. His father had never been this intimate with him before. Chris knew he could grab the rock and crack the man's skull in one move.

Hunt put his finger on the wormlike vein in Chris's neck. How alive and how delicate. In another time, another place, how different this might seem. But the wheel had spun on its ancient axis and this event was determined. No more anguish about lost times—the abandoned selves had merged and were formidable, despite vestiges of old memories. Like lovers, they adhered together and the inchoate pleasures of the beast were theirs. To be his. Love's debt would be repaid with a single stroke of the hunting knife—and a new era of terror would commence. As he envisaged the magnitude of the freedom before him, a note of dissatisfaction blunted it. Why not continue as he was? He had never felt such power. But then, not even the cunning annihilation of the world would be compensation enough. His thumb pressed the throbbing vein. Just like the boy's mother. She could be cold and impassive, but that thread of purple gave her away.

He turned to look behind him. A sea of vermilion wattles punctuated the shimmering heat waves. The birds had silently regrouped behind him. They had come to him. A golden dust haze hung around them, obscuring the dark, two-toned bodies.

He could see others in the sky, coming to join their brothers. Some were still so far off, they appeared headless, so small were their heads compared to their bodies. Three giant birds were descending together: Father, Son, and Holy Ghost, Hugh mocked. Their broad wings, all of six feet in extension, seemed to touch one another as they closed into the golden cloud. Hunt rose and his cold eyes looked over the flock, like a deacon surveying his congregation. His white shirt and tan breeches complemented his handsomeness while giving him an air of a missionary conquering some forbidden place. They had all gathered, the birds' fiendish eyes fixed on the human who was about to reward their ravenous hopes.

"Ai-yah! Ai-yah, O Monarch of the Unknown," the baritone voice extended its range upward. "Come! I command you. Come. Feast. Feast." The high snarling command ricocheted through the canyon pass. He raised his arms in an avid invitation, and the ritual of death could now begin. He would wait for the abbot no longer.

Behind his back, Chris moved his arm forward and touched the rock.

David reached the mesa and saw the shotgun sticking up out of the rocks at the base of the slope. He examined the chamber and saw that it had not been fired, and the telescopic sight was unscarred. He passed his revolver over to the padre, who refused it, and then on to Laurel. Without saying a word, he continued to follow the birds' flight past the eastern ridge.

The buzz of a chant reached Chris's ear like a tremor in the earth. The sound suggested someone about to regurgitate. Cautiously, Chris turned his head in its direction. Hunt was exhorting the creatures, jumping up and down before his vast audience, which now extended beyond the length of the valley onto the adjacent mountainsides. They were stacked in tiers. It was like being back on the mesa again. Suddenly, Hunt squatted on the ground and his head went down between his legs. *Move,* Chris said to himself, and grabbed the stone. What was he thinking of? That man doing all those strange things out there was still his dad.

David arrived at the eastern ridge seconds before Hunt's chant began. The whining melisma echoing hollowly through the pass riveted David to the spot. Laurel, supporting Padre Dominguez up the incline, was less than fifty feet behind where David stopped, shotgun in hand. She saw him dart forward and pull himself up the side of the small bluff separating them from the plateau below. David's perspective from that vantage point permitted him to see the whole panoply without hindrance. The monster rally of birds to his right, Hunt and Chris to his left.

As if in deep transport, Hunt raised himself from the ground and started toward the boy. The chant had become leaden and came in spasmodic gulps. Spittle whitened his lips and his eyes rolling back in his head appeared sightless. This final distortion of his father's features was more than the boy could handle. Frightened witless, all he could manage was to continue to slide away in crablike fashion. Hunt paused and, leaning over, picked something up off the ground. He brandished it over his head, waving it about as his whine reached fever pitch. A hunting knife glinted in the dying sun.

"No. Dad! Don't," Chris whispered. The hand holding the

knife paused in its descent. David had raised his shotgun in anticipation. He steadied his hand and waited till the hairline cross in the sight covered Hunt's hand. He thought of nothing before pulling the trigger.

A circle of blood whipped into the air, already polluted by the scavengers. Round and round over Hunt's head they squawked their bloodlust. David, his jaw gone rigid, did not move. Laurel, unmindful of her safety, dashed past him crying, "Chris! Chris!" The boy, dazed, lay hugging the ground. Hunt's arm was still thrust skyward, gushing blood.

"No, señora! Stop, please." Padre Dominguez hitched up his soutane and ran past David in pursuit of the foolhardy woman.

Crazed by the sight and smell of the pulsing blood, the carrion dipped down in renewed frenzy. David fired another shot into the air, keeping his eyes on Chris, as Laurel ran down into the valley. The carpet of creatures lifted higher despite the banquet that bubbled below them.

Chris turned and saw someone who looked like his mother rushing toward him. He saw her hat fall off and knew the sun would harm her. He tried to rise, but found he had no strength to do so. The padre was the first to witness the extraordinary phenomenon that followed. Hunt's blood was suddenly staunched in its flow, and out of the torn tissue and cartilage, a gray, taloned hand emerged, its nails clicking together furiously. Caught midway between the mother rushing toward her son and the awesome sight of this instant transplant, the padre reached protectively for a small crucifix he carried in his inside pocket.

David saw Laurel reach Chris and fall to the ground beside him. Hunt turned and watched David racing toward mother and son. The only thing between him and them was a ridiculous-looking fat man in dark clothes. He was holding something up in front of him as he advanced.

With his taloned hand, Hunt struck the padre straight in his face. The blow smashed the priest's nose and drove the metal icon into his forehead, where it lay embedded. Dominguez fell to his knees as blood oozed out of the wound and blinded him.

David, out of breath, but anchored between Laurel, Chris, and Hunt, stood as the fiend continued to press toward them.

"Don't look," David yelled, and gestured to the woman and child behind him on the ground. It was too late. All David could do was try to block their view. They saw nonetheless. The advancing specter was changing shapes as it plodded forward. Like an explosion of identities it became a Catherine wheel of personae: Palfrey. The Tolos demon. Laurel. A monk, a wild dog—each dissolving and evolving out of one another, and still it kept advancing. The vultures, aware of this supernatural transformation, halted in their flight. Their huge wings outspread as if paralyzed, they coasted between the shifting air currents while remaining rooted to the area. The carpet had become a rooftop that obliterated the sun and cast a premature darkness over the plateau.

David waited as the thing approached. Laurel started to scream and reached for the pistol David had entrusted to her.

"Put that away," David said. "Do what I tell you." Hysterically, she ran out into the open ground, toward where her hat had landed, with Chris following her. The psychedelic horror show was winding down like a film that's jumped its sprockets, and David stepped forward to intercept—the Kunma. Through all the transitions, Hunt's green eyes had remained his own, steely and bright. These David engaged with a determined effort of will. The Kunma's left arm moved, covered the taloned right arm, and he came to a halt. His roar forced the carpet above to break apart. The sound he made was a gibber in the old tongue from a tongueless mouth. But to David, the intent of the wounding sound was real. "You have betrayed me. You protect the 'Holy One.' You have betrayed me"—a scalding accusation, made more vivid by the clawed hand, clicking and slicing the air, as if to rend the elements. In one swift move the creature attacked David—his abbot. The two figures inter-twined and toppled to the ground. As their figures locked, a strength welled up in David that was both unexpected and in-toxicating. The claw was trying to wreak havoc, raking the air as it attempted to gouge David's flesh. They thrashed in the raw silt of the desert beneath. Hot crystals burned David's mouth and he rolled wildly to the side, to avoid the descending claw. As he rose, he saw the padre stumbling toward them, mumbling a prayer. Suddenly David felt pain shoot through his back and legs. Its intensity shriveled him to his knees, then onto his face in the shifting sand. The claw had done its mischief. Prone on his face, he awaited the final blow. The Kunma was standing above him, its spittle flowing from the sides of his mouth onto David's back, adding insult to the injury he had perpetrated.

The man on the ground turned slowly round and attempted to rise—the abbot glared at the Kunma in disbelief and con-tempt. There was a long silence as the abbot lifted himself from the ground, deliberately moved toward the Kunma, and struck him across the face with a backhanded gesture. The Kunma registered the impact of the blow and bellowed with an infinite sorrow, as if announcing the end of the world. He fell to his knees before the abbot, then shuddered as an ectoplasmic change spooled out of its substance and materialized into Yonger, a Mongol lad, barely eighteen as he had been when the abbot and he had last parted in the temple at Dorje. In self-abasement, the Mongol acolyte slithered in the sand in a reptilian frenzy as its tongueless mouth guttered, "Forgive, Gomchen, forgive!" Finally, he stopped his thrashing and crouched at the abbot's feet, panting, exhausted. His body, covered with sand, resembled some totemic figure trapped and deserted by nature itself. The abbot had remained motionless, measuring the pain that had seized his body while exerting the power of his will to subdue it. The creature at his feet had dared to attack his master—for that act alone there was nothing but the direst punishment. Whatever measure of control the abbot still had over him would be shattered and there would be no reasoning, no power to stem its fury. His own life, as well as the others', could be extinguished if he made the wrong decision. He turned his head away and saw the boy incarnation looking at them from a distance. His blond hair caught the last light of the fading sun. Even from this distance, the abbot could feel the boy's compassion reaching out toward him—the victim absolving his intended assassin. Chris's mother was attending to the guileless wounded priest. Her hat was askew over a face already marked by the sun's punishment of her skin. Stealthily above, the feathered canopy had lowered itself and was gyrating within twenty feet of the stricken padre's head.

"Fire the gun," the abbot called out to Laurel. "Fire. Quickly," he repeated his command. Laurel picked up the .38

revolver, raised it, and pulled the trigger. Yongen's body twitched in response. The carpet zoomed skyward again. The padre's outstretched fingers found Laurel's hands as she dropped the revolver. The priest's nose had swollen to a blue-purple discoloration; still blotting his forehead with the last of her Kleenex, she saw the crucifix buried in his forehead. The padre raised his fingers to the wound. Blood oozed as he touched the crucified form. His lacerated mouth formed an idiotic smile. "Have we stopped the devil? Yes? *In nomine Patris et Filii et Spiritus Sancti.* Amen," he sighed with relief. The abbot watched the boy approaching him, unseen by his mother.

"*Gyalwa Rinpoche,*" the abbot said. The boy's eyes blinked rapidly while searching out the abbot's intentions for the now silent beast.

"Go—do what you can for your mother and the old man," the abbot said with a trace of reverence.

The boy remained rooted.

"Leave the Kunma to me." The abbot, forced to action, picked the rifle off the ground, gave it to Chris, grabbed the boy under his arm, and hustled him toward his mother. Simultaneously, he realized the pain had slowly subsided in his back. He watched as Chris removed his jacket slowly and tore off one of its torn sleeves to create a temporary styptic round the prelate's head. The abbot moved slowly toward them. He was determined to keep his back away from them to prevent their seeing the slit with its bloodstained fringes.

"You've got to get him to a hospital. Is there one in Toledos?"

Laurel nodded. Above them, the birds had begun a croaking chant. They had been denied their pound of flesh too long.

"There's one shot left in the pistol—and two in the shotgun. I'll take the pistol. Use the shotgun if they get too close and keep the padre in the backseat."

"What about you? We can't just leave you like this," Laurel pleaded.

"Like hell you can't. Besides I'll take the Seville. I think there's some life in her yet. We'll meet in Toledos." He touched Laurel's shoulder. "You'd better have them look at you, too. You're burned. You're beautiful, but you're burned." They embraced tenderly, her arms round his neck. Over her shoulder, she saw Chris standing by the creature. The boy was looking at his father. In this brief span of time, Hunt had been reclaimed by the Kunma. Hunt's face turned toward Laurel, who stepped back in astonishment. "Oh my God," she uttered with revulsion. She watched as her husband smiled at her, then slowly turned his face away. He seemed unaware of his son standing by his side—at eye level to one another. Laurel cried out to Chris, but the abbot prevented her going to the boy.

"Let him," he said gently but firmly.

Chris put his hand out to touch his father's shoulder—the one without the claw. He would not cry for him as he knew his father would disapprove. He could feel the heat of his father's body under his fingers. Hunt looked at the boy, then turned away. Chris understood. There was no helping matters—what was their former life had spiraled out of hand. Chris stayed by his father's side nonetheless, then turned and ran quickly back to his mother, taking her hand in his own.

"And don't look back," David continued. "Remember what happened to Lot's wife." Chris looked up at the abbot with a curious smile, then said, "Come, Mother." Then taking the padre's hand, he led them out of the valley. The padre hesitated and called out, "Señor, take this, please. It will help." Padre Dominguez pressed a small, black prayer book into his hand. The abbot looked at the slightly soiled icon and nodded. "Thank you, Padre."

"Go with God's blessing," Dominguez said, and made a limp sign of the cross in the air. The abbot led him back to Chris and Laurel, who silently continued their journey back to the mesa. David watched as they disappeared in the distance. At one point Laurel turned and, with an odd gesture of coquetry, waved back to him. As he suspected, the darkened heavens swooped silkily above the departing trio, the sound of their hunger flaming the heavens. *Where there's blood, there's hope*, the abbot joked feebly. He heard the first shotgun blast from beyond the ridge. Only then did he turn and advance thoughtfully toward the kneeling figure. If it were not for the claw on his mismatched right hand, one would not suspect a demon's presence inside this now disheveled, but still comely, man of the world. A sudden breeze played with his fair hair and a cowlick arched and fell.

"Do now what must be done," Hunt spoke, his baritone rich with its original luster.

The abbot froze in his tracks. What must be done? You cannot kill the Kunma itself, he knew that. It could abandon Hunt, go out into the world to the world's destruction. He knew too well by now the laws of the bardo governing those who emerge from it seeking revenge on mankind. It could find another chrysalis, another spokesman. And what would that spokesman seek? There was only one way left and he would have to take it. He spoke in the old tongue.

"*Om—Argham Tsargham Bimanese—Utsuma maha, Korodh Humphat.*"

"I will do what you ask. Gomchen—love for love—there's no other way." It was said with such love that the abbot's knees almost went out from under him.

Even before they left the valley, the abbot's wound had ceased to throb and ache. The blood had staunched its flow, and his sense of invigoration, first felt during the Kunma's attack on him, had returned while accepting that he was walking within two time zones. His recognition of this willingness to live within those parameters was the balance his soul had desired and demanded. The therapist self could characterize this as a form of enlightened schizophrenia. Peter Mendoza experienced it. Now he—the abbot, David Sussman, and many unknown others—considered the experience as fully living within dharma—the blessings of many lifetimes. It was as good a way of putting it as any.

The two travelers in time left the valley and prepared to meet the next turn of the wheel.

The abbot, determined to his task, drove with a steady concentration down the canyon pass. Hunt sat next to him, his eyes closed against what lay in store. The Seville, damaged on the right side, was otherwise none the worse for wear. Chris's hunting pack lay neatly bound together on the backseat. It contained, among other things, a large army canteen, a thermos, and a small fold-up pup tent with anchoring spikes. It would do, the abbot speculated—crude, but providential. When had the supreme being ever provided in kind?

They spoke only once, at the start of the journey down. The

abbot removed one of his last cigarettes from his carefully hus-banded pack and started to light it. At the sound of the striking match, Hunt opened his eyes and looked at the tiny flame. The abbot passed the packet over and Hunt removed a cigarette with his left hand, waiting for the Abbot to oblige him with a light. The action was over so quickly that the single match did double duty. It reminded the abbot of their first meeting at Immaculate Hospital—eons ago it seemed.

The abbot exhaled. "Where did you go after you escaped from the monastery?"

"My first thought was to find my mother. She and my father had vanished over the Butasi Pass, after leaving me at the gompa those many years before. It was a foolish thought, but I was delirious. Your death agonized me beyond description. I kept calling out to you, but only the wind answered. So I thought of her, my mother. I wanted her to know I was worth something after all. I staggered about in my unhappiness. I passed chorten after chorten, desecrating them with my piss in your name. How the holy relics inside them must have screamed." And his jaw slackened in pain.

"What then?"

"I lost my way. Somewhere in the high pass, I saw a dim light moving against the snow. It was a nun heading back to her convent. She'd been out to fetch herbs for one of her ailing sisters, and I'd come upon her accidentally. She took me back with her and there were six others. In my excitement, the ab-bess appeared to me like Dorje Pag-Mo herself, but in reality, she was fat and smelled excessively."

Hunt paused and drew on his cigarette. Catching whiff of the carnivore's dung off Hunt's boots, the abbot turned up the air-conditioning—for once blessing what man hath wrought.

"That night I did not sleep. The sisters were generous sharing their food with me. I could not explain my plight. I had no tongue with which to speak. Without a tongue, I would spoil part of their pleasure. Not even my torn clothes could convince them otherwise. They disrobed me and each took from me what she needed. As I was unable to satisfy them all, they turned against me and tossed me out into the night with my robe the only defense against the gathering snow. I kept moving as fast as I could. Overcome with fatigue, I sank to the ground and slept. After that I can remember nothing."

They drove on in a heavy silence in the slow-gathering dusk. From the periphery of his vision, the abbot saw the ashes drop from Hunt's cigarette. When he looked sideways, Hunt's eyes were closed again. The abbot reached over and removed the stub from Hunt's lips. It had burned down to its filter tip and hung like a yellow fang. What welled up in the abbot next was indescribable. The man—this thing sitting next to him—was alive. Whatever it was, it was alive. Living, like himself, in a fantastic interplay in time and space. It was a dreamworld made reality. Yet within—what?—an hour or so, this entity was willing to give it all up. To die—and be reborn—that was the essence of what had to be done. A return to the eternal cradle of life, swaddling hope to all who entered there.

Salvation. That word again. Another illusory state? Or an adventure beyond, into a dimension as yet unknown and unpenetrated?

Hunt had read his thoughts, and the abbot heard him mumble, "Gomchen," in the most reassuring way. Pity and a strange admiration rose in the abbot. *The devil always yearns for heaven,* he echoed Mendoza. To extrapolate divinity from the devil's beastliness was to make him the most modern of heroes, he concluded himself.

The expanse of grassland appeared through his windshield like a trick of the waning light. Except for an occasional giant cactus, there had been no vegetation, coming or going in the region.

The abbot stopped the car at the edge of a field and looked around. He wanted to be sure it would not suddenly vanish. The grass was more than knee-high and now—close up—was yellow and dried out by the sun. An overgrown path to his right led to the mountains. The grass rustled and cracked underfoot: it would go up like a matchstick. When he turned back to the car, he saw that they'd been riding alongside a precipice all the while. Five feet from Hunt's side was a sheer drop. The mountainside was now a filmy blue shadow, as was most of this grassy slope. In the reaches beyond, a Morse code of lights twinkled hesitantly. A small cluster of houses? A filling station? The sky was clear of foul pursuers. Somewhere on the descent, the pack following them had gradually given up and returned to their rookery.

When he touched Hunt's shoulder, the claw reared protectively and the abbot jumped back. He was about to light another cigarette when he realized he had only two matches left. He heard Hunt sliding across the seat toward the only operative door.

When Hunt emerged, he seemed tranquil and even stretched luxuriously. The nails clicked softly against the twilight sky, as if to extol its beauty. His eyes took in the scene and brightened for the first time since leaving the mesa. David reached into the backseat and removed Chris's camping equipment. He flung it over his shoulder and, without a word, started moving through the grass. Behind, he could hear Hunt following in his footsteps. He must remember the words exactly or the transition would not be effected. It had been so long since the abbot had helped the dying cross over. Then he'd been a novice, and he believed in the promise of nirvana at the heart of the bardo. But he had renounced it for the puling thing it was—a dying man's grasp for consolation, a last play for power really, with no power left to recognize the Buddhists' sugar teat for the extortionist's trick it was. He had turned Bon Po to fight such weakness and excess. Or had he, then, regressed in favor of another panacea? The shamanists' illusion of power and invincibility. Living in the moment—alienated—with no thought of redemption. In that lexicon the Supreme Powers were all demon gods—equally bloodthirsty and demanding as their earthly progeny. Buddha was the invention of cowards to gain power through passive enslavement—and what greater shackle than this hope of heaven through good works. He had not flinched or called for mercy or forgiveness, even as his screams mingled with the bursting of his flesh among the flames. No, he had reveled in his mastery in extremis. Yet, this thing he had saved from obscurity and lifted up in the light of his own brightness—this "Kunma" demanded the promise of the enemy's heaven.

How could he explain what was about to take place? On one level, the act was a form of metaphysical justice. On another, it was murder. He would have to live with it. And what of all this and its repercussions on the lives of Laurel and Chris? This man was her husband, the boy's father, but that was on a plane of life fast receding for him.

The abbot turned to find Hunt's eyes on him. The abbot sank to his knees and Hunt followed. The grass now stood over their heads.

"Love for love," he had said. For the first time since the abbot had looked for Yongen in the courtyard full of his enemies, he felt helpless and simultaneously in deepest sympathy with Hunt/Kunma. The force flooded him. It was above and beyond any and all factions—religious, political, or otherwise. The words of all philosophers were irrelevant before it—they meshed here—and for the creature, the flames were to restore him to the deepest sense of order he craved. There was an immense simplicity in its savage cry for wholeness and acceptance. Did God reside in this crucible—this imponderable seesawing between darkness and light?

"Tell me," the abbot spoke in some last desperate call to his own humanity. "Even if I had not arrived, would you have killed your son?"

"But you did arrive."

The abbot carefully scrutinized Hunt's face.

"My turn will come," Hunt said, and looked at the abbot, the Mona Lisa smile on his lips.

"Remember him—remember my son. Protect him. And her." Hunt's final words bound them together for all time. The two travelers through time slowly embraced. When they rose, Hunt disengaged himself first and disrobed until he was totally naked. He knelt on the ground again. David then circled behind his creature and placed his hands on the man's shoulders. The muscles tightened under his fingers as Hunt slowly assumed the lotus position.

The abbot intoned quietly, "Give in. You are about to be released. Hear my words and follow." He moved in front of the naked being. Kneeling, he placed his palms on the other's thighs.

"Give up the consciousness of life in this flesh." He felt the legs trembling under his palms.

"The first day is for Varrocana, who has no back or front and whose four faces shine with the white light of consciousness. Open. Open. To him offer your limbs. Upwards and dissolve."

The abbot massaged the flesh gently as he chanted. The claw clicked feebly. The shaking diminished as the energy moved up into the arms and torso. The abbot felt the thighs sink downward until they rested against the ground.

He moved his hands up to the lower abdomen. He could feel the heat trapped inside like electric charges sparking one another. Again he massaged slowly.

"Give up the consciousness of life in this flesh. Upwards and dissolve." Again the inner agitation and the energy gathered against the pressing palms.

"The second day is for Vajrasattva, who sits on his elephant throne. His eye will open and awaken you to the new consciousness. The gray light around him is hell. He will guide you through." He moved his palm up and down the torso and out along the arms. The whipcord energy followed like a current.

"Upwards. Upwards. To him offer your torso. Your arms. Upwards and dissolve."

The haunted heart hammered under the instruction and the

lungs pumped laboriously. The palm rested over the heart a long time until it quieted down and adjusted itself to cessation.

"Upwards and dissolve."

With a high, plaintive singing sound, the energy moved into the cranium.

"Give up the consciousness of life in this flesh." The abbot's fingers pressed the two sides of the nose.

"Upwards and dissolve. The third day is for Rat Nasambhava, who sits in yellow light, ready with his bodhisattva ksitigarbha to establish your space in the next order of things—upwards and dissolve."

Hunt inhaled deeply through his nostrils and exhaled explosively. Under the abbot's touch, the bridge of the nose collapsed and the nostrils felt pinched. The abbot's two middle fingers pressed through Hunt's lips. Hunt's mouth closed and gripped the two fingers tightly. The saliva was warm with the energies of the abandoned parts.

"Give up the consciousness of life in this flesh. Upwards and dissolve. The fourth day is for the purification by the divine fire. Amitabha awaits you in all his compassion. He holds a lotus in his hand and will guide you through the demands of the other bodhisattvas in his rank. You will struggle most here. As you left this life, so you must find your life. Upwards and dissolve."

The tongue pressed madly round his fingers, as if to expel them. The heat gathered in the cavity and the fluid thickened as in epilepsy or rabies. The abbot could feel the bone structure of his index fingers and he ceased his massage and clamped the tongue downward. The churning meat wrapped round the fingers as if to absorb them whole. The abbot waited till the throbbing flesh had quelled itself and slowly loosened its grip.

"Upwards and dissolve."

Hunt's mouth opened and the abbot removed his fingers. A cascade of fluid dribbled down to the ground. A breeze rippled through the high grass. The stalks waved and shared their secret with the two interlopers. The abbot's fingers now covered the eyelids.

"Give up the consciousness of this flesh. On the fifth day of air and wind, Amog Hasiddhi will appear in a green light—from the realm of the accumulated actions. He is holding a crossed vajra in his hand, and, raising the thunder rod, will strike it, announcing his presence. He and his consort, Samaya-Tara, will instruct you toward fulfillment. But the jealous gods who inhabit this region will instruct otherwise. You will see. You will suffer. Upwards and dissolve."

The eyelids fluttered once and the fluid left in the sockets fell in two gushing lines on either side of the face. An emptying out that looked like tears of sorrow. The ears were last.

"Give up the consciousness of this flesh. On the sixth day, you will be lost in the rush of all the peaceful divinities, which number forty-two. And from the four directions you will be forced to face the six realms of the world. The Buddha of all the gods—of the jealous ones—of the human beings—of the animals—of the hungry ghosts—and of the realm of hellfire. The seventh day will be the longest and complete what is left to do. Upwards and dissolve."

The abbot rose and looked down over the body and prayed.

"O Buddhas and bodhisattvas. You in the ten directions. Have compassion on the person known as Yongen. He is leaving this body for the other place. He is dying out of choice.

But he remains alone, suffering without refuge. He is about to return into the bardo—the mighty gap between existences. He yearns for your protection, your understanding, your mercy. He is terrified and abject because he fears his dharma deserves nothing but the condemnation to a nethermost place in hell. Yet his yearning goes upward. As a Kunma he has lived like a herald of death—mourning even as he dispensed death. Now in death, he exchanges love for love"—the abbot's voice broke as he spoke this—"and offers that exchange in remission of his sins. O compassionate ones! Seize him. Be his refuge. Do not let him fall again."

A popping was heard in either ear and they were closed against sound forever.

Finally the abbot placed his hands around the head. "Upward and dissolve." The energies of the spirit had ascended to the top of his skull where they bristled—poised for exit. The abbot lay his own head against the other's. From the depth of his being, he shouted the word "Hik," immediately followed by the sound "Phat!" He released his hold and stepped back.

Through the crown of the cap a thin, grayish smoke escaped—a thread that gathered round itself till it resembled in miniature the person it was about to leave behind. It rose swiftly into the air—until it stretched like a long silver cord, umbilically attached. It detached suddenly and disappeared.

The wind soughed roughly through the grass and the tops of the stalks banded together in groups and beat against their neighbors in an internecine struggle.

David felt a massive chill and found himself facing a corpse sitting upright. He had accomplished it—even in his unbelief, the abbot had carried the seed of belief. David saw Chris's pack resting in the grass. Deep twilight was closing in as he finally loosened the straps. He'd have to get out of here before he was incapable of finding his way down. A flashlight was in the glove compartment of the Seville. It would help. He removed the canteen from its slot and shook it. He emptied the warm water and then took out the thermos. Holding the receptacles in either hand, he headed toward the car. He was halfway when he realized he'd forgotten the tent spikes. Without them, the operation would become futile.

He tore off the paper they were wrapped in and removed two nails. He ran back to the car. Over the edge of the precipice, the distant ring of lights shone more assuredly. He'd use them as a guide. He set down the canteen and the thermos, then picked up a rock that filled his palm completely. He slipped under the chassis and reached across for the canteen. He set it beside him and placed a spike against where the gas tank lay. He drove the rock against the spike in five solid strokes until it punctured the tank and the contents began to spill on the ground. He placed the canteen under the leak and listened as the fuel dribbled into the gray-green container. Three minutes later, it gushed over the top and David reached for the thermos.

"Shit," he cursed. He'd forgotten to unscrew the top of the thermos. He was losing precious gasoline, but what could he—stupid he—do? Finally he was forced to hold the thermos at an angle to catch what fluid there was left. When that container was half-filled, he started to back out from under the vehicle and inadvertently hit the canteen. He scrambled to arrest the spillage and scraped his back against some stones. He felt the pain again as he rose. He picked up the two vessels and ran to where the body awaited the final rite. The shadows were rushing to thicken, and David could see the red aura glowing round Hunt, even as he watched, diminishing in brightness. The thing was still alive. Oh, God! The pain, push it back. He knew that an aura lingers on after death. Without ceremony, he emptied the canteen over the body, then the thermos, until the body was soaked from head to foot. The aura faded to a pale pink, sputtered, and quickly vanished. He reached in his pocket for the matches and realized his hands were soaked. He wiped them on the grass till they were dry, then struggled to light the first match. His fingers were shaking and the rising wind did not make it any easier. He knelt behind the body, using it as a shield and tried again, succeeding on the third strike. No sooner did the flame spark into life than the wind whisked it away. Panic seized him. One more match.

His eyelids closed in revulsion as he dropped the lighted match. He felt himself the vessel of chaos incarnate—the expanse around him a silent mockery of his pretensions. Behind his closed eyelids, he felt a vibration. A bright glare forced his lids apart. The edge of the field had burst into yellow flames. Guided by the rising wind, they licked rapidly forward. Fixed in his gesture of repudiation, the abbot watched dazedly as they rushed like lemurs toward destruction. The burning path rushed directly to Hunt's recumbent figure and the animal flames leaped over his back, turning him into an instant torch. They shot beyond him and spread across the open field.

The abbot ran to the car and found the flashlight in the glove compartment. From where he stood, Hunt's hair was a medusa of red-orange snakes—a writhing whip that fissured downward demanding vitals to feed on. Hunt's shirt, lying by his side, fanned like a burning kite into the air and shredded. It patched off tiny incendiaries that started combustions in all areas of the field. Hunt's head snapped backward as his body became a blackening outline against the mounting conflagration. The abbot saw the eyelids picked clean and the eyeballs exposed. Two glass marbles, fixed upward. As the retinas sizzled, one eyeball loosened in its socket till the eye swiveled round and appeared to be looking directly at the abbot. The thief of souls was rushing to find his own again. The orbs popped, lavishing their juices on the pyre.

The abbot was hardly fifty yards down the road when the car exploded and he fell to the ground. The glow filled the night sky and then quickly doused down. He rose and ran farther from the scene of immolation. He ran and ran till he was forced to stop—panting wildly.

The flashlight maintained its intensity until he made it to the bottom of the pass. Somewhere below was the road leading onto the highway. He had to keep his eyes on the small group of lights out there. From them, he could gauge how far he'd come down the mountains. Suppose he ran into a mountain lion, or whatever predators inhabited these parts? What then?

Was he not the abbot, after all? Besides, he still had his .38 revolver with one good shot left. It would be like being back in Pune once more.

He felt something like grains of sand striking his shoulders and matting his hair. The wind was picking up velocity as he descended. If it kept up, there would be no ashes for stray birds to pick amongst. The roar behind him could now be the muffled sound of distant thunder. He was finally alone with the night and the ever-beckoning lights.

PART EIGHT

November 1982

The wind hurdled across the river and shook the window-panes. Winter would come early again this year, but its shock troops were already outside. The impact resounded on all three sides of the Eagle's Nest and David was startled out of his deep reverie. The bedroom suddenly became chilled as the hidden crevices filtered the blast. Once more David wondered if he should sign the lease ensuring him ownership of this white elephant with its majestic view. He felt something rubbing up against his ankle and looked down. He saw Sam mewing for attention. He lifted the cat and cradled him.

> *Blow. Blow thou winter wind—Blow*
> *Ye hurricanes that do buffet*
> *the world about—Nuncle Lear.*

He looked fixedly at the window by his bed as his inner eye clouded and he saw the Kunma suspended outside. An aureole fire framed him, as his talons clicked in anticipation of David's flesh. The eye slipped and fixed him again. Ever since his return, David had lived in fear that somehow he'd bungled the ceremony and that the Kunma would seek revenge. He turned his head away and the day vision was gone. Using a cane, he moved into his bedroom and started to dress. The back pain he felt from his encounter in the valley still inhibited his movements.

David lowered the kitten to the floor and removed his terrycloth robe. After leaving the mountains, it had taken him almost three hours to reach the flatlands. By then he was chilled to the marrow. The batteries in the flashlight had held all the way, and he'd sworn never to mock the Duracell commercial on television. The plastic wonder was lying on a shelf in his clothes closet, nestled among the woolen scarves and gloves. A memento mori. His luck had held out, for he'd been picked up on the highway by a truck hauling citrus fruits from California—"Thanks, mister, my car broke down"—and deposited on the outskirts of Taos. The driver, a garrulous Irishman in his late thirties, discoursed on the perils of picking up hitchhikers.

"I could tell you was okay when I saw you."

"How could you tell?"

"Your clothes. You look a wreck, but I saw the alligator decal on your shirt. I knew you'd been in some kind of upper-class trouble."

David had reached Taos by 10 P.M. An hour later, he was at the Buena Vista Hospital in Toledos. There, he felt the startling impact of his back pain in full force. A nurse found him lying flat, with his face against the linoleum floor. The abbot had conceded to David. His sciatic nerve had been severely damaged in his encounter with the Kunma. He had remained hospitalized for over a month while he recovered.

Except to attend Papa Champ's funeral, Laurel and Chris had remained in Toledos till David was mobile enough to travel. The mountains had swallowed up the secret of Hunt's death and it awaited discovery by some intrepid mountain climber if there was anything left to discover—only McGraw's death received homage in the national press.

During all this, Chris remained by David's side, wrapped up in a deep silence and speaking little. His eyes, at least, told David he understood. What he actually thought and felt about the extraordinary experience was yet to be revealed. For a boy nearing his thirteenth birthday, he showed unusual stoicism and fortitude. When the time came for the boy to verbalize his grief, David would be there to guide him through it.

David returned to New York, to a dirty, stuffy apartment and two months of accumulated mail. He called Anita first thing on arrival. She said hardly a word while David described the intricate skeins of karma leading to the eerie ritual in the Sierras. David reclaimed Sam from his neighbor and set about reconstructing his life. That was on September 18. Today was November 16. In nine days, he was due to be in Baltimore for Thanksgiving on Crelow Street. He would take Laurel and Chris to meet them—Laurel would be scrutinized and questioned. Mama might be getting her bride after all. A shiksa. But what a shiksa.

He had decided that his visit to Mendoza would take place without the use of his cane. He'd tried several times to venture out without it, with varying success. On those occasions, his pockets always contained his Nuprin tablets. He planned to meet Laurel and Chris for dinner at the Café des Artistes. There they would decide on the concluding element hanging there like a dangling participle in their mountain adventure. According to the Buddhist calendar, the time had arrived for disclosure of the Kunma's progress within the bardo. A brief twinge in his left leg registered his anxiety.

Peter Mendoza had reveled in his visit with his daughter, Amy, in Michigan that summer. The prodigal had not returned, but he had gone to her. He'd rented a small cottage by Lake Erie where he relished playing grandpa to one-year-old Rachel. God had been merciful in his usually inscrutable way: Amy's husband had abandoned her and the child, and Peter's reunion was a triumph of fatherly love over the vagaries of wayward youth. He had promised to see them again during Rosh Hashanah when they would celebrate and make future plans for her restoration to the family seat in New York.

Peter opened the door in a festive mood to admit David. "How do you like my shirt?" was the first thing Peter said, and he spread his tapered fingers over an orange Hawaiian shirt, decorated by a parody of Gauguin's jungle lilies. It hung loosely over a new pair of chino trousers. He was barefoot.

David's dark shantung silk shirt and tan trousers were in shocking contrast with his friend's attire and gave his good looks a weathered cast. Peter discerned a slight limp as they retreated into his apartment.

Two pots of tea later, Peter tossed the aromatic leaves into the garbage can, and asking to be excused, he headed back to his bookstore. "Should I come with you?" David started to rise from his chair.

"Stay put. I won't be a minute." Peter carefully slid into a pair of weathered slippers. Before he returned, David was forced to take another Nuprin.

Peter reentered carrying a large tome and placed it on the Dutch table in front of David. Peter opened the book with a kind of reverential flourish. The book was an old, much worn, leather-bound antique—written in Hebrew. Peter turned to a lithographic print dominating one page. Peter placed a finger on the caption beneath it and silently traced the words.

"Peter," David said with a perplexed smile, "you don't expect me to read this—do you?"

"Davie, someday you will. In fact, I'm sure of it."

"Please, Mr. Chang, when will the porters arrive?" David pleaded. "They must arrive this time." Peter chuckled, recalling the moment in the Capra film. "Who is this and what's going on here?" David asked, peering closer at the print.

"Whom do you see?" Mr. Chang continued benignly.

"Here we go again. An old bearded prophet raising his arms to heaven, and a dark, rather sinister figure retreating into . . ." David sat back, knowing without being sure.

"The old prophet is Abraham," Peter spoke in a quiet drone.

"Then this is a copy of the Bible." David nodded. "I thought so."

"Only the Old Testament," Peter droned on in wonderment. "It's a very rare edition, 1784 to be precise, printed in Cádiz. It's one of my treasures—and not for sale."

"Abraham." David savored the name.

"Yes, fighting the Angel of Death—the figure here. The workmanship is not exactly Goya, but it will do."

David's fingers strayed and cupped his chin. "How long do you think it took Abraham to grow that beard?" he asked with a merry effort to dim his own prescience.

"Mythological figures like Abraham come into the world with beards already, if you catch my meaning, but not all who do share his anguish." David vaguely recalled his father telling him this story back in Baltimore—eons ago, it seemed.

"The Angel of Death appeared to Abraham to prevent him from sacrificing his son Isaac to God. The angel retreated, but not before inflicting a great wound."

"How?" David stared hard at the reproduction.

"The angel lacerated Abraham's sciatic nerve and severed it." Peter's voice had dropped.

David stood up, the quickest move he'd made in months. "Where's Isaac in this picture?" he demanded. His heart was racing.

"He's gone. Run away. Glad not to be sacrificed," Peter said evenly, stroking his chin. For a moment Peter's eyes reflected the inner judge who carefully weighed his evidence. "You know, or maybe you don't know, that's why kosher dietary laws stipulate that one cannot eat the hind leg of a slaughtered animal."

"Because the Angel of Death resides there." David could hear his father's voice again, telling the tale at some long-forgotten seder.

"You're perhaps thinking Bubbamansa—big fairy tale," Mendoza posited grandly. David chuckled for a moment before breaking into tears. He just sat there and let them flow. "Not on the book, please," Peter admonished gently, and moved it to the center of the table.

"I've been like this ever since—it happened." David's shoulders went slack.

"Do you wonder"—Peter put his hand on his shoulder—"what we need now is a drink—and I don't mean more tea." As Peter brought down the old brandy bottle and glasses, he chattered on, "There's a young rabbi friend that you might like to meet. He's at the head of a new synagogue, about to grace this graceless neighborhood. You might, as they say, hit it off. His name is David, too. Coincidence? No? David Newman. I don't think he's ever met a Buddhist Jew before." Filling the glasses, he perked up. "Now it's my turn to tell you about my summer."

David, Laurel, and Chris sat in a circle in the living room. The East Side apartment was cheery and cozy—an incongruous meeting ground for the day's ritual, which would terminate in Central Park. Laurel's face had responded well to treatment in Toledos, but it was apparent she would bear signs of her ordeal in the valley for some time to come. She had decided to close the house in West Haven and live in the city. Her main concern was for Chris, who would have to start a new life in New York and lose contact with his old friend Tripp at school. That couldn't be helped, like so many other things. She sat now, a radiant, anxious smile on her lips, dressed in blue slacks and a matching turtleneck sweater, watching David, seated by her side. He was staring down at the outlines of a mask—a simple if crude representation of Hunt's face drawn by him on a large sheet of white paper, placed on a porcelain platter. Under the outlines of Hunt's features was the one of the adamantine

Kunma. The time allotted for the passage of the Kunma through the bardo had just come to an end.

According to legendary practice, one could determine from the way the paper burned where the wandering soul of the dead man would alight in his next incarnation.

If the flames were white and shone, then he would be reborn in the highest regions of the perfect one.

If they were white and burned quickly with rounded tops, then he would be reborn in a happy incarnation.

If they formed a lotus, he would be reborn in a religious service.

If yellow, he would become a figure of importance in religion.

If they were yellow and burned quickly with much smoke, he would be reborn as one of the lower animals.

Red would see him reborn humbly.

If it burned in a shifting combination of the above, the incarnation was as yet undetermined, but offered hope within the aforementioned categories.

If the paper would not burn, but crumpled to blackness, it would signify he had been eternally damned and all hope for incarnation blighted.

"Are we ready?" David asked. Laurel and Chris nodded.

"Repeat after me, three times." He intoned the sound "Om," which they imitated with their palms locked together. David nodded, handed Laurel a box of matches, and striking one, she applied it to the paper. The edge crumbled under and a black spot began to spread across the top. Laurel gasped and grabbed David's hand. The blackness spread but suddenly broke into flames that raced across the drawn faces—its color vacillating continuously—white, yellow, red, to a faint blue before the paper steeled into a large bubble of ash. They sat and watched till it flattened out.

"David, what does it mean? It went blue even."

David spoke quietly, "Give me your hands. We'll pray for him." And they all bowed their heads in silence. Chris was the first to break the chain and left to go to his room. The two adults looked at one another. Almost instantly, he returned with a large orange kite. He put it at David's feet. "I made it. It's for you, Gomchen." David's and Laurel's hands separated and they stared at Chris. The boy was now sitting in a lotus position— smiling.

Ralph had returned to Ranch House immediately following the burial and resumed his duties. He had instructed all in McGraw's employ who had been privy to the truth to keep their mouths shut or else. He listened, paid mouth honor to the press, read the newspapers, and bided his time. He ordered Tomito to clear up the junk in the attic, which he accomplished in three hours with his ten-year-old daughter, Manuela, in tow. She saw the tarnished gold trinket as she was playing in the old child's rocking chair she'd discovered in one of the attic's corners. The ring lay there by itself, a wedding band at her feet, as if it had rolled away on its own from the rest of the debris. The inscribed name "Marianne" was still legible. She put it on her thumb and continued to rock—singing to herself. Three weeks later, after the reading of Papa Champ's will, Laurel designated Ralph as master of Ranch House.

———————

The orange kite with its long green tail had caught the stiff breeze and quickly ascended beyond the trees' grasp.

"Bare, ruined choirs," David thought, *"where late the sweet birds sang."* He and Laurel, seated on a boulder, watched as Chris carefully maneuvered the kite over the empty Wollman Rink. The kite, flapping strongly in the wind, would help guide the spirit to its deserved place. The Kunma was lucky. At least he'd have a chance to start all over again. David had calculated Yongen's and the Abbot's deaths to have originally taken place during the year of the Iron Ape—according to the Tibetan calendar. Peter had calculated the dates correctly—that would make it midway in the fourteenth century. He had traced the lineage of the various Dalai Lamas and corroborated the time period. Hunt's destiny was inevitably intertwined with Yongen's—one's fate would disclose the other's.

As David buttoned the top of his raincoat, he saw the kite bob and dip. "Chris," David called out, and pointed skyward.

Laurel stood up. "David, he's crying."

"Don't go to him. Let him mourn by himself." She sat back on the stone and moved closer to David.

"Gomchen," Chris had called him. The responsibility facing him in the future caused his heart to do its usual thing. He would lift the veil—slowly—till the boy was accustomed to his knowledge, and the process would go on. He would be in touch with the proper Tibetan authorities.

While they watched, the kite recovered and soared even higher as Chris tugged at the string in sure strokes of encouragement. The wind buffeted the boy. His blond hair swirled and his coattails flapped. He resembled a large bird, trying to

maintain his balance in the wild order of things. He held on
to his cap with the left hand as the right continued to tug.

Tatyata gate
gate Param gate
Parasam gate
Bodi Svaha

Consciousness Beyond Consciousness
Beyond consciousness
All things are known by the omniscient one—
Om mani Padme hum

EPILOGUE

David's encounter with the young rabbi at Peter's apartment was the start of a new and surprising turn in his life. The two Davids took to meeting several times a week. David's agnosticism, blown apart by the turn of the kharmic wheel, was now edging him toward the religion of his forebears. He started to wear darker colors, which accentuated the blue of his eyes as never before—lending him a more piercing manner. The "Buddhist Jew" Peter had called him. What new concept of the face of God would that engender. Pleasure had been his calling card in the art of therapeutic support. But is not all pleasure ultimately rooted in the acceptance of all things—good and evil? Surely at the center of that vision would emerge the profile of a new god—in all his merciless goodness. His pleasure principles would require emendations that would embrace a spiritual horizon only dimly intuited in David's perceptions before.

As for Peter Mendoza, he began putting together notes for a metaphysical thriller that his daughter, Amy, now ensconced back in New York, neatly typed up for her father.

While she worked, Peter took care of Rachel, having become most adept in the art of changing Pampers. Maybe this time the resulting book would not be rejected. The display at Spectra was already ensured—complete with a picture of the author. Eventually it might even turn out to be a book something like this one.

Shalom!